Fay Weldon

was born in England and raised in New Zealand. She took degrees in Economics and Psychology at the University of St Andrews in Scotland and then, after a decade of odd jobs and hard times, began writing fiction. She is now well known as novelist, screenwriter and critic; her work is translated the world over. Her novels include, most famously, *The Life and Loves of a She-Devil* (a major movie starring Meryl Streep and Roseanne Barr), *Puffball*, *The Hearts and Lives of Men*, *Darcy's Utopia*, *Growing Rich* and *Life Force*. She has four sons, and lives in London.

FAY WELDON

The Cloning
of Joanna May

Flamingo
An Imprint of HarperCollins*Publishers*

Flamingo
An imprint of HarperCollins*Publishers*
77–85 Fulham Palace Road,
Hammersmith, London W6 8JB

Published by Flamingo 1993
9 8 7 6 5 4 3 2

Previously published by Fontana 1990
Reprinted three times

First published in Great Britain by
Collins 1989

Photograph of Fay Weldon © Mark Gerson FBIPP

ISBN 0 00 654593 9

Set in Sabon

Printed in Great Britain by
HarperCollinsManufacturing Glasgow

The Cloning of
Joanna May

1

This has been a year of strange events: some wonderful, some terrible.

In the autumn a great wind swept through my garden one night, and toppled two oaks, three maples and a chestnut tree, all top-heavy with wet leaves, rooted in sodden earth. Had the gale come a week later the leaves would have been gone and the trees no doubt survived: a week earlier and the earth would have been dry and the roots steadier, and all would have been well. As it was, the chestnut crashed through the conservatory and set off all the alarms, which joined with the sound of the gale to frighten me out of my wits, so that I would have telephoned Carl, my ex-husband, and forthwith begged for his forgiveness and the restoration of his protection, but as the chestnut had brought down the wires I couldn't. By the morning the wind had died down and I, Joanna May, was my proper self again, or thought I was.

I went out into the garden and studied the sorry fallen giants, their earthy boles pointing unnaturally skyward, their scuttling insect population stricken by sudden cold and light: and wondered if there was any way of yanking them to their feet again, resetting them in the soil, making good what had been spoiled, but Oliver, my gardener and lover, told me there was not. The truth had to be faced – the trees were finished. That was the end of them: now all they could do was slowly die. I found myself weeping and that was very strange, and wonderful.

And that evening when preparing for bed I looked into my mirror and saw the face of an old woman looking back at me, and that was very strange and terrible. I attended to this apparition at once with astringent masks, moisturizing creams and make-up, and by the time Oliver padded into my bedroom on bare young feet with earthy nails, I, Joanna May, looked almost myself again; but there is no avoiding this truth either – that the task of rehabilitation will get more difficult year by year. Most things get easier the more they are done – but not this. The passage of time makes fools of us all.

I said as much to Oliver and he replied, 'Well, you're sixty, and should be used to it by now,' which is easy enough to say when you are twenty-eight, as he was. Personally I had expected to live for ever, frozen in time at the age of, say, thirty. 'I don't mind how old you are,' said Oliver that night, 'let alone how old you look. It's you I love.'

'Love' I could understand, but what did he mean by this 'you'? Small children (so I'm told) start out by confusing 'me' with 'you'. Addressed so frequently as 'you', their clever little minds work out that this must be their name. 'You cold,' they say, shivering, as the wind blows through the window. 'Not you,' comes the response, 'me.' 'Me cold,' says the child, obligingly. Presently the little thing progresses to the gracious 'I am cold.' But is the 'me', the 'I', really the same as that initial 'you' with which we all begin; the sudden bright consciousness of the self as something defined by others? Perhaps we did better in our initial belief, that the shivering cold is jointly experienced, something shared. I wonder.

Well, well, we will see. And as so often happens, the events that ensued ensured that I did see. Any enquiry, however primitive, this 'you' of ours manages to formulate in its mind as to the nature of reality, is met at once by such an eager response from that reality, such a convulsion of events, as to suggest that its only function is to provide us with examples, illustrations, of propositions that occur to the mind. Like Directory Enquiries, existing only to be asked, there to be consulted.

By the end of that year of strange events, I can tell you, when I looked in a mirror, I saw a face that would need a great deal more than a jar of wrinkle-cream and some exfoliator to bring it back to order. I was indeed old. Having children makes you old. It is the price we pay for immortality. God's last laugh, imposing this extra penalty on mankind before he flew off, leaving time the murderer behind, just waiting.

2

The great October wind frightened Jane Jarvis, aged thirty. It howled and raged outside her attic window, and quivered the panes until one of them actually cracked and shattered; then it swept in and around the room, bringing wet and cold with it. Rain spattered the TV screenplay she was sitting up late to read for Home Box-Office, and the wind somehow pried the sheets loose from their binder and swept them into the air and fluttered them round the room. Jane Jarvis thought the wind was alive: that it was some kind of vengeful spirit: that it whined and whinnied like the ghost of her aborted baby, long ago. She went into her bedroom and shut the door on the wind and the manuscript – not one she would recommend, in any case – and tried to sleep, but could not. She considered the temporary nature of all things, including her own life, and panicked, and rang her live-out lover Tom when she heard the clock strike three to say she'd changed her mind, he could be a live-in lover, they'd have a baby, but no one answered and by the morning prudence and courage had re-established themselves in her head and heart. She tacked strong polythene over the broken window; there would be a long wait for a glazier. The streets of London glittered with slivers of broken glass.

'You don't need me at all,' said Tom. 'You're self-sufficient.'

'I need you for some things,' she said, in the lingering sensuous voice that came so oddly from her rather thin, ladylike lips, 'of course I do. It's just I'd be mad to give all this up.' By which she meant freedom, independence, control over her own life.

'You're cold,' he said. 'Cold and over-educated and selfish.'

'Just rational,' she said, but Jane Jarvis was hurt. She took care not to show it. She had her pride. She did not want him; she did not want to lose him. She did not know what she wanted

– except her career. Soon, if she played her cards right, she would be head of the London office of HBO.

'Where were you last night at three in the morning?' she asked.

'That has nothing to do with you,' he said. 'How can it?'

———◦◦———

The wind lobbed someone else's chimney through the neat suburban roof of the home of Julie Rainer, aged thirty, and spoiled its perfection in many ways, and broke the round fish-bowl in which Samson the goldfish spent his timeless, circling days, and Samson died on the wet thick pile of the carpet. Julie was frightened and wept and in the morning rang the vet and asked him, in her lingering bedroom voice, why she brought death to so many small lives and he said they died in the glare of her perfection; and she puzzled over the answer for days. When he rang her the following week and asked her out to dinner she accepted the invitation. She liked the smell of antiseptic on his fingernails and her husband was away.

———◦◦———

The wind not only frightened Gina Herriot and Gina's three children Ben, Sue and Anthony (ages twelve, nine and two) but crashed an oak tree through the bonnet of the car in which they were sleeping. None was hurt, but the frame was bent and the doors were jammed and had to be opened up by the iron claws of the emergency services, as if it were a can of beans and they the can-opener. The car was parked in the road outside the house where the Herriots lived. The children's father, Cliff Herriot, had been drinking, and it was sometimes easier, as Gina explained to the social worker in her gentle, sexy voice and using language of a violence which issued oddly from her rather thin, ladylike lips, to lock him in than lock him out. Gina seldom confided so much of the detail of her situation to anyone, having her pride, indeed too much of it, but the violence of the wind had frightened her, more than her husband ever did. Fortunately the report went missing, since it was made out at the time the contents of all Social Service file cards were being transferred to disc: or perhaps because fate has a propensity to behave in the same way to people of similar nature. Events fall out, this way or that, beyond our apparent control, yet in keeping with our expectations.

Gina was thirty, but born seven weeks prematurely, and this initial misfortune, this first hard, grating sharpening of the knives of fate, echoed like a sound, a siren song, through her life. 'Trust Gina', her neighbours said to each other, 'to be in the car when the tree fell,' but they didn't say it to her face. They feared her calm, quick look of disapproval: she did not like personal comments or appreciate advice. Her nose was broken but she remained chilly in her beauty: like Grace Kelly, they said, in that old film. 'Why doesn't she leave Cliff?' they asked. 'The brute!' But they didn't ask her to her face. Anyway, they knew the answer. She loved him.

———◆◆◆———

As for Alice Morthampton, aged thirty, in the womb a week longer than her mother-apparent had expected, the great wind bypassed her: of course it did. Alice was smiled upon by different stars than were Jane, Julie and Gina. The storm cut a swathe through southern England, passing from east to west, taking in London on its way, but Alice was not in London at the time, but in Liverpool, where she was engaged in a photo session: smart clothes against demolished warehouses.

'Smile, damn you, smile!' Angus the photographer had implored her during the day, but Alice Morthampton would not, saying in her languid, croaking voice that she knew better than he; she had surely been employed to actively not-smile, since that was her speciality. She spent the night in bed with him, however. 'You don't care about me,' he complained. 'You only do this for the sake of your career.' And she sighed and said she wasn't sure why she did it, she certainly didn't enjoy it: her career would get on well enough without him, probably better – and as she felt his assault upon her, as it were, weaken and tremble within her at least had the decency to apologize for her habit of speaking the truth, even when least welcomed, so he felt man enough to continue.

9

'I love you,' he said.

'Whatever that means,' she said, apparently unmoved by either desire or emotion, or perhaps too proud to show either. The storm caused a short delay on landing at Heathrow the following morning, true: aircraft were slewed across the runways and took time to move: but on the whole the fates were on Alice's side.

Jane, Julie, Gina, Alice: these were the clones of Joanna May.

3

After Carl May divorced his much-loved wife, Joanna May, for infidelity and had her lover killed, he lived celibate for several years (as did she) concentrating upon his business interests, which were many and various. But nature abhors a vacuum, in particular one to do with sex, and presently a Mr Hughie Scotland, aged forty-five, a TV and newspaper magnate, fleshy, vigorous and wilful, reached for his address book and ran his finger down the M's. Then he called Carl May on his personal number, not even leaving it to his secretary to do. She was crying anyway. His staff often did: tears dropped into the word processors, doing them no good at all. But Hughie Scotland was rich enough not to worry.

'Let me be blunt and to the point,' he said.

'You always are,' said Carl.

'I'm in a fix,' said Scotland. 'My wife is screaming at me all hours of the day and night –'

'I thought she was in Iceland,' said Carl. Susan Scotland, born in Alabama, had recently been appointed US Lady Ambassador to that chilly, prosperous country.

'She is,' said Scotland. 'I don't mind her screaming in person, but she screams over the international telephone system, and causes me embarrassment, for nothing is private to a man in communications who has enemies; you have no idea the language she uses. I don't want it to get about, for her sake.'

'I have to be at a meeting in ten minutes,' said Carl, 'or I'll have enemies.'

'I'll be brief,' said Scotland. 'I want you to take this bimbo of mine off my hands. These girls topple presidents and bishops, and I don't want this one toppling me; she could be on the phone to the gutter press day and night; she'd upset my wife.'

'Hughie,' said Carl, 'you *are* the gutter press,' but Hughie took no notice. Susan Scotland's recent distress had been caused by press photographs of her husband and a young woman named Bethany bathing and sporting naked in the waters of a trout farm: they had been published not only in rival newspapers but throughout his own extensive syndicate. 'You'll shit in your own nest for a profit,' she'd wept down the line from Reykjavik, thus shocking and alarming her husband.

'Hughie,' said Carl, 'I don't need a bimbo. I am a serious person. I am not like you: I am not in the habit of splashing about naked in trout tanks.'

Hughie said, 'Carl, those were free-range trout, it was a pool, not a tank, and a hot day, and a man can surely do as he wishes on his own property. You know I've diversified into fish farms? If my wife wants to see more of me let her come back from Iceland.'

'I'm sorry,' said Carl, 'but no. Pay the girl off. Isn't that what people do? What's the worry?'

'You're a dry old stick,' said Hughie, 'and getting worse since your wife left.'

And Carl went to his meeting. But presently he was tempted out to lunch by Hughie: few people can resist the lure of an inside story. Even Carl May could be affected in this way. Hughie, rather disappointingly, chose an obscure restaurant.

'I can cope with governments,' said Hughie, 'and monstrous taxes and creeping socialism but I cannot cope with women. Take this bimbo off my hands. She keeps crying. Why do women spend so much time in tears?'

'Why me?' asked Carl, picking at a lemon sole. He ate little, and drank less. He preferred his fish unfilleted.

'These girls have to move upwards,' said Hughie, 'or they get offended, and that's when the trouble starts. And you have class. I have style but you have class.'

'Me?' asked Carl, surprised. 'Me? Class?'

'How many women have you slept with in your life?' asked Hughie.

'One,' said Carl. 'My wife.'

'That's class,' said Hughie. 'Why don't you leave that fish

alone? It comes from the North Sea; it will have died of pollution, caused by your outfall.' Carl May was Chief Executive of Britnuc, a corporation which had become involved with the rehabilitation of the old Magnox nuclear power stations, two of them sited on North Sea shores. 'Freshwater fish are the meat of the future. Do me a favour, I'll do you a favour.'

'What?' asked Carl.

'I'll hold the story on the plutonium leak last March at Britnuc A. No one else has got it.'

'They haven't got it,' said Carl, 'because there wasn't one.'

'The public's too sanguine about nuclear power,' said Hughie. (How was he to know Chernobyl was to blow?) 'They need stirring up. So do you. Bethany's the girl to do it. Those press photos didn't do her justice.'

'I only read the financial papers,' said Carl.

'Out of touch,' said Hughie. 'You don't want to lose your touch. What you need, mate, is a bit of pain to stir things up again. You're slipping.'

It seemed to Carl that he would use less energy obliging Hughie Scotland than disobliging him, and so he agreed to take the girl Bethany on to his personal staff, Scotland paying her wages. The rich stay rich by staying mean. Fish with the bones in cost less than fish with the bones removed.

4

'I dreamt that I dwelt in marble halls,' Carl May whispered to himself and sang,

'With vassals and serfs by my si-i-de,
And of all the assembly gathered there
You were the joy and the pri-i-de.'

And well might he sing, and thus, as some months later he stepped from the back of a limousine and his sneakered foot touched conquered ground, while the Thames ran by as busy and significant as the ancient Euphrates.

Bethany Turner stepped out from the other side of the limousine and a different tune ran through her head. 'Shoo fly,' she whispered and hummed, 'shoo fly don't bother me, for I belong to somebody.' And she thought, of course, if she belonged to somebody, that somebody must be Carl May, her rich grey man, but she was wrong. Bethany loved, like a million million other women, someone who existed only in her head, who would never, in all her life, materialize. She loved a phantom, in whose image Carl May stood.

'What are you singing?' she asked Carl.
'Tunes from the dog-house,' he said. 'Tunes from the dog-house, that's all.'

It was a joke. For Carl's mother had kept him much of the time, when he was little and hungry and stole, chained up in the dog's kennel in the yard, to teach him a lesson. His father was a dead dog: his mother was a bitch. That much he learned. 'Marble Halls' would drift over the neighbouring fence, from

14

next door's wind-up gramophone, and sustain his assaulted spirit. The child Carl shivered, he wept, he slept, he dreamed, and later he made the dream come true, as a few, just a few children, can.

'And you?' he asked. 'What are you singing?' For Carl heard everything, however soft, especially soft.

'Tunes from a childhood,' she said. 'That's all.' As for her, she'd been brought up in a whorehouse. Thrust people down when young and most stay down. A few rise up, like Carl and Bethany, and then if they're lucky they find each other.

He took her arm in his and they walked off to inspect this especially poignant part of his empire, there beside the Thames, and were happy for at least this one hour: he had found someone he truly desired, whom he could mould to his will, and she had found someone she truly admired, who would do as she wanted; the past, they thought, was now well and truly over. None so dangerous as those who believe they are happy, and are not. They flail around them, laying waste.

How at home they felt, young Bethany, old Carl, in this wasteland of razed warehouses and mean streets. Her high crocodile heels caught in crevices where weeds and grasses still found temporary hold, just enough dusty soil to live. His spongy-soled sneakers made light work of cracked, uneven surfaces. Soon builders and container-gardeners would move in and a new People's Park spring up all around: fast-food concessions in ferny precincts; disco dancing in leafy glades; Goofy and Peanuts and Garfield fighting it out in flowery pastures. Miniature sheep would graze on new enriched turf for the delight and wonder of young and old; there would be fireworks by night, TV stars by day, entrance £5 per head and few extras, and all thanks to the ingenuity and enterprising thrust of Riverside Gardens plc, the funding of the DTI, the involvement of local government, and Riverside Developments Inc.

Carl May was on the board of both Riverside Gardens and Developments. Six months after its no-doubt-royal opening,

Riverside Gardens was destined to pack up its container plants, crate its miniature sheep, fill whole lorries with stacks of well-watered turf and move on to the next inner-city waterside site. Then Riverside Developments would move in, all planning permission and social grants agreed by the local housing authority, to erect high-price housing for those young professionals who wanted a river view and easy access to the City, and who were prepared to pay for it.

In this way everyone would benefit: not only the people who flocked to the part Disneyland, part Garden Centre of the People's Park – in particular a thousand thousand dispossessed fathers who needed somewhere to take their children on access weekends – but those who would obtain a minimum of six months' employment in its running: that is to say craftsfolk, fast-food concessionaires, builders, painters, waitresses, gate-keepers, security men, artists and artistes, cleaners, hedgers and ditchers, occupational therapists and so on. And after they were gone there would be permanent employment for the servicing agents of the young property-owning incomers – janitors, hair-dressers, manicurists, dress designers, drivers, dentists and so forth. Yes indeed, all would benefit, and not least the profit and status of Carl May himself: Carl May of Riverside Parks plc, Riverside Developments Inc., and many other interlinking business concerns beside, including the one of which he was Chairman – British Nuclear Agents, Britnuc for short.

Bethany was twenty-four. She wore high crocodile shoes, ginger stockings, suspendered beneath ginger woollen jodhpurs held by leather bands at calf and waist, a not very clean white cotton shirt, highwayman's style and well unbuttoned, chains of gold butterflies round neck, waist and ankle. Her red hair had been untidily pinned up with a Spanish amber comb: she wore emerald-green contact lenses in her eyes. The look of the wanton was intentional, and as fake as her orgasms: she could do student, or executive wife, or lady doctor just as well. The only school exam she'd ever taken was Drama and she'd got a credit for that. But she could think of easier and livelier ways of making

16

a living than being an actress, and recognized it as folly to waste her father's training in being what men wanted.

Carl stood 5 foot 10 inches in his shoes, or had done last time he was measured, thirty years ago, in the days when he still needed life insurance to set against mortgages. Suspecting that time might have shrunk him, thinning the discs in his spine, as time does, he now wore elevated shoes. He knew the value of height when dealing with other men: but also that height is in the mind of the observer, it is a matter of bearing rather than actuality. He saw no deceit in the elevated shoes: he would have reached at least 6 foot 3 inches had it not been for severe malnutrition in early childhood, or so he had been told: he knew he was in essence a tall man. He wore carefully casual clothes for this outing with Bethany: he had a natural tendency to be dapper, to wear carnations in buttonholes, which he was at pains to overcome. To dress too carefully was to display nervousness. He had the well-developed chin of those accustomed to telling others what to do. His hair remained thick, though white.

The gap in their ages, the gulf in their manners, their way of dressing, the sense of his wealth in proportion to that wiliness born of helplessness in her, the very place in which they walked – exploiter and exploited (but which was which?) – made their perambulation altogether disreputable. People looked after them puzzled and not altogether pleased, as if expecting something sudden and terrible to happen any minute – as if a bulldog and a kitten, not a man and a woman, were out walking together. But Carl and Bethany saw in their looks only admiration and envy.

Carl and Bethany returned to their limousine to drive over rough ground to a site of special interest, where a brass plaque was to be set into the ground: a place of pilgrimage for future generations.

'Perhaps,' said Carl, modestly.

'How can you doubt it!' said Bethany, as expected of her.

The mythology of Carl's past had become familiar to the public, and even to himself: his childhood had indeed, by constant reference, been all but sucked dry of pain, drained of poison. Yet this pain, this poison, he knew well enough was the source of his energy, his power.

'Let there be buildings!' Carl May had only to cry, pointing to an arid landscape, and lo, so there would be. In the beginning, it is true, unlovely stubby concrete profitable blocks arose, but then, confidence breeding confidence, came the glassed towers and steel pinnacles of the finest architectural imagination. And all at Carl May's command – he, who until he was ten had lived in a shed down here by the river, chained with the dogs.

'Let there be beauty!' Carl May had only to murmur, he whose stepfather had battered and abused him, and lesser men would scurry forward with trees and flowers – albeit grown in container pots with soil substitute, well sterilized against all insect pests – and yes, there would be beauty, of a sort.

'Let there be light!' Carl May ordained, and nuclear power stations sprung up at his command and pumped their power into the National Grid. He, who was rescued by a teacher at the age of ten, half-dead, passed into council care, thence to foster parents and public school, Cambridge, business school and the Institute of Directors. He, who had everything except what he wanted – that is to say that which was not to be bought with money, that cluster of blessings which trip off the tongue as faith, hope and charity.

'See,' said the world, 'anyone can do it. It is perfectly possible to rise above circumstances, however dire those circumstances may have been. An unhappy past can be no excuse for the actions of murderers, sadists, child abusers, wife batterers, criminals of any kind. Carl May did it – so can you!'

It was to revive the pain and thus maintain the level of his achievement that Carl May took green-eyed Bethany down to the banks of the Thames. So, on this very pilgrimage, he had on occasion taken his blue-eyed wife Joanna. But that had been in the days when the mean and horrid streets still stood, before Carl May had conceived the idea of Riverside Parks plc, and Riverside Developments, and the main area of his fame and accomplishment (apart from his notable capacity to overcome the rigours of the past) was seen to be in the new world of nuclear power, the harnessing of the atom for mankind's advancement, that peace, happiness and prosperity might reign henceforth, and so forth.

'Without my wife,' Carl May had said for all the world to hear on radio and TV, 'I am nothing.' He was brave enough to bare his soul in public, or at any rate such part of it as he wished the public to know. 'The love of a good woman', he had joked, 'behind any great man!' only half-joking, and popular psychologists at once put pen to paper. 'You see,' they said, 'the wife can do for a man what the mother did not. No one should give up hope: no personality is irredeemably lost, destroyed. The narrow eyes of the tormented, anxious child, the thin mouth of the frightened child – they need not be permanent. With time, and love, those eyes will open wide, the mouth fill out. Fear not.' Carl May believed it too.

5

A couple of days before Chernobyl went up, making a large world into a small one, by reason of our common fear of radiation – the invisible enemy, the silent murderer, that which, like age, creeps in the dark – in this case consisting of a myriad, all-but-immortal particles, too small for the eye to see, of one man-made radioactive isotope or another (selenium, caesium, strontium – you name it, we invented it) flying through the air and causing death and decay wherever it fell, at any rate in the popular imagination – I, Joanna May, read of another strange event.

A girl in Holloway, doing three years for cheque offences, plucked out her eye. The technical term for this is '*orbisecto de se*', and very nasty it is, for those who have to clear up afterwards and put flesh and head back together. The human eye, if you regard it without emotion, is a glob of light-sensitive jelly attached by strings of nerves and muscles to the convoluted tissue mass of the brain, in itself a fine ferment of electrical discharges. But it works, it works. The 'you', the 'me', the 'I' – behold, it sees! The soul in the dark prison that is the flesh looks out through the senses at the world: the senses are the windows to that dark prison. And what the soul longs to see is beauty; smiles, grace, balance – both physical and spiritual – love in the maternal eye. It longs to see evening light over summer landscapes: crimson roses in green grass: birds flying, fish leaping, happy children playing – all that stuff. Yes, all that stuff.

What the contemporary eye gets to see on a good day is Mickey Mouse: it can just about put up with that, some joke is intended in the ugliness. The white lacy Terylene of a wedding dress makes up for a lot. A nice strong erect penis, viewed, can reconcile a lustful girl to some grimy back alley. But three years in Holloway! What is the eye, the I, to make of that!

Three years in Holloway, three years of grey concrete, the stuff of anti-life, the stuff that keeps radioactivity in (at least temporarily) or out: three years of looking at old Tampaxes in corners and cigarette stubs and grime and grey tins holding the brown slime of institution stew, and any sane person would be tempted to pluck their eye out, let alone the mad, who more than anyone proceed by punning. The word in action. The deranged pursue their sanity down the only alley known to them: giving language more meaning, more significance, than it was ever meant to have.

If thine eye offend thee, pluck it out. And quite right too. Broadmoor's a handsome place, set grandly in the wild hills: a great sweep of dramatic sky; old bricks not new concrete. One eye in rural Broadmoor's better than two in suburban Holloway, any day. She plucked her eye out and got transferred to Broadmoor. That's where one-eyed girls go.

I wanted to write to Carl to say, 'Carl, Carl, did you read about the girl in Broadmoor who plucked out her eye?' but how could I? I had betrayed Carl, spoiled the achievement which was his life, made of him a murderer (how could one doubt Carl's hand in Isaac's death: as well believe that Kennedy's assassin – and his assassin's assassin, and his assassin's assassin's assassin – all died of random acts) and Carl May had divorced my mind as well as my body – of course he had. And that was the hardest thing of all to bear.

Instead I rang for Trevor and asked him to fetch me the *Yellow Pages*. I turned to 'I' and there found Investigation Agencies, and ran my finger down the list, passing by the Acme and Advance and Artemis (they cluster their names in the A's, these places, and advisedly) all of whom I had used in the past and from whom I had sucked all possible juice of entertainment, and presently came to Maverick Enquiries, an agreeably innocent

21

name, I thought – and dialled their number. It is my experience that the cool appearance of any Investigative Report, the comings and goings, contacts and activities of the investigatee neatly and impersonally described, acts like antihistamine ointment on a wasp sting to soothe the obsessional and tumultuous mind, if only – like the ointment – for a time.

I did not report to Oliver what I had done. Oliver thought I should just forget Carl. Oliver thought such a thing was possible – of course he did. Oliver was a nice guy, and young with it. But I had been married to Carl for over thirty years, and Carl was intertwined in my mind and body like the strands of dry rot fungi in the damp bricks of an empty house.

Let Oliver say as often as he liked, 'Forget him, Joanna, as he's forgotten you,' the simple fact was that Oliver had not been alive as many years as Carl and I had been married. But I liked to hear him say it. The young find everything so simple. That is why their company is refreshing. The young, moreover, see it as their duty to be happy and do their best to be so. I was brought up to be happy to do my duty, and so tend to equate happiness with boredom.

I would say to Oliver (or words to this effect), 'If Carl May has forgotten me why hasn't he found himself a wife, or even a girlfriend; why does he stay celibate?' and Oliver would reply (or words to this effect), 'Because he's so busy making money.' Oliver was kind. He could have said, 'Because he's in his sixties; too old to get it together,' but he didn't, in case I was reminded of my own age, and suffered. Isaac was kind, in the same way as Oliver. He too tried to smooth the path that ran before my thoughts. Too kind, when it came to it, to live in the same world as Carl May. My fault.

If thine eye offend thee, pluck it out! I wait for the arrival of the soothing ointment, the person from Maverick Enquiries. I want to be told, as I have been told so often in the past, that Carl still lives as a celibate, in memory of me.

6

How had it come about that Joanna Parsons, that English rose, had married Carl May, this upstart from a kennel? Why, because she fell in love with him, of course, and he with her, and her father was too busy and her mother too complacent to interfere with the course of true love. Nor were Carl's natural parents in any position to object to the match, being dead, and his foster parents were only too happy at this sudden uxorious turn of events: proof that the trouble they had taken with the boy, and the love and money they had expended upon him, were to be rewarded as they had hoped. He had joined the ranks of the achieving middle classes.

Little Joanna – for this is the way fate often works; sealing in our memories what is yet to come – had, when she was a child, read about the strange case of Carl May in a daily newspaper. The image of the abused and abandoned boy stayed in her mind, waiting, as it were, to pounce. The one to whom she, who had so much, could give so much!

How was it possible, thought little Joanna at the age of ten, weeping (unusually for her) into her porridge and cream, served by a maid, the plate so prettily laid on the white linen cloth, how was it possible that a world that contained so much excellence, pleasure and refinement should be the same world in which a boy could be kept in a kennel, beaten and abused, all but starved to death, have to teach himself to read from scraps of newspaper; a boy whose mother would then kill herself and whose stepfather be battered to death in prison at the hands of a vengeful mob? What, all this, and porridge and cream and dab your mouth as well? What a strange and upsetting world it was turning out to be!

'That child should not be allowed to read the newspapers,' her father said, observing her tears. The Parsons lived in Harley Street, above the shop: that is to say his consulting rooms. It was Dr Parsons' joke. Joanna's father was a physician: his speciality ear, nose and throat; two windows from the soul's prison on to the outside world, one organ of communication. The doctor's function was to keep all three bright, clean and properly receptive. Dr Parsons smoked a good deal, and coughed quite often, and presently was to die of lung cancer, but never made the connection between cigarette smoke and his ill health.

'The newspapers should print only what is happy and good,' said her mother, 'not upset people the way they do.'

Dr Parsons had disappointed a family of generals and majors to go into medicine. He was a man of moderate height with regular features, fair hair and bright blue eyes – the latter a recessive gene. He came from the North East – he was of Scandinavian stock.

Mrs Parsons, daughter of a West Country solicitor, had pleased her family by marrying a man a notch or so above her in the social scale, three inches taller, four years her senior, and well able to support her. She was slightly built and reckoned beautiful, with high cheekbones, wide green eyes, and the red hair sometimes inherited from two black-haired parents. She was of mixed Norman and Celtic stock. The strands of the different races met in their child, Joanna: she was beautiful, strong, healthy and bright, as if to encourage just such a blending.

'Do stop that child snivelling,' said Dr Parsons. 'Take away that newspaper.' The maid did so.

Mrs Parsons dabbed Joanna's eyes tenderly while rebuking

24

her crossly. 'You have no business crying,' she said. 'Remember there are others far worse off than you!'

It is the custom of intelligent and competent men to marry women less intelligent and less competent than themselves. So mothers often have daughters brighter than they, and fathers have sons more stupid. It does not make for happiness. Nature looks after the race, not the individual.

Joanna stopped crying the better to puzzle it all out. But she did not forget Carl May. She saved him up, as it were, till later: stored him in her mind. One day she would make it all up to him. In the meantime she learned her letters and presently Latin and Greek, at an all-girls' school, and amazingly nobody stopped her, for the more a girl knows the more trouble she has finding a husband who knows more. But then prudence prevailed and she went on not to university but to a finishing school in Switzerland, where, in the interests of a future marriage, she was taught the mastery of flower arrangements, the organizing of dinner parties, the proper control of drunks (speak firmly but politely), servants (likewise), and the finer points of deportment. She 'came out' gracefully, being presented at Court, in the traditional way, when the ceremony was revived at the end of the war, and at her very first dance just so happened to meet Carl May, a pale, intense, not very tall but good-looking young man who worked at the Medical Research Council in Hampstead. He had not been on Active Service: his was a reserved occupation.

Carl May was famous already as the young man who'd started life in a kennel. Joanna Parsons' heart went out to him at once: she saw him as the solution to a puzzle which had worried her all her life. His body went out to her, in trust and confidence; and though his head regretted she was not of the titled, moneyed classes, he thought he could put up with that. He needed a wife to look after him and he needed one now. He did not need children, but he did not tell her that, not at once.

25

'I love him so much, Mummy,' said Joanna. 'I do so want to marry him. I want to make the past up to him. I want to make him happy.'

'If you love him you should marry him,' said Mummy. 'After all, I loved your father.' It was 1949, the nation was three years into socialism, everything was upside down. The young man had fought through heavy odds to end up well educated and well spoken: what were a few years in a kennel? They would make him appreciate her daughter the more. It was time the girl was out of the house: she made her mother feel faded, dusty and stupid. Mrs Parsons wanted Dr Parsons to herself again.

'I want to marry him, Daddy,' said Joanna, waiting for opposition. But none, to her disappointment, came.

'Why not?' was all her father said. He'd rather she'd married a doctor and perpetuated a race of physicians; he'd rather the young man had faced up to Hitler directly, but those few hard early years should at least help keep the young man's feet on the ground, and besides, Dr Parsons was busy. Men had brought back odd diseases from the African deserts and the jungles of the Far East; ears heard wrongly, noses smelt falsely and words came strangely from tortured throats. And it was time the girl was out of the house. The vivid presence of the daughter made him discontented with the mother.

Only Joanna's Aunt Anne was against the match: she said, 'the child who's beaten grows up to beat,' but she was years ahead of her time and regarded as an hysteric. What a hopeless doctrine it would be, if true! That we never recovered from our past! What price progress then? For what applied to individuals applied to nations, and societies too. So much the world was beginning to see.

Now Joanna was sixty, and disgraced: she had failed, in the end, to make the past up to her husband, failed to make him happy. And Carl was sixty-three. Age wears out the resolution of youth: or look at it another way – the past seeps through into the present, as the garish colour of underlying old wallpaper,

26

left unstripped for one reason or another, but usually financial, will eventually show through to the pale expensive layer on top and spoil everything.

7

'She should be thoroughly punished for making you so unhappy,' said Bethany to Carl, when he ran through his life for her, the way new lovers do.

'My mother is dead,' he said, surprised.

'I didn't mean your mother,' she said. 'I meant your wife.'

'Oh that old woman, that Joanna May,' said Carl, 'who cares about her?'

Bethany had heard that kind of thing before, for all she was so young. On the night she met Carl, she turned over in bed and said, 'I'm twenty-four going on forty-two and you're sixty-three going on thirty-six, so who's counting?' And Carl stopped counting there and then, though of course the world did not.

That first night he said to her, 'You're the second woman I've slept with in all my life,' and she said, 'I don't believe you,' and he did not care if she believed or not: he just got out of bed to make some calls to Australia, and so she believed him.

'I was totally faithful to Joanna all my married life,' he said, when he had finished his calls and got back into bed. He had skinny white hairless shins but she did not care. 'That was my folly.'

'What happened?' asked Bethany, though she knew pretty well; these things do not go unnoticed, even in circles of power, where policemen seldom enter in.

'I found her with another man,' said Carl, easily, though this was the first time for several years he had found words for the event. Well, who had there been to speak to? And in so saying, he bound Bethany to himself, or so she thought. She was safe with him now, she told herself: he would not, could not, surely, pass her on to some subordinate.

'What did you do?' asked Bethany audaciously, and audacity was rewarded, as it so often is.

'I killed him,' said Carl, even more easily. 'That is to say, I had him killed. But it amounts to the same thing.'

Bethany wondered how the deed had been done, but did not like to ask. Screams in the soft suburban night had many a time disturbed her childish sleep; she had never liked to ask. Once she did and her mother slapped her. 'What you don't know can't hurt you,' Mother said, and Bethany had believed her.

'Why him not her?' Bethany enquired further, now, of Carl. 'Most men kill the woman and leave the man.' Twenty-four going on forty-two, no doubt about it, reared in a whorehouse! The things she knew for all she never asked.

'I left her alive,' said Carl dreamily, 'to suffer from the loss of me.'

'Most women left alone for that reason,' said Bethany, 'just find someone else.'

'Not when they're old,' said Carl. 'Don't you want me to tell you how I disposed of her lover?'

'No, I don't,' she said, so he didn't. Confidences are dangerous. Witnesses get killed. Those who know too much disappear. The world is not a safe place, even for the well intentioned; especially the well intentioned.

'Why did Joanna betray me?' asked Carl May, that first night, he who so seldom displayed ignorance or doubt, thus suddenly loquacious. 'I don't know much about women. What did my wife need that she didn't have? I still can't understand it. We'd been married nearly thirty years. She was never much interested in sex; what did she want with another man? She had more than enough to do – the house to look after and so forth; I was good to her: attentive when I had the time: generous – she could spend as much money as she liked on clothes, though she never would: ask Joanna to choose between Dior and Marks & Spencer and she'd choose Marks & Spencer. It was her background – middle of middle. Revenge of some kind? Insanity? She liked animals more than people: she said so: it hurt me. She had a little grey cat which died. That upset her. And then of course the dogs – it's true I got rid of the dogs. But she never found out about that. It can't have had anything to do with that. No, it was just in her female nature, buried deep, but there it was. The need to betray, to spoil, to turn what is good bad. The bitch goddess, at it again.'

'How do you mean, Carl? Got rid of the dogs?'

He was not in the habit of explaining himself, and she knew it. But still she asked, and he replied, as she knew he would. As he trusted her body, so he began to trust her mind.

'I was jealous,' said Carl May to Bethany. 'I didn't like the way she stroked the dogs. I didn't like the way they nuzzled her, as if they'd been there many a time before. Or how she'd talk to them instead of me. It upset me – a kind of spasm attacked my throat: such a lump in it I couldn't swallow. Once, looking at her with them, I almost fainted. A lot of people depend upon me. I have to keep myself steady for their sake. I had the animals stolen: I was going to sell them; then I realized I'd have to have them poisoned. You know how dogs will find their way back home. But enough of all that.'

'You did the right thing,' said Bethany, who felt quite safe, having no dogs to poison, no lover (so far) for Carl May to destroy.

Bethany knew well enough the value of the benefits she offered her new lover; how hard, once enjoyed, they were to do without: the sheer surprise, the sudden joyful restoration of self-esteem, as conferred by the sexual act when performed with the right (even though unlikely – especially the unlikely) person. Moreover, Bethany surprised even herself: she had never known the magic work so well before: not in the many sometimes profitable, sometimes distressing couplings of her adolescent days; not even when she moved away from home and the suburbs to the nightclubs of the fashionable world, not even then had she and whoever come even near it; no, not even with Hughie Scotland, Carl's predecessor, not for all his fame as a media stud. Those others had not seemed to notice any lack of anything. Those others had given her money, cars, racing tips, sexual satisfaction, all kinds of things – but what Carl May gave Bethany, in return for his pleasure, was confidence. And what she felt he felt too. Oh yes, she was safe enough. He wouldn't want to do without her. So Bethany believed. So Joanna had believed.

'You be careful,' said Patsy, Bethany's mother, when Bethany reported back to her that she was moving on from Hughie Scotland to Carl, and rather liked the new arrangement. 'Don't go falling in love. Love's all misery and muddle and never any profit.'

'Don't talk like that!' said Bill, Bethany's father, to his wife. 'You and I are in love, always have been, and look at the profit we've made! Look at the child we made! Our Bethany, child of love. No wonder she's sought after; and fate is on her side, it's obvious. Carl May! That really is the big time.'

Patsy and Bill, ex-flower-folk, kept a house of moderate ill fame in an outer-London suburb, halfway down a very long quiet street. They went together to local pubs: he brought home lonely men, she brought home lonely women. They brought them together in the upstairs bedrooms of the large suburban house, charging an agency fee. Bill mowed lawns for the neighbours; Patsy would meet their children out of school if they were ever in a fix: they were an obliging pair, they took care to be, no one ever complained. Where did altruism stop, self-interest begin? Hard to tell. Whoever can, of other people or themselves?

Patsy and Bill met in the fifties, at the cinema. *Gigi* was showing: Audrey Hepburn of the wide brown eyes as the girl reared in the brothel who found true love, Maurice Chevalier as her protector. 'Thank heaven for little girls,' he sang, with all the faux-innocence of that sickly decade. There at the cinema, to that tune, Patsy and Bill fell in love, and reaffirmed that love at a rerun in the sixties, at a half-empty local cinema, while they were trawling for custom amongst the dispossessed and empty-lifers at a Tuesday matinée, and there, in the back row, Bethany was conceived in a fit of wholesome life-trust. How else should they rear her but as Gigi was reared? So the beauty advice came from women's magazines, and the style was suburban not *fin-de-siècle* Parisian, but never mind, never mind! Bethany was created.

And Patsy and Bill, proud in their achievement, while valuing the joy of sex, all sex, and perhaps overvaluing Bethany their daughter, for a time all but priced her out of the market; many was the boring night she spent alone: lying empty, as a house may lie empty while its value increases. That was when she was fifteen. Noticing what was happening, they brought the price down.

All things are chance, thought Bethany, who bore no malice against her parents, no resentment for the manner of her upbringing, or thought she did not. I might have been born in Africa in time of drought, she thought, and had stick arms and legs, and a stomach which stuck out: I might have been born an Eskimo, and hardly seen my legs and arms at all, so cold would it be to undress: as it was I was born to Patsy and Bill, and if they had not been so foolish, so trusting, and so adored Audrey Hepburn, would I have been born at all? And now here I am with Carl, and happy and safe, so what's the point of complaining? But he still hasn't got his wife out of his system. Something must be done about that.

'Well,' said Bethany, 'it seems to me your wife lived an empty life and was a shallow woman and you're well rid of her. But perhaps her life was boring. Perhaps she was just bored. Some women will do anything not to be bored.'

'She could have gone to classes,' said Carl. 'She had no reason to be bored. She had me. Boredom is no excuse for infidelity.'

'She should have had babies,' said Bethany, 'with all that time to spare. Why didn't she?' Not that she wanted or anticipated children herself, belonging to a younger generation, one which did not define women as people who had babies.

'She did,' said Carl, cunningly, 'but she never knew it.'

'That's impossible,' said Bethany. 'How can you have a baby and not know it?'

'In the same way,' said Carl, 'as you can have an hysterical pregnancy and be convinced you're growing a baby when you're not. That's what Joanna did to me when she was thirty. She got morning sickness: her belly swelled up. She looked terrible. I took her to this doctor friend of mine, Dr Holly; a very clever man. He just looked her over and sent her out of the room and said to me, "Your wife and Mary Queen of Scots! There's no baby there, only air and wind." "What's the cure?" I asked. "Love and kisses," he said, "or failing that, a mock abortion, a ceremony of death." Almost nothing he didn't know about women. So that's what we did. Told her she was to have a termination, anaesthetized her, and whee-e-ee, like a balloon going down, went Joanna's belly. When she woke up she was cured. My lovely wife, slim and fresh and all for me again!'

'But that's not having babies and not knowing it,' said Bethany, 'that's not having a non-baby.'

'Oh so clever she'll cut herself,' said Carl May, his old finger running sharply down the skin between Bethany's breasts, where she should have buttoned her blouse, lifting the white nylon rosebud in the centre of her bra and snapping it back so she jumped. 'Wait! Joanna knew well enough I didn't want children: I told her the day before our wedding: she accepted that when she married me. I took that phantom pregnancy of hers badly, an imagined one seemed to me worse than the real thing; let her conscious mind be loyal and loving, in her unconscious, in the depths of her being, Joanna May betrayed me, went against me.'

'You were to be all in all to each other! Just you, just her! I think that's sweet – my mother and father were like that, in the beginning. Then they had me, and felt differently.'

'How could Joanna and I have had children? Do you understand just what sort of inheritance I have? What do you think it's been like for me, knowing what kind of parents I had, what sort of bestial blood flows in my veins?'

'Your parents were mentally ill, Carl, that's all. They must have been.'

'That's all? Insanity? All?'

How white he suddenly was. She ran her finger over his lips. They were dry and trembling. He calmed. She had not known he could be upset. She felt privileged, and powerful. Carl May,

33

Chairman of Britnuc, power in the land, TV personality, calmed by Bethany's young finger.

'I had myself sterilized when I was eighteen,' he said. 'A vasectomy. I would be the end of the line: that particular experiment of nature's. I chopped down the family tree.'

'Joanna didn't mind?'

'Joanna didn't know,' he said. 'Why should she? What difference did it make? She understood my mind when we were married; we would have no children. There'd be just the two of us.'

'Tea for two,' said Bethany dreamily. 'Just me and you. Two for tea and baby makes three.'

'Baby makes five,' said Carl sharply, and nipped her finger suddenly with teeth made sharp and fine by the passage of sixty-three years. 'While she was opened up we took away a nice ripe egg; whisked it down to the lab: shook it up and irritated it in amniotic fluid till the nucleus split, and split again, and then there were four. Holly thought we could have got it to eight, but I said no. Growth begins so quickly: there wasn't time. A truly vigorous egg, that one. We kept the embryos in culture for four whole weeks, had four nice healthy waiting wombs at hand and on tap, for implantation. All four took like a dream: there they grew until they popped into the world, alive and kicking and well. Four nice assorted ladies, desperate for babies, got four very pretty little girls: little Joanna clones. Not cloning in the modern sense, but parthenogenesis plus implantation, and a good time had by all. We kept it quiet. So quiet one of the mothers didn't even know we'd done it. What passive creatures women are: they just lie there, trusting, and let the medical profession do what it wants.'

'That's two for tea and four babies make six, Carl, not five.'

Carl bit Bethany again. 'Wrong!' This time she yelped, and quite reminded him of his younger days. 'There wasn't anyone to tea. There ain't a father in the whole wide world,' crooned Carl May, 'that gave help to my poor old dutch. All on her lonesome ownsome. Her DNA and hers alone. She was thirty. She was growing little hairlines round her eyes: so I gave time itself a kick in the teeth. It seemed a pity to let it all go to waste, when you could save it so easily.'

34

'Like an old Magnox power station,' said Bethany; he looked at her sharply.

'Don't be so cutesy,' he said, not even bothering to bite, so she desisted.

'Well,' said Bethany, 'all I know is if it was me I'd have told her. I'd never have managed to keep it to myself. I can't keep the smallest secret, let alone cloning someone and not telling them!'

'It's sensible to keep things in reserve,' said Carl May. 'Information may not be wisdom, let no one tell you it is: but knowledge – ah, when it's secret knowledge is power.' And Carl May looked at Bethany hard, until she wondered which of her secrets he knew and wasn't saying.

'No,' said Carl May, 'she'll never get it out of me. Let her go to her grave not knowing. She chose loneliness: let her be forever lonely.'

'But now I know,' Bethany said, 'what about me?' and wished at once she hadn't opened her mouth.

'You'll keep it to yourself,' Carl May said, and she thought, yes, I will: on the whole I better had. I can see I better had.

'One day you might tell her,' she said. 'You never know what's going to happen next. One day you might, to punish her. To take away her singularity.'

'A long word for such a little girl,' he said, and pinched her with sharp-filed fingernails – she'd given him a manicure: he enjoyed that: he on the chair, she crouched on the floor, red hair falling – better, she could see, in future, to file his nails less sharp or use words that were less long, or both.

'What can happen next,' asked Carl May, 'that I don't know about: what can surprise a man like me? I win. I always win. I need to win, as other people need sex, or food, and that's all there is to it.'

Bethany shivered, and hoped Carl May hadn't noticed, but of course he had. So she looked and spoke as bright as could be. 'I wouldn't like to have a lot of little me's walking about,' she observed. 'One of me is quite enough,' and the jabbing nail turned into a stroking hand, a pressing mouth, and she felt safe: yes, she felt safe enough. One of her, she told herself, was more than enough for him. Besides, she wasn't perfect, not like Joanna: on the contrary, she was flawed; she knew it: people had told her so often enough. Now she was glad, not sorry, Carl May had noticed. If the penalty of perfection was reproduction she could do without it. Her bone structure was not good: she was pretty rather than beautiful – she had her mother's chin: it would droop and double by the time she was thirty: she was all artifice: she inspired lust not love: she was cunning not wise: bright not clever: could memorize well but not categorize easily: was a good guest but an over-effusive hostess: affectionate but not constant – being able, at will, to switch that affection in the direction which most suited her, and often tempted to do so. These things Bethany knew about herself. She was in fact too vulnerable to the passage of time. She was the kind who went off early. Never mind, when she lost her capacity to charm she would start a business: an employment agency: a chain of them perhaps: Carl May would help her, pension her off: she would be powerful through money, that safe and snazzy stand-in for sexual pleasure. She liked to be safe. She didn't like to be bored. It was difficult to keep a balance between the two.

'What a pity you can't have babies,' she said, quite forgetting to whom she was speaking. 'I'd like to have your babies. Then I'd always have something of you to love!' Men liked to hear that kind of junk, but Carl merely shook his head impatiently, as if some gnat had bitten him, so she shut up and let him get on with it.

8

The day they went down to the river, Carl May returned to the subject of his ex-wife, and his secret knowledge. He and Bethany sat side by side in the back of the limousine. Perhaps he thought she was too confident: he liked to have her a little frightened. He knew how to frighten her. It's always pleasant to do what you're good at doing: hard to refrain from doing it. Anyway, Carl May had said, 'You could always give birth to one of my clones. I could use your womb to implant me.'

'What a lovely idea!' said Bethany, in her best and politest voice. 'They can't really do that, can they?'

'Oh yes they can,' said Carl May. 'I'll take you down to my friend Holly. There's an advance on freezing now: the rage is all for drying: keeps the nuclei intact. It used to be just frogs and below: now it's sows and upwards. Shall I take you down to Holly? Prickly Holly?' He pinched the tip of her little finger, and they watched it turn blue between the bloodless nails of his thumb and third finger.

'He must be rather old by now,' said Bethany, and wished she hadn't.

'No older than me,' said Carl May, but added kindly, 'Lost his nerve, lost his bottle, you're quite right,' and he let her finger go. She sucked it. He liked that.

'One of you,' said Bethany, 'is more than enough for me. I'd be exhausted. I want you, not your clone. What would be the point of a clone?'

He nipped her neck. She was covered with little bruises in tender places: mementoes of Carl, he called them. She loved them.

'It would come in handy,' he said. 'It could stand in for me here and there — at banquets, for example, when all anyone needs is my presence; when my opinion counts for nothing. It would save my digestion.'

'But what would you do while you stayed home?' asked Bethany, whose idea of pleasure it was to be out, not in.

'Learn not to need to win,' he said and, as if to make up for a lifetime of over-controlled Joanna May, flung himself upon Bethany, digging his teeth vampire-like into her neck, tearing her blouse, his hand approaching her crotch from the top, not the bottom, down between her clothing and her skin, forcing her belt to give and break, without any thought at all for the presence of Philip the chauffeur in the front seat. Philip was indeed embarrassed by their moans and groans, but Carl May paid well: it was a privilege to work for such an employer, who had led a lonely and prudent life far too long, and the girl was not reluctant, on the contrary, so he put up with the embarrassment easily enough. He had faced worse in the course of his job – the poisoning of Joanna's dogs for one thing, the backing his car into and over Joanna's lover Isaac for another, as required of him by Carl May. Who was he to object to anything? What kind of moral stance could he take? What outrage would now be justified? Once a servant, an employee, has decided that loyalty to the one who pays him supersedes all other moral obligations, and has acted upon that decision, to change the mind becomes impractical, not to say dangerous. Reason and self-interest must be called upon to counteract the pangs of sensibility.

Philip kept his eyes on the road and drove slowly beside razed warehouses, over broken tarmac, where the weeds kept bursting through.

'You know far more about me than you should,' said Carl to Bethany, after his final climactic gasp.

'It was all just a story anyway,' said Bethany prudently. 'All that about clones. Just to frighten me.'

'Of course,' he said. Then he added, 'But just think, if there were more of me, and more of you, how much pleasure we would bring into the world!' and he actually smiled, and she remembered that she loved him and was pleased to give him pleasure.

He slept a little. Bethany stared out of the window on to a broken landscape. Philip parked the car. His employer woke up with an old man's start: a shiver: where was he? The river air was in his nostrils: the air of his childhood: a flowing tide of soot and despair mixed: there in his mind for ever, lying low but always there. He got out of the car. Bethany followed. The sun went in and a cold wind blew across the river.

'I brought you down here,' said Carl to Bethany, 'so you could see for yourself how I began. Of course it's all gone now – but where we stand used to be the corner of Jubilee Road and Bosnia Street. This is where the brass plaque is to be.'

And Bethany said, 'If it was all so nasty, why do you want to come back? Or is it like a loose tooth? You want to jiggle it even though it hurts?'

And Carl knew he had been deceived in her: she was not after all what he hoped. He was disappointed in her, hurt; he had forgotten what it was to be disappointed, hurt. Bethany did not begin to understand the significance of his achievement. She belonged to the TV age: nothing surprised, nothing impressed: real life rolled off a scriptwriter's pen. To have started here, yet come to this! Magnificent, but she could not see it.

The chauffeur buttoned his coat and straightened his cap, feeling the alteration in his master's mood: though if you'd asked him he'd have said, 'Just something in the air, that's all: just something in the air that chilled me, reminded me of this and that. I wouldn't work for anyone else: not for twice the wages and half the hours. It's an honour.' He'd been in tanks in the war and killed men for less reason than he killed for Carl, which was from loyalty, obedience and self-interest mixed.

'But it's all such a long time ago,' said Bethany, compounding her error. She felt the cold wind in her hair and round her chin and cutting down against the white and tender skin of her still partly unbuttoned bosom; harsh against the grazed skin where he had sucked and bitten her neck. Had he told her where they were going she would have worn boots and brought a scarf. With almost every step over the uneven ground she caught the leather on her high heels; they would be badly snagged: she

39

would have to have them rewrapped. He was thoughtless.

'If you're not interested we can go home,' said Carl. She understood then, too late, too late, that the cold wind was somehow his doing, and said, 'Of course I'm interested,' and then, 'They say one's childhood is never over. Do you think that's true?' But it was no use: the cold wind whipped and zapped through her red hair, and that was the only answer she got.

'You are not sufficiently interested,' Carl May said, 'for me to waste any more of my day on you.'

They rode home in silence, to the big boring house at 20 Eton Square, Belgravia, where the May collection of Egyptian art and artefacts was housed in what used to be the stable block, open to the public on the first Wednesday of every month. Very few of the public in fact took the trouble to attend. The windows had been blocked up to save specimens from the dangers of direct natural light; the ceiling rose to a central peak: the single door was arched: the room, though vast, was for all the world like a kennel. It was a dismal place. But Carl liked it, which was all that mattered.

As the chauffeur pulled up outside 20 Eton Square, a small group of reporters rushed to meet the car. Microphones were pushed under Carl's nose and flashbulbs popped. News was coming through that the power station at Chernobyl had blown, and in the light of the fact that two of Britnuc's plants, like Chernobyl, were WCRs, water-cooled reactors, could he make a statement? Was the public in any danger?

'Making electricity is not like making a sponge cake,' he said kindly in his soft gravelly voice. 'It is dangerous and things go wrong. When I know exactly what has happened at Chernobyl, if anything, I will be in a position to make a statement. Not before.'

'But, Mr May, the public is worried.'

'The public is right to be worried,' he said, smiling, and closed the front door, swiftly, and upon Bethany's right foot. The picture of the snagged and torn leather upon the six-inch heel of her shoe was upon the front cover of a tabloid newspaper the next day. 'May Faces Snags,' it said, going on to speak of the unseen killer which now stalked Eastern Europe. Other newspapers relegated the item to the middle pages. It was one of those stories which was to grow and grow, as wind patterns in the upper atmosphere made nonsense of national boundaries.

Carl went straight to his study to make telephone calls, his face still set cold against Bethany.

Bethany was a practical young woman. She dumped her shoes in the bin, feeling that since they brought her no luck they might as well be discarded, changed into more restrained clothes, dabbed ointment on her neck and, in the cold light of the bathroom, brought her hair under better control. She did not like the bathroom. It was too large, too full of marble, too brightly lit, and the washbasins were antique and their porcelain, being finely crazed, never looked quite clean. She did not like the house; Joanna's house. She did not like the servants; Joanna's servants – who did not like her, with her tiny knickers left everywhere and her strewn junk jewellery and hairpins, and her waterproof make-up smeared on sheets and cushions: but that was her role; how Carl liked it; they would just have to get used to it. In fact Bethany came to the conclusion she did not like Joanna, whose ladylike presence in the house was still too clearly felt for comfort.

The woman had no natural taste, that was apparent. She had re-created her father's consulting rooms in her husband's house: dark, highly polished mahogany furniture, dusty pale-green velvet curtains, over-plump greeny chintzy sofas and blue-and-white encrusted Chinese jars of arguable value standing on every available ledge. Twice a week the housekeeper would arrange fresh flowers – unnaturally large blooms – in the bleak white fluted floor-standing Italian vases which stood boringly in each corner of the room.

Bethany assumed, and rightly, that the twice weekly arrival of the peculiar flowers was an expression of gratitude from whatever container-gardener firm had been granted the contract to supply the Thameside Garden Park – a gift, of course, not a bribe. Bethany well understood the difference. Many a gift had she received in her life, before or after a favour. But she could not be bribed – that would be an indignity.

Bethany bent to smell the flowers, which seemed to occupy some point between gladioli and chrysanthemum and withdrew her face at once. They had been sprayed with a strong flower perfume somewhere between violet and rose. It was not her place to comment or improve. She thought longingly of her parents' suburban garden, filled with nothing more exotic than pansies and roses, and settled down to read *The Layman's Guide to Nuclear Power*. It was one thing to appear ignorant; quite another to be so.

9

Carl was on the phone to a certain Gerald Coustain. This is how their conversation went:

Gerald Coustain said, 'What you're telling me is that there is no indication of additional radioactivity from any outside source at either Britnuc A or B?'

Carl May said, 'That is correct. I would add that this is hardly surprising since our instrumentation is not designed to pick any up.'

There was a short silence from Gerald Coustain, who worked for the Department of Energy.

'You're being remarkably frank with me,' he said.

'Why not?' enquired Carl, who was still in what Joanna had learned to call 'a mood'. Bethany had failed him. It was not his time he feared to waste, so much as his emotion – and what were referred to in a booklet he had recently received through the post on the subject of AIDS as 'bodily fluids'. He was aggrieved. He had made himself vulnerable. It was dangerous. If, as he felt, the experiences of his childhood energized his present, a fire to be fanned and nurtured back to life, that fire was as like as not to go out altogether under the thwack of cold water delivered by Bethany. There was a lot at stake here. A long time ago! What had that to do with it?

'I have done everything the inspectorate required,' said Carl May. 'I have followed its instructions to the letter, no matter how absurd those instructions were. Nowhere could I find regulations appertaining to the upper limits of instrumentation.'

Again there was a pause.

'Nuclear power is a new industry,' said Coustain, his voice receding as if he held the receiver further and yet further away.

'It is essential that the spirit of the law rather than the letter be followed.'

'Come off it,' said Carl May. 'You don't want Britnuc A and B off line every time instrumentation shows a rise in local activity any more than I do. You fellows have your own information-gathering network. Don't come bleating to me every time the shit hits the fan.'

Coustain, thinking he should perhaps make a virtue out of necessity, asked Carl May if he would make some reassuring statement on TV the next day: along the lines he had sketched out: and so Carl May did, in the programme seen by his ex-wife, Joanna May.

10

'God's last laugh,' I said, 'before he flew off,' I, the original of the clones of Joanna May. I said it, of course, more for the sake of a neat phrase than anything else: my way of vaguely invoking the name of God whilst yet dismissing him. God was there once, I safely maintain, thus explaining away some intimation of immortality, some general notion we all have of 'more to this than meets the eye' whilst disposing of him, whoever he may be, for all practical purposes.

'Joanna, define your terms!' – Miss Watson, 1942. A certain Miss Watson taught me English language when I was a school-girl. She was in her eighties. Young women were at the time busy making explosives in factories to blow young men up: they had no time to teach their juniors anything. The old were brought out of retirement to be of some use, while the young finished each other off. No wonder the war was so popular with everyone. A long, violent, riotous, disgraceful party! Miss Watson died of a stroke on VE day; and quite right too – the party was over.

If I'm forced into a corner by the ghost of Miss Watson, who returns to me often in dreams, I would define God as the source of all identity: the one true, the only 'I' from which flow the myriad, myriad 'you's'. We acknowledge him in every 'I' we so presumptuously utter. Now what could be more all-pervasive than that?

Carl once told me God flew off the day Fat Boy was exploded in the Nevada Desert, when man entered the atomic age (though of course man – and woman – had in fact entered it long before,

45

when Pierre and Marie Curie first started sieving and filtering their dusty mounds of pitchblende), leaving the field to the likes of my husband. But I prefer to think He flew off when the first flicker of television appeared upon the screen. He knew he was beaten. For Lucifer read John Logie Baird, inventor of TV, toppling the Ultimate Identity from his seat of power: spoiling the currency of 'I' forever. The 'you' that is the real 'I', the one perceived by others, the one understood by the child in that initial bright vision, now watches the 'you' that that you perceives. There is no end to it. Our little shard, our little divine shred of identity, so precariously held, is altogether lost as we join the oneness that is audience. My clones and I. After I found out about the clones I began to worry a lot about 'I'.

As for evil – which everyone knows is the absence of God – what could it do when God took off but take up residence in the source of its trouble. The minute parents, those stoical folk, look away, evil creeps out of the TV set and settles in the wallpaper. The children ask for sneakers now, not proper shoes. Why? Because sneakers have long laces, long enough to hang a person by. And every year the laces get longer and tougher, the better to do it; to hang, to dangle yourself or others. Why bother to preserve the 'I'? It's seen too much of sights not fit for human eyes, it is not fit to live. It no longer believes in life: all it gets to see is corruption, seared, torn and melting flesh. There is no 'I' left for any of us. The great 'I' has fled, say the eyes in the wallpaper: only the clones remain, staring.

If the I offend thee pluck it out. Idopectomy.

My children who are myself pun too. Bloody clones. That was Carl's doing.

On hearing the first news from Chernobyl, I sent Trevor the butler to the Post Office with a telegram to Carl May my ex-husband saying, 'Yah boo sucks, signed Milly Molly Mandy', but Trevor came back saying the Post Office now sent only greetings telegrams – Happy Birthday, Congratulations on your Wedding, and so forth – and I decided silence was the better policy. One must go with the flow of events. If waves slap against your face, turn back to shore.

The next day Carl made a statement to the press saying (or words to this effect), 'It can't happen here. Our reactors are constructed on a different principle from theirs. Children may safely drink milk though sheep may no longer safely graze on the uplands.' His lies were soft and persuasive, as ever: and his face calm and handsome. It had the tranquillity of a death mask: as if someone had placed a waxed cloth over his corpse's face – after it had been composed by the undertaker, of course – and moulded it into shape and propped body and mask up before the cameras and used puppet strings to work the mouth and eyelids. Carl was dead, pretending to be living. That is what a diet of lies does for you – and now I am no longer with him what else will Carl choose to eat but lies? There is no nourishment in them, the spongy junk food of the mind. The soul dies from malnutrition.

I longed to tell him so – yah, boo, told you so – to ease the itch of spited, spiteful love, watch the pale dead face suffuse with the living pink of rage, but I didn't. Let him stay dead. It was what he chose when he threw me out: it is why he lived without a woman after I was gone.

I dedicated my life to Carl: I threw away the children I could have had, for his sake, to keep him happy. Isaac was nothing; a side-show, a weak man: he died and I scarcely noticed. Oliver is nothing either, when it comes to it: a pet which curls up alongside, by a warm fire, or on a forbidden bed, to be indulged. Better than nothing, that's all, poor Oliver. Of course Carl is dead, dying: so am I, without him. But Carl is at least able to blow up the world while he waits. I'm not.

11

The clones of Joanna May also blamed their nearest and dearest for the accident at Chernobyl, with rather less reason than did their original.

In their case, of course, near did not necessarily or permanently mean dear, and this was either an affliction ironed into their genes, or the common cross of humanity, as may be decided by events. Nor was the tendency to blame irrationally peculiar to these four women, of course: it afflicts all mankind. When the weather is fine on polling day, the sitting government is returned. If the weather is wet, it gets thrown out. And that's that.

———◦◦◦———

Jane Jarvis listened to the news on the radio and slammed her attic windows shut to keep the radioactivity out. A pity, because it was such a fine spring day, but to keep out the bad you had to keep out the good. Then she returned to the brass bed where her lover lay. It was Saturday, and lunchtime. Presently they'd get out of bed and walk into Soho for something to eat. Her flat was in Central London: she had the whole attic floor of a big house in Harley Street. She could afford it. Such was the reward of beauty, intelligence, education, and the capacity for making decisions others feared to – saying, simply and firmly, 'this is good but not profitable' or, 'this is bad but commercial', or 'this is neither good nor profitable', or, just occasionally, 'this is both good and commercial' and having the results bear her out. Tom designed book jackets and lived in half a house in Fulham, and earned a quarter of what she did, for eight times as much work. He would take her out to lunch, so she would have to eat spaghetti, not oysters.

Jane Jarvis was 5 foot 7 inches tall; precise and orderly in mind and body. She measured 36 inches around her chest, 24 inches at the waist and 36 round her hips, as had her original at the same age. Her nose was straight and perfect; her eyes widely spaced: her cheekbones high, her top lip a little short, the bottom lip a little thin: her gaze was direct. To wash her hair she dunked it in a basin of soapy water, rinsed it and towelled it dry. It frizzed out round her head. She belonged to some new, insouciant age. She walked like someone who knew herself to be free. She lived at the top of No. 30 Harley Street. Her original had spent her childhood in No. 34.

'I want the windows open,' said Tom, when she got back into bed. 'I can't sleep with the windows shut.'

'I didn't realize you had come here to sleep,' she said.

'Besides which, why bother?' he asked. 'If there is radioactivity out there glass isn't going to stop it.'

'It will stop alpha rays,' she said.

'Smarty pants,' he said.

'You can't bear it if I know things you don't,' she said.

A row was approaching through the window: no glass could stop it: the hideous black cloud of the spirit: tumulus and cumulus fighting it out: lightning flashes of dire perception, thunderclaps of rage, hail storms of battering distress; every passion and woe of the past returned to plague the present, bent on turning love to hate. They knew it, Jane and Tom: both looked uneasily out of the window: they could see rooftops and sky: no sign yet of the storm they expected to see, but they knew it was coming, in spite of there, in the real world, a blue sky, a few white clouds. On the bed the grey cat Hattie sensed their unease and stopped purring. Tom put his hand on Jane's thigh, the better to forget what was going on out there, seen or unseen.

'I thought you wanted to sleep,' she said.

'This is crazy,' he said. 'Why don't I live here? Then we could use beds the way other people use them. We wouldn't have to be in bed in the middle of the day.'

'I like it like this,' she said.

'You don't love me,' he said. 'It's obvious.' He removed his hand. 'You don't know the meaning of the word love,' he said.

'You're over-educated. What do you think I am, some kind of stud?'

It really made no difference what they were arguing about. Her reluctance to marry, settle, wash socks, have children – which he saw as just a habit of thought, a pattern of belief, an ongoing fear of change, something more to do with the ascendancy her mind had somehow gained over her body than anything to do with her essential nature; his failure to match his sexual desires to hers, which she registered as a hostile act; his intention to punish and humiliate her for earning more than he did; his fear of giving voice to his feelings; his inability to offer reassurance and comfort; his failure to acknowledge her equal status; her lack of taste, as he saw it; his lack of understanding, as she did. One way or another accusations and insults began to crackle in the air, feelings no longer contained but given voice to. You did this and you said that. Wimp and harpy, bastard, bitch. Unfaithful! Gutter slut and macho pig and the simple, friendly, curing pleasures of desire fulfilled denied – and just as well, perhaps, lest sex itself become the weapon, and then indeed there'd be an end to everything, and neither in their heart wants that. But spite and rage preferred – preferred, that's the shocking thing, the self-revelation that hurts and wounds – chosen above love and kindness not just by the other but by the self. Not so much the other hurt, humiliated by the other, as the self by the self. The row is with the self, the other stands witness, accepting the bruises: it is some kind of horrid, magic, contrapuntal duet: variations on a theme; how can the unloveable, my self, be loved by you; your fault that it cannot. Projection. Simple! He accuses her of his own deficiencies: he hands them over. She does the same to him. Outrageous! How can I be expected to put up with this? And what is more, and have you forgotten; accept this evidence, accept it or I'll kill you, that you do not love unloveable me! Unforgivable!

The row is vaporous: it circles blackly, out this window, into that: it never stops; when you make up others begin: their turn next; always someone's. It feeds on itself, it feeds on you, the

50

more you give in to it, the bigger it grows, the more powerfully it affects your neighbours, down here in the shameful gutter world, up there in the reeling attic sky, breeding every ill that flesh is heir to.

Keep your mouth shut, keep it shut, take a pill to knock you out. How gently, silently, this ire crept, the first cold wet breath through slammed shut windows. *You* shut the window: *I* want it open: Why? Because *you* want it shut. *I* shut it, knowing *you* didn't want it. Why don't *you* love *me*? Why, because *I'm* unloveable, but not as unloveable as *you*. And what is radiation compared to this virus already in the bloodstream?

Oh yes, a virus. The row comes like a virus. Unseen, unheard, unknown. It comes in a droplet, through a break in the skin, the brushing of flesh, a flavour in the air, a particle inhaled. Once in the blood it's there for ever, an infection; a lingering, debilitating disease, flaring up from time to time. Once you're sensitized, the first time you succumb, there it is, yes, for ever; a spiritual TB, before the development of antibiotics; sometimes it kills, sometimes it doesn't: it just doesn't go away; it merely hides to wait its triggering. Can't wait! AIDS of the spirit.

In the end Jane Jarvis scratched and clawed Tom Jeffrey and he left the house saying he'd rather die than return to face the virago, and they didn't make it up till Sunday, when they went out to supper and she ordered oysters and he let her pay. He was growing a beard. Lemon juice trickled amongst the black bristle. He had a square jaw and even teeth. He was a good-looking man, a sensitive man, a talented man. One day the world would recognize him. He would make a good father. He wanted to be a father.

Oh yes, indeed a virus, caught somewhere along the way by Jane Jarvis, at Oxford perhaps. He certainly thought that was where she'd picked it up.

It could not be in the genes, could not be in the nature, must be culturally induced, caught. Joanna May suffered a severe attack at the age of sixty, but had not been previously afflicted. Her relationship with Carl had ended with the murder of a third party, true, but that was Carl's doing and coolly done; no one had ever shouted, screamed or clawed. No, there was this to be said for Joanna and Carl – they never descended hand in hand, step by step, into that shocking desert landscape where the air is rent with whining and spiteful complaint, and the self stands isolated and terrified in all its snarling, scratching fury.

Jane Jarvis said to her Tom as he left, in the rain, 'With people like you in the world, how can it be anything but doomed. I hope you inhale beta particles and die.'

And this was the man she loved, or tried to love, or hoped to love, and knew if she didn't love, who else would there be?

Julie Rainer heard on the news that a radioactive cloud hovered over the country, and blamed the Russians, since her husband was away on business as he so often was, and there was no one else to blame. She closed the windows and poured away the milk. She stalked her lonely, perfect, tasteless house and filled in yet another form for yet another adoption agency: checking her lies against a note of previous lies in a booklet kept solely for this purpose. Her husband could not have children: he was infertile. She had spent hours, hours of intensive life with doctors' fingers and spatulas inside her, investigating, before they turned their attention to him: it was her fate, her destiny, she felt, to have these prying feelers there. She despised herself. She lacked the courage to be artificially inseminated, she lacked the courage to leave her husband, though she did not love him, whatever that meant. She felt she would gain courage in the end: but by then it would be too late to have babies.

Time was against Julie, as it is against all women, in such gynaecological matters. In the meantime, she loved her animals, who gave her work in the way that babies do: removing dog hairs from a sofa, replacing chewed seat belts, nursing aged cats, cleaning up after kittens, discouraging algae in the fishbowl – these things gave her pleasure, a sense of achievement . . .

'You love those animals more than me,' said Alec, closing his leather briefcase, off again, mini-computer in hand.

'I expect I do,' was all she said. She only told lies on forms.

She called up the vet to ask him what to do with the animals in view of the radioactive cloud and he said he doubted they would come to much harm, no one seemed to know how much radiation was about, or indeed what radiation actually was, but it would also do no damage to keep them in, and even perhaps to bath the dogs.

'But supposing the water's radioactive?'

He thought she was the most beautiful woman he'd ever met, but over-anxious. He thought her husband neglected her. He had the sense that she waited for her life to take its proper direction, and that also, if she was not careful, she would wait for ever. She was lost: in the wrong place: with the wrong fate: making herself neutral.

'Shall I come over?' he asked.

'No,' she said sadly.

'It's a pity your husband's away at such a time,' he said. 'Chernobyl has made everyone nervous, probably more nervous than they need to be.'

'You can't see it but it's always there,' she said, 'like my husband. I'll just call the animals in, shall I?'

'Good idea,' he said, and went to deliver a calf which had two heads. These things happen, with or without radiation. The farmer was inclined to blame Chernobyl, all the same, and however irrationally.

Gently, Julie Rainer, aged thirty, 5 foot 7 inches, 36–24–36, wiped the paws of Hilda her grey cat with a damp cloth, but Hilda took offence and scratched her. Julie watched a line of blood ooze along her white inner arm and threw the poor creature – the one she loved – across the room.

'Bloody animal,' she shrieked, 'bloody animal! It's all Alec's fault.' Later of course she stroked and cosseted the cat, who fortunately had not seemed to take deep offence, and then she went out into the night and breathed deeply, to punish herself.

———◦◦◦———

Cliff came home on time and Gina did not realize he'd been drinking until too late.

'Isn't it terrible about this thing at Chernobyl?' she said, when he came in. She was 5 foot 4 inches, 38 around the chest, 28 around the waist and 40 around the hips. Well, she had been seven weeks premature and reared in a less fortunate environment than Joanna May, her original.

'Don't give me any of that fancy stuff,' he said. 'Where's dinner?'

'Not quite ready,' said Gina. 'I had to get the kids back home from the park. It was raining; supposing what they say is right: the rain's radioactive?'

'I want some straight talking round here,' he said. 'Dinner is either ready or is not ready, and if it is not this is what happens,' and he hit her.

Now, the kind of row that occurred between Gina and Clifford was of a rather different genus than the one that slowly developed between Jane and Tom. It was not a black cloud that little by little took over a clear sky: not a virus sent to blight the life of the potentially happy. No, this was the kind of domestic discontent that runs like gutter sludge through the houses of the depressed and desperate, be they smart new bungalow, palace or slum – and once your children get their feet wet there's no drying them out. Mothers' noses get broken, eyes blacked, kidneys damaged, unborn babies killed; the little witnesses have a hard time of it; thwarted in their desire, their passion, to love someone, anyone, who is worthy of their love, they grow up to lay about them likewise. It is never over. Parents must be worthy of their children's love, and that's all there is to it. And whoever grows up, properly, finally? Not *you*, not *me*, not *him*, not *her*.

'Where's my dinner?' he says. He might be four. 'Not ready,' she says. She might be six. Wham he goes: he's all of fourteen.

'How can you?' she wails; fifteen if she's a day; and to the neighbours, grown-up at last, 'I walked into a lamp-post,' denying truth, so what sort of grown-up is that? And not so different in essence perhaps, just more swift, more desperate, more dangerous than Jane and Tom. Where's my dinner means did you care for me in my absence, did you notice I was gone, Mum oh Mum, how can I trust you? Not ready means no actually I didn't, I don't care about you one bit; wham means I can't express this sorrow, this grief, this disappointment, in words, you self-righteous bitch, you cow: the wham arrives reinforced by a great communal strength, the sudden surge of the male's hatred of the female who will not be possessed, will not be owned, will not be all body but will have a soul, and who in the refusing suggests some unattainable, other ideal. And then her tears, her silly tears of resentment mean see I knew you were like this, you've proved it again; her loyalty acknowledges that if I am punished it must be my fault, things will get better, you my neighbour can't possibly understand the complexity, not his fault, mine, I have failed, I have failed – the whole thing's impossible . . .

If there's no one around for Gina, and no one around for Cliff, either will kick the cat. There! Told you after all that I was unloveable. See what you've done?

In the next room the children turn up the TV – they'd have done better to stay in the park, in a different kind of fallout. Presently Gina comes in to say, 'Sorry about the explosion. It's all over now.' Except her nose is bleeding, so it clearly isn't. Why does she tell such lies? Why doesn't she leave? She doesn't leave because how can she leave, where can she go, she hasn't got the courage: one day perhaps she will, she says, leave. But leave what? Who? Herself – that's what she fails to understand, late with his dinner because Chernobyl exploded. How does she leave herself behind?

He is the product of her imagination taken flesh: she married him to make him flesh, he is what she deserves. She stood there and said, 'I will, I will!', knowing his nature, the strength of his backhand, the cheap wine reddy-brown upon his teeth.

Those who have rows are more alive than those who don't: make better friends, more interesting companions. They may wreak havoc but they understand their imperfections – witness how they project them upon others – they cry to heaven for justice. They believe in it.

———••◦••———

Alice had a row with her agent. He was her nearest and dearest. Other men came and went, but he was the voice on the phone, unsweaty, unsmelly, a man firm and strong upon a letterhead.

He rang her to say Kiev was cancelled. She'd been going to do a show there.

'I don't believe it,' she said. 'You're doing it on purpose.'

'Alice, be reasonable,' he said. 'How could I make a nuclear power station explode?'

'You're using it as an excuse. You didn't want me to do this show. You don't want me to represent my country abroad. You want me to do some cheap swimsuit for some cheap mag because there's more in it for you.'

Alice was 5 foot 8 inches tall, 33 inches around the chest, 22 round the waist and 32 around the hips. She'd spent a week longer in the womb than Jane or Julie, and eight weeks longer than Gina. She exercised and dieted. She was in love with herself: she would stand naked in front of a mirror and run her hands across her body: she would do anything for herself.

'There's never anything in it for me,' he said. 'Ten per cent! A tip. That's all it ever is, a tip.'

'Perhaps it's time I got a new agent,' she said.

'Perhaps it is,' he said.

There she went again. Prove *you* love *me*, before *I* prove *you* don't. Later *he* called to apologize. *She* knew *he* would. *He* needed *her* more than *she* needed *him*.

Sometimes Alice felt alone in the world. She wished she'd had a sister: all she had for company was her little grey cat, and that was often left for neighbours to feed and so was cantankerous. Nevertheless the penalties of continual companionship, that is to say marriage, seemed too onerous to contemplate. What did she need with a husband in the flesh when her agent on the phone cared so much about her – how she looked, how she felt, where she'd been, what she earned – and all in exchange for a tip. Sex she could take or leave – and often left, for the sake of her looks. Not just because of the necessity of early nights if her eyes were to stay bright and large, but because sex made her screw up her face and that encouraged wrinkles.

One day she might marry, one day. Not yet. One day she might find the courage to marry.

So thought and felt the clones of Joanna May, before they discovered each other and themselves.

12

After his conversation with Carl May, Gerald Coustain put down his cordless telephone and said to his wife Angela, 'The man's a monster.' They sat in the garden. She was setting examination papers in A-level European history: she had lean academic fingers. He was potting out delphiniums: he had plump and clumsy ones: he was a civil servant of the stout complacent kind. She did not reply: what was the point: she knew Carl May was a monster. The sun went behind clouds; the wind was suddenly cold: there was rain in it.

'I think perhaps we should go indoors,' he said.

'Why's that?' she asked, absently, lost somewhere in the Boer War. 'It will stop in a minute: it's only spitting.'

'There is a possibility the rain is radioactive,' he said.

'Don't be absurd,' she said. 'Things like that don't happen.'

But she gathered up her papers and they went inside. He left the delphiniums to take their chances.

'Perhaps we should change our clothes and shower?' he said.

'I would rather die than do anything so extreme,' she said.

'Death itself is extreme,' he said.

'If you envisage this alleged radiation as life-threatening,' she said, 'shouldn't you be measuring it to find out? Or something?'

'Our organization is a little sketchy,' he said, 'and I am not getting much cooperation where I had hoped to find it. I can't get through to the Department. The lines are jammed.'

'Perhaps you should go in to the office,' she suggested.

'On a Sunday? I spend Sundays with my family.'

'All the same,' she said.

'Besides which,' he said, 'it's safer indoors. Bricks and mortar offer some small protection. No one would expect it of me, to go in to the office through radioactive streets on a Sunday.'

He felt her disapproval and stood out against it. He must be allowed to make his own decision, surely.

'How is poor Joanna?' he asked, to change the subject. Angela had been Joanna's best friend, until the divorce. After that, of course, the relationship had become difficult.

'Joanna was never poor,' said Angela. 'Nothing poor about Joanna. Her house would make two of this, she has a park rather than a garden, her month's alimony is my year's housekeeping.'

'In the circumstances, Carl May was generous. I would not be so generous, if I caught you at it.'

She laughed. It was hardly likely that he would. She was plain as a pikestaff, warts and moles all over the place and hairy legs. People were amazed at the match. He'd been a good-looking man when young: he could have done better for himself. But he hadn't wanted to: he'd wanted her: and as for her, she didn't give two figs for her looks. Their children, surprisingly, were all handsome, in a tall, strong-jawed way, and being male, their facial hair was not a matter for concern.

'That way he can control her,' said Angela. 'If she accepts his generosity.'

'I suppose it is better to be controlled than ignored,' he said. 'Poor thing.'

'She has a young friend,' said Angela. 'The gardener: the man who pots out her delphiniums.'

'You're making it up.' Gerald Coustain did not want to know this.

'But I saw him when I went round the other day. She was looking wonderful. Not quite so perfect and clear-cut as she usually is – a little blurred around the edges. Swollen-mouthed. Sex, I suppose.'

'What were you doing round there, in any case? I'd rather you didn't call on her. Meet for lunch, of course, in town, if you insist. But not too close, Angela. No home visits: especially not if what you say is true. Carl May might see you as an accomplice. Be prudent.'

'If your promotion depends on my prudence, you've had it anyway,' said Angela. 'Hadn't you better be getting along to the office?'

'There are no trains to speak of, not on Sundays.'

59

'Then get a taxi.'

'Certainly not. It is not a question of my promotion, Angela, but of your safety. God knows what Carl May might do next. He had his wife's lover written off, blanked out, knocked off the perch, however you want to express it –'

'Murdered. But there were special circumstances. One can't condone it, of course.'

'It has hardly reached "condone", Angela. One doesn't even know about it! Just don't get involved, that's all. I hope she has the sense not to boast about her lover to you ladies, or this one won't last two minutes either.'

'You ladies!' she scorned him. 'You ladies! Where has your courage gone? Can't say boo to Carl May, can't get to the office in case the rain's radioactive –'

In the end he went, as she knew he would. Angela served as her husband's conscience. Women who play this role are often as plain as pikestaffs – indeed, the plainer the better: Angela had a grey skin, a double chin, short grey greasy hair and wore belted navy blue around a waist almost larger than her hips, and her husband was never rude to her, or tried to make her unhappy.

13

The next day Angela called Joanna.

'How are you, darling?' she asked.

'Do you really want to know?' asked Joanna.

'Yes,' said Angela, settling in to listen. Angela had undertaken to see Joanna through her divorce: so much one woman will often do for another, although with luck the service may never have to be reciprocated. But you never know, you never know! The burden of guilt, indignation, upset, and general sense of injustice must be handed round, communally shouldered: it is too much for one person, one 'I', to bear. The 'you' must take a hand. At first the phone calls come at any time of day or night: the woman wronged, the 'I', has no idea of time, place or pertinence: then the notion of the otherness of the recipient, the sharer of distress, the *you* reasserts itself: the calls are at least prefaced by 'is the milk boiling over? the toast burning? is Hollywood on the other line? have you a minute?' and it's clear the healing process is under way. Joanna was by now far down the road to recovery: whole conversations could be held without mention of Carl. But of course Chernobyl and his face on the television screen that morning had stirred up what Angela saw as a good deal of muddy sediment: nasty little insects crawled again in and out of slime: they had only been playing dead: they were back again, spreading disease and discomfort.

'When I think how Carl has behaved to me!' said Joanna, and it was clear to Angela she had had quite a relapse. 'When I think how I wasted my life, simply threw it away! Why did my parents allow it? Carl May was a completely unsuitable match: it was unforgivable of them. They just wanted me out of the house. I was born to have children, but no, Carl May wouldn't have that: the day before we were married he told me he didn't want

61

any. What could I do? Everything arranged: all the guests: the presents: I had to agree. You know what he's like. I was so young I thought it didn't matter. Infatuated! His unhappiness had to be loaded on to me; that was what it was. He denied life, made me deny it too. He turned me into some sort of snow queen and when I made just one small attempt to thaw myself out he used it as an excuse to throw me out of his life – he set it all up, I swear he did. He was just waiting for the opportunity to be rid of me.'

'Yes, but Joanna –' said Angela, cautiously.

'I'm sorry, am I boring you? You do agree, don't you? I am right?'

'Carl may look at it a little differently. Carl came into his art gallery one day and found you and that Egyptologist together.'

'For heaven's sake, Angela, I was over fifty.'

'What has that got to do with it?' Angela sounded really interested: she really wanted to know.

'Obviously I was desperate and Carl should have understood that.'

'But Joanna, I'm over fifty and I'm not desperate.'

'But you're happily married!' Joanna's normally quiet voice was suddenly quite loud.

'And now you're not married at all,' replied Angela.

Joanna was silent. She sniffed a little.

'I don't know what's the matter with me today. Why did Carl choose to come into the gallery at that particular time? He never went in, normally. Besides, I thought he was away: he usually was.'

'Perhaps he suspected something. Perhaps you seemed unusually happy.'

'Oh, I was. Isaac was so much the opposite of Carl. But he had to put paid to that, didn't he? And then that accident – if accident it was.'

'Of course it was, Joanna.' Though nobody believed that for one minute – Isaac, crossing the road outside the Eton Square house, in too much of a hurry, knocked down and killed by Philip the chauffeur, reversing into the garage. Oh yes!

'Carl was so hard and cold about it all: not an ounce of sympathy for me.'

'Could you expect it?'

'Yes I could! We'd been married for thirty years and it was always me looking after him, worrying about him, listening to tales of his dreadful childhood; didn't I deserve anything in return? We were supposed to love each other.'

'I think that's what Carl believed, Joanna. And then you went and had an affair with another man; not even someone more important, or younger, or richer than him, but some penniless librarian with straggly hair. What an insult! Of course he reacted. I know you think he over-reacted, but men are like that, especially men like Carl, who are used to having their own way.'

'Whose side are you on, Angela?'

'Yours, Joanna, you know I am. But Carl did have a point of view.'

'Well, I don't see it. I suppose you're busy.'

'I am a bit.'

'Your children are about to visit you, I suppose.'

'Yes.'

'And the grandchildren?'

'Yes.'

'You see, you have everything and I have nothing.'

'Joanna,' said Angela briskly, 'you have a house worth two million pounds –'

'It's falling down, and Carl won't pay a penny for repairs.'

'You have a butler –'

'He's gay. Carl will only let me have gay servants. I'm surprised he doesn't have them castrated as well, just to be on the safe side.'

'And a gardener who shares your bed. Perhaps Carl is right. You are simply not to be trusted.'

'How do you know about Oliver?' asked Joanna, after a short silence.

'It's obvious.'

'Don't tell Carl,' said Joanna, 'or he'll kill me.'

'Or the young man, judging from past form,' said Angela, quite bleakly, and quite seriously.

'I'd thought of that,' said Joanna.

'And you let him take the risk?'

'If I do,' said Joanna, 'so can he. It's worth it. I don't care any more. I don't mind being dead. What have I got to live for? Next year's crocuses?'

Angela said, 'All I can say is, Joanna, keep your young man out of the garden for the time being. His parts might begin to glow in the dark, and you wouldn't like that. Gerald seems to think we're getting quite a lot of radioactivity over here.'

'How lucky you are,' was all Joanna said, 'to have Gerald.'

14

Angela is a good friend. She is a Doctor of European History, but she pretends to be less than Gerald in all matters because thus she preserves the domestic and marital peace, and she reckons those are of all things the most important to preserve, above dignity, truth and honour, and who is to say she is not right? She is married and I am not, and I am sufficiently a child of my generation to believe a woman who has neither husband nor children is scarcely a woman at all.

I, who revealed the truth one day, and lost everything, including dignity and honour, should be the last to suggest that she is wrong. Isaac of course lost more in a similar revelation; that is to say his life. But he had often told me he'd die for me if he had to. Fate listened, that was all: happened to be passing by, as he spoke, with its ear-muffs off. Alas, by dying, Isaac did me no good. He stepped without looking into the path of a reversing car just outside the May Gallery. There were no witnesses, and it was known that Isaac had left the gallery early with a migraine, and a man who has a migraine does not look carefully where he is going, so who was to doubt the driver's word – he being chauffeur to Carl May, and with a clean driving licence, and doing nothing more sinister at the time than backing into his own garage, albeit across the public pavement? And Isaac King had no family to dig away at the matter, to fling up dirt and dust until some nasty scandal was revealed, some bleached bone of unfleshed-out truth discovered.

Isaac was one of those rare and valuable people who are, or appear to be, totally innocent in their life's work: who, by pursuing their own interests, do no apparent harm to anyone.

An academic, an antiquarian, an Egyptologist, his imagination fired by Rider Haggard's Cleopatra when he was a boy, his fervour fanned in various university departments; and then, discovering the civilization of Ancient Egypt to be a culture of the wholly benign, the unmalicious, thereafter lived by sifting the desert sands for scraps and shards yet undetected, nodding politicly at museum curators, with impossible care and patience deciphering the all but indecipherable, piecing together fragments, writing up, collating, publishing papers only a handful of people anywhere in the world would understand. He wanted to bring the past to life. A benign and beautiful past, like no other.

'Is there any money in it, this Egyptology of yours?' asked Carl, at the interview. He was looking for a curator first and a collection second. He had a gallery: he wanted to put something in it: he wanted to be known as a cultured man. An enviable opportunity for the right person. I was there at the interview. I was to be involved. I was to be cultured too. I rather fancied Meissen, but Egyptology turned up.

Isaac smiled at Carl's question. He had a kindly but melancholy air. His smile was somehow forgiving. I understood then for the first time that Carl needed to be forgiven: the understanding cracked wide my wifely love and admiration, and through the crack all kinds of emotions and sensations came rushing unannounced.

'Twelve chairs of Egyptology in all the world?' Isaac King enquired. 'Six hundred devotees at most, turning up to the occasional conference, to compare notions and theories? Of course there's no money in it.'

And Carl, I knew, was both impressed and horrified by such selfless dedication. And as for me, I thought this Isaac King was just wonderful. A good man. So kindly was this man, so generous, so trusting, that coming across the embalmed mummy of a newborn baby, and discovering no body inside, but only sawdust, he concluded not that the embalming priests had cheated the grieving parents but, being too enthusiastic with their fluids, had disintegrated the body by accident, and decided to go ahead with the funeral without telling the parents for fear of upsetting them.

Carl May would never have reached such a conclusion. Nor would my father. Nor indeed did I. But I loved Isaac for believing the best, and not the worst. We were in each other's company from time to time, in that musty vaulted room, the May Gallery, and the pleasures of ideas exchanged became the pleasure of emotion shared, and eventually touch as well. We were as close as we could get.

Carl had me locked in my room so I couldn't go to Isaac's funeral. It would not perhaps have been proper: in giving evidence at the inquest it was I who told the world Isaac had complained of a migraine. He had complained of no such thing – merely that I would not leave Carl there and then, discovered in flagrante delicto as we were, and go off and live with him in his bedsitting room in Ealing, which smelled of gas fire and tooth powder, for all his goodness and generosity. But I was guilty and afraid. I had betrayed Carl and been discovered. Yet I still hoped for Carl's forgiveness. Indeed, I expected it. I had made my demonstration of discontent: now I wanted things to be as before. But how could they be?

And so I moaned and groaned about the unfairness of it all to Angela, while trying not to acknowledge that, of the two of us, Isaac had had by far the worst deal. And she, to her credit, kept pointing it out, waiting for the day when I would have ears to hear. How *good* she is. This practising of so prudent a doctrine, of course, that of female subservience, does have some drawbacks. It renders Angela catty in her conversation: occasionally, one feels, out of sheer desperation, giddy in her behaviour and desperate in her undertakings. The unplucked whiskers on her chin, the straggly hair and wrinkled stockings, suggest some kind of revenge upon the world in general and on her husband in particular. But Gerald, dear Gerald, the amiable fool, seems not to notice, or care: they enfold each other happily enough at night, she tells me, her bulges against his paunch; her feet, untreated bunions and all, tangling with his softer, whiter, smoother ones. Gerald is a civil servant, he drives a car, his shoes are softest leather – his feet are in good shape. I saw his feet once, when the couple kindly asked me, the sorry divorcée, out to the local lido one weekend, to share with them the pleasures of an unexpectedly warm summer day: on littered grass crowded with suburban folk and children eating hot-dogs. Gerald and Angela are not smart at all: Carl couldn't abide them: once I too looked down on them; now I am grateful for them.

(Now Angela knows I am not so alone, of course; that Oliver leaves his nettle-pulling and rose pruning to slip into my bed, I may not get asked to the lido again. Pity may give way to envy – or so I pride myself.)

Something is going to happen. I can feel it. It is so quiet and orderly here in the house, it is unnatural. It is the lull before the storm. Even Oliver feels it. He makes love silently, as if afraid of disturbing someone, something. I am in the habit of being quiet in any case: Carl required very little sexual response from me, and seldom got it. Well, that suited me. Sex between us was a kind of formal dance: a ritual performed in the presence of my beauty, his power: confirmation that the one could be owned by the other. There was little sweaty enjoyment here, little ecstasy of the flesh – but it had its compulsion; like any rewarding habit it had become necessary – as going to church on Sunday might be for a religious-minded person. Or so it had seemed to me. Perhaps I was wrong? Perhaps it was central to his very existence – in which case I had indeed provoked him. How could I, when it came to it, feel on Carl's behalf, any more than I could think for him? I should have allowed him, even after thirty years or so of marriage, some independence of emotion.

Oliver has dirt under his nails, both finger and toe: his broad working hands assist me in altogether new pleasures: I daresay I should be too old for these responses but I find I am not. Does he love me? I don't know. Why should he? I think he likes the thought of screwing the rich older woman who employs him: kicking off his muddy boots at the door and walking barefoot (he seldom wears socks, finding them constricting) along thick

68

carpets on his way to my room. I don't think he laughs at me or reports on me to his friends.

I am fairly sure Oliver likes me. Carl never liked me. But then I didn't like him. I loved him. I admired him and was awed by him: Lord of the dark domains, as he was, and myself the Ice Queen, having dominion over many secret things.

A woman may go out to work, earn her independence, spurn suitors, decline marriage, and be in every way her own mistress. But she will never wake in the morning with this particular gratification – she will never open her eyes to tranquillity and luxury, as I so often did, with the agreeable thought, 'Good Lord! Little me! All this, and just because I look the way I do, am the person I was born.' Enough for this woman just to *be*; not like the other to be forever proving, convincing, striving, placating, buying the comforts and respect of the world. Let someone else, for this fortunate, idle woman, do all that: let he who loves her, maintain her.

Of course it may all come to an abrupt end: the husband's, the lover's, favour may suddenly and dramatically be withdrawn. All the same, the flavour of that confidence remains: it is not forgotten . . . See how I crook my finger and young Oliver comes to my bed. The Ice Queen may be deposed, but she still knows who she is, and so does her subject. She who rules with the divine right of the old-fashioned female, she-who-must-be-obeyed, whose bag must be fetched, lawn mowed, glass kept filled. Someone has to do it.

I like Oliver. I like him for his implausibility, his trust in the future. He means to be a rock singer. He is getting it together. He has been doing this since he left college ten years ago. He lives by odd jobs; he can dry-stone-wall, dig ditches, lop trees, wire houses, clear blocked drains; he can paper and plaster, tell a comfrey from a borage leaf – the kind of things snow queens are not so hot at. Oliver looks like a young Elvis Presley and like him might presently run to fat. When things don't turn out right – the drummer loses his drums (how can anyone *lose* drums; they are so plentiful and bulky: still it's done) so the one

gig of the year can't be set up – his girlfriend sends the engage-
ment ring (such a *little* diamond!) back. She lives in Scotland:
he only sees her at Christmas and Easter: of course she sends it
back! Oliver simply smokes a joint or two, and ceases to worry.
I join him. We pass the magic weed from hand to hand, enjoying
– as no doubt they will presently say in the ads – a special
languid intimacy. I find simple things move me. When Oliver
rolls a joint for us both, unwraps a boiled sweet for me, my
heart turns over. Such kindness! I am unused to it. Carl would
mix me a gin and tonic before our dinner guests arrived and
hand it to me, smiling with his lips, but barking in his heart, a
high-pitched non-stop frantic bark: the gesture did not really
register as love, or kindness. Poor Carl. Poor me.

I try to forgive Carl: try not to burden my friends with
these sudden spasms of anger, misery and resentment. It is my
experience that a quiet mind is gained only by forgiveness: when
you cease to see the other as enemy, as merely yourself in another
guise, see the 'you' as perceived by the other, forget the notion
of 'I' – *I* shiver, *I* suffer, *I* bleed; *I* hate, *my* head will burst with
my resentments; *you* whom *I* hate for not acknowledging this *I*
– then peace descends. Our lives are our own again.

Until the next storm bursts.

15

Those who fear a storm breaking have it in their hearts to whip one up. So Joanna did, forthwith. She too had seen the press photograph of her own front door (or so she regarded it) closing upon the high heel of young Bethany, but shut her conscious mind to its significance, putting aside the yellow press with conventional murmurings of 'rubbish' and taking up *The Times*, who contented themselves with a ten-year-old library shot of her ex-husband at the opening of the May Gallery, the bearded face of Isaac in the background, just discernible. These things combined – the conscious, the barely conscious, the unconscious – to send winds both hot and cold, feverish and chill, through her mind to brew up a veritable hurricane. Well might she fear the lull before the storm.

Joanna paced her marble floor and then went out to find Oliver pruning and digging out rhododendron bushes.

'I mean to sell this house,' she said. 'I hate it.' The King's House stood on the edge of the Thames, near Maidenhead. The river divided around it, to form an island.

'It's a very special house,' he said.

'Oh yes,' she said, 'I know. Some king kept it for his mistresses. Now it does for discarded wives.'

'George the Third,' he said, 'had it renovated for Priscilla Evans. Part of the kitchens dates back to the sixteenth century.'

'Oh, you would know,' she said.

'Yes I would,' he said, 'because I am interested in what goes on around me, not just what happens in my head.'

'Does that make you better than me?'

'No. Just different.'

71

Clip, clip went the secateurs, firmly and sharply. He took care not to bruise the wood he cut. She found his concern for the bush insulting.

'I think it's a very vulgar house,' she said, 'but you wouldn't understand that. You think because it is old that justifies everything.'

It was true that the house was an uneasy mixture of the cosy and the elegant: much balconied, pink-washed outside, a nook-and-cranny effect inside, suggestive of weighty lovers chirruping at one another, peeking round corners. Successive purchasers had added marble floors and gold taps, and green watered-silk ruffled curtains of such expense Joanna had been reluctant to take them down, though only ever truly at home with crimson velvet curtains, round shiny mahogany tables and sideboards, patterned carpets and Chinese vases.

Oliver put down the secateurs and carefully brushed each small wound with bitumen paint.

'All that trouble for a bush,' she said. 'I mean to put this house on the market, I'm not joking.'

'I don't think you'd be wise,' he said. 'It would be a lot of trouble for nothing. If you're not happy here where would you be happy?'

'Somewhere far far away,' she said, 'and don't tell me wherever I go I'd have to take myself with me or I'll scream.'

He laughed, and took up the spade and began to drive it into the stony ground beneath the largest of the bushes. His arms were bare; the muscles moved beneath brown skin.

'I'm sorry about this,' he said.

'About what?'

'I was talking to the bush,' he said. 'I'm digging it up. I'm apologizing.'

She fretted and tapped her foot.

'Why are you digging it up anyway?' she asked.

'Because it's old and keeping out the light from the others,' he said, 'and because purple rhododendrons very easily become a pest.'

'Well anyway,' she said, 'I'm going down to the estate agents now.'

72

'Look,' he said, 'this is a perfectly good house with a fine garden which had been allowed to go to rack and ruin and I'm just about getting it into shape again. I like it here very much.'

'Well, I'm bored and lonely here,' she said, 'and since I pay, what I say counts.'

He raised his eyebrows.

'You're just in a bad mood,' he said.

'Of course I am,' she said, scornfully. 'And I'll do what I want, when I want, with my own house, my own garden.'

'Joanna,' he said, 'the garden can't be yours. Gardens are like children, they belong to whoever takes care of them.'

'Then stay round here and weed it for some other employer,' she said. 'Because it won't be me.'

'You need me, Joanna,' he said, and put down his spade. 'You have a very jealous nature. You're even jealous of rhododen-drons. Why don't you help me dig them up? You'd feel much better.'

She looked at her long idle nails, her well-kept hands: she looked at his grimy and hardworking ones, no longer gardening, and felt better . . .

'It isn't in my nature,' she said, 'and besides, the air is full of radiation. Angela says it isn't wise to be out.'

'Perhaps I'd better come in then,' he said, 'or perhaps you'd better come under the bushes.'

And he would have pulled her under them there and then, and she would not have objected, or minded sharp stones against her back, her front, or twigs in her hair, or dirtying her purple dress, only the postman chose to come up the path at that moment, with a packet from the Maverick Enquiry Agency, which she could not ignore.

She left Oliver digging in the drifting outfall from Chernobyl and went inside, to read the report.

Fifteen minutes later she came out and said, 'I'm going to see Carl right now.'

'Why?' he asked.

'Because it's all too much to be endured,' she said.

'Don't go,' he said, and had she been listening, had she really

73

cared about him, she would have heard that tone in his voice which is used by bit-part film actors who know that a sudden fatal blow is about to fall, in the next few frames, and try not to show it. But she wasn't listening; she didn't care; she was going to see Carl.

16

'Yet each man kills the thing he loves,' murmured Carl May, as he paced his elegant office in the tower block in Reading which was the hub of Britnuc's empire. The building had been designed to dominate the city skyscape, and so it had, but not for long. No sooner had the foundations settled, no sooner the first window cleaner toppled to his death – always the mark of a properly finished office building – than all around arose the thrusting towers of usurping empires – leaner, taller, glassier – but doomed to crumble and collapse, built on the hot and shifting sands of finance, not the rock of industry, the cold power of the atom. Carl May was neither shaken nor dismayed, though the arch of sky he loved was now the merest tent of blue, so high and near the false towers crowded. He knew they would not last.

'What is that you said, my dear?' enquired Bethany, looking up from her VDU, upon which she played computer games. He'd had the contraption carried up from a lower floor. In this calm and spacious room all was grey and pink and empty surfaces: uncluttered: all that was needed here was mind: no tools of trade, no paper, pens, or telephones: he was too grand for that. But Bethany must have her toys.

'I was quoting,' he said, 'from *The Ballad of Reading Gaol.*' It was Carl May's joke. His empire, his prison! Oscar Wilde, once imprisoned for imprudence in Reading Gaol – still there, that gaunt grey building, still used, not a quarter of a mile away from where Carl May now had his throne – had through that imprisonment received his immortality.

'Do you think,' asked Carl May of Bethany, 'anyone would have taken any notice of Oscar Wilde if he hadn't gone to prison?'

But how was Bethany to answer a thing like that? She shrugged, and went on playing. He sighed. Carl May was restless. In the outer offices phones rang and minions ran; press officers dealt with queries concerning outfall and infall, becquerels and watertables, cladding and coolants, leukaemia and bone cancer, prevailing winds and drifting particles. Head Office personnel took calls from Britnucs A and D where staff threatened action over the recent tightening of various safety regulations, and from B and C where there was some anxiety that the tightening had not been sufficiently extreme. PR withdrew distribution to better facilitate the instant re-editing of an entire series of linked film for internal, external and educational purposes: no one could say Britnuc was not on its toes since Chernobyl went up; and the External Services division within the day had liaised with Concrete Casings – of which Carl May was also a director – to tender to the Soviet Union so many tonnes of special-grade radiation-resistant (though so far untested in the field) concrete for immediate shipment to Kiev.

Carl, confident in the efficiency and dedication of his staff, reserved his energies for the highest level – that is to say ministerial dealings; but the Government was, on the whole, wisely quiet, until such time as ignorance, panic and bad judgement in the lower levels were either cured, or covered up.

One female journalist did get through to Carl May that day by impersonating the Prime Minister's voice, but that was the only entertainment in an otherwise boring morning for Carl May. Those who have perfected the art of delegation tend to suffer, in emergencies, from too much peace.

In Carl May's childhood kennel, there had been a lot to do. Not only had he soothed the savage heart of Harry the bull-terrier but trained him to fetch him scraps of newsprint from the streets around: Carl May himself, being chained by a collar, was in no position to do so. Those were the worst days. But they had not been boring.

'I never saw a man who looked
  With such a wistful eye
  Upon that little tent of blue
  Which prisoners call the sky'

said Carl May to Bethany, but her hand was upon the control
stick, her eyes upon the screen, and she seemed not to hear. In
theory she worked upon a special personal project of his, an
Open Day for Britnuc two years hence, thus avoiding bad feeling
amongst his other secretarial staff; it was an arrangement which
he could safely cancel nearer the time. He liked to have her close.
He realized he had been lonely, and resented his ex-wife Joanna
for having by her behaviour rendered him thus, so sadly and for
so long. With what great effort had he, Carl May, brought
himself to trust a cruel world, and how she had destroyed that
trust, completing what his mother had begun.

He wondered, as he sometimes did, whether to trace the clones
of Joanna May, and see how they had turned out, and whether
one of them might not do instead of Joanna, but he could see
the folly of it. The capacity for infidelity, Carl May suspected,
ran in the genes; it could not be in the rearing – for surely Joanna
had had a calm, tranquil and orderly rearing; she had seemed
neither too fond of her father nor too antagonistic to her mother,
and yet she had succumbed – and all he would do was set himself
up again for the same shock and sorrow. Joanna at half her age
would still be Joanna.

Bethany, thought Carl May; now Bethany was a different
matter. She knew where her bread and butter lay. She had been
bought. She acknowledged the transaction. He had taken, as it
were, an option out on Bethany, body and soul. When it ran
out, he would either renew on his terms, if he so chose, or let it
lapse, and she would be free to go. He felt well disposed towards
her. She gave him pleasure. He told her things he never told
anyone. It would not last.

He did not want it to last. He felt humiliated as well as
pleased, lessened as much as augmented. She was less than him
in everything but youth.

'It is sweet to dance to violins,
When love and life are fair,
To dance to flutes, to dance to lutes,
Is delicate and rare:
But it is not sweet with nimble feet
To dance upon the air –'

said Carl May aloud.

Bethany hummed a little song as she worked upon her game: little
trills and tweets rose round her, as if flocks of tiny birds flowed
from her machine: her red hair fell enchantingly upon her face.

'Do you understand that?' asked Carl May.

'Understand what?' she asked. Carl May felt a stab of displeasure: it cut between his ribs like a knife.

'To dance upon the air is to hang,' he said. 'Love is a hanging
offence.'

'Why's that?' she said, not caring.

'Because each man kills the thing he loves,' he said, 'which
was where we began.'

'You didn't kill Joanna,' said Bethany, 'only her boyfriend,
so what are you going on about?' On her screen, in search of
paradise, she dodged monsters and beheaded and delimbed her
enemies with a sword which flailed every time she pressed the
space key.

Carl May thought if he had Bethany cloned, he could perhaps
undo the effects of her upbringing. If he got Holly to remove
one of Bethany's eggs, fertilized it *in vitro* with any old semen,
removed the resultant nuclei and reinserted the nuclei of any
one of Bethany's DNA-bearing cells (which the new dehydrating
technique had made just about possible), and then had the egg
implanted in a womb as stable and orderly as that of Joanna's
mother – and such wombs could be found, now as then; their
owners crying out for implantation – why then Carl May might
create a perfect woman, one who looked, listened, understood
and was faithful. If he reimplanted the egg in Bethany herself –
but no, that would be hopeless; she was spoiled, sullied, somehow she would reinfect herself.

'Shoo fly,' murmured Bethany. 'Shoo fly, don't bother me,'

78

and ping, ping, wimble, doodle, cheep cheep, splat went the little fluttering doves and ravens, the electronic sounds of victory and defeat – he'd made her turn the volume right down but still the small inanities, the false excitements, trembled and hovered in the air, insistent. He decided the cloning of Bethany would be more trouble than it was worth: it would require more time and energy than he had available. She made him feel tired, and that was the truth of it. Old King David's maidservant may have warmed his bed but she sure as hell carried him off quicker. He would be too old by the time Bethany was reissued, as it were, to get the benefit of it.

Now, if he had himself cloned, as he'd threatened Bethany – then the two younger versions of themselves could indeed pair off. But what use would that be to Carl May? Another body would feel the pleasure: another mind register it. Odd how the notion kept reasserting itself – that what one clone knew, would be known by all: what one felt, the others would feel; that to make clones was to create automatons, men without souls – soldiers, servants, deprived of will, decision. How could it be so? Did the common misconception suggest that the soul, what-ever that was, would be split, divided out fairly amongst the repetitions – as if nature and God were indeed in some kind of partnership? For every new exercise in human diversity – a quarter of a million of them every day – God would dole out only one soul? They were in short supply? Nonsense! He wanted to talk to Joanna about it. Joanna the faithless, the betrayer: Joanna who mocked him, whispered about him behind his back, trapped and tortured him. Joanna Eve.

'Shoo fly,' murmured Bethany. 'Shoo fly, don't bother me!'
'What are you singing?' he asked.
'Just something that goes through my head,' she said.
'What's that?' he asked.
'It has no words,' said Bethany, but she lied. The words were clear in her head. If you went on from 'Shoo fly, don't bother me, For I belong to somebody,' you got to:

For an old man he is old,
And an old man he is grey,

But a young man's heart is full of love,
  Get away, old man, get away.

Bethany stopped singing. She felt sad, to be so young and yet so old, twenty-four going on forty-two.

17

The clones of Joanna May would have been faithful if they could, but fate was against them. Like their master copy, Jane, Julie, Gina and Alice, for good or bad, were of a nature which preferred to have the itch of desire soothed, settled and out of the way rather than seeing in its gratification a source of energy and renewal. Here comes sex, they said in their hearts, here comes trouble! But trouble came. There was no stopping it, for them or anyone.

———◦◦———

Of the four, Jane Jarvis made the best and closest approach to monogamy. Her chosen parents, Madge and Jeremy, were academics – chosen by Dr Holly of the Bulstrode Clinic in conjunction with Carl May, of course, rather than herself, but when did any infant have the choice of its environment? No, the child is landed with what it gets, albeit sharing with its natural parents a characteristic or so – his brown eyes and her crooked little finger and a tendency to sniff, not to mention the bad temper of a maternal great-grandmother, the musical ability of a paternal great-uncle – which may or may not make the family placing easier when the baby erupts into it. But little Jane, long awaited, painfully implanted, was eagerly received into the world by parents who knew she was nothing to do with them, and didn't care, and never said: she was cherished, taught, instructed, cosseted, pressured and expected to pass exams, which she obligingly did. At sixteen she appointed – or so her manner suggested – an unkempt and unsuitable lad as her permanent boyfriend, much to his surprise and gratification and her parents' initial dismay. While other girls moaned, giggled, sighed, heaved, chopped, changed, got pregnant, gang-banged,

81

gossiped and groped themselves out of any hope of further education, pretty little Jane Jarvis sat studying, her faithful and besotted Tom beside her, making coffee and replenishing pens and paper as required.

When she was seventeen, her quasi-father Jeremy the economist, the most steady and rational of monetarists, owl-eyed, unimpassioned, kindly and distant, startled his family and the campus by making one of his junior lecturers pregnant. He seemed sorrowful that the event had caused distress and concern; he announced the news at breakfast the day after Jane sat her English A-level and the day before her Sociology exam, thus greatly compounding his offence. 'Surely it could have waited,' wept Madge the Eng. Lit. structuralist. 'Are you trying to destroy her as well as me?' Jeremy seemed puzzled: he said he was going with Laura to the ante-natal clinic so he would be late home for tea. Laura had been a frequent visitor to the house and had coached Jane in Economics, since Jane somehow cut off when offered instruction by her father.

Jane got a B in English and A's in Economics and Sociology. The results arrived the day Laura gave birth to a boy. 'You see,' said Jane to Tom, 'adversity just makes me concentrate the more.' Oxford let her in: she'd done the three A-levels in one year.

Madge wept and said to her husband at breakfast, the day the letter came from Oxford, 'I don't want you, I don't need you, go to her if that's what you want.'
'Look here –' he said.
'Go, go!' she screamed, so he went. Perhaps that was when Jane caught the row virus: her quasi-mother, rushing out of the room, beside herself, brushed one bare ageing arm against Jane's young one.

'It was their timing that was so awful,' Jane lamented to Tom later. When she went up to Oxford, leaving her mother alone in the big house, with its many bookshelves and bicycles and good prints, she found she was pregnant. Madge offered to have

82

the baby; she needed something, anything, and Jane almost consented, but in the end she couldn't, she didn't, she had her future to think about. She had a termination at twelve weeks: a boy. A couple of years later Jeremy returned home: so that was just as well. It had been a kind of convulsion in all their lives, that was all. Everything smoothed out again. Laura married someone her own age and went to Sweden with the child. Madge became Professor of American Studies. Jeremy just seemed somehow older, and more tired, as if he'd tried something terribly important, and had failed at the last hurdle.

At the degree ceremony – she got a First in Eng. Lit. – he kissed the back of her neck with dry tired lips and said, 'I'm proud of you. I wish you were mine,' and she did not understand that, or pursue it, as she would have had it been some puzzling line in *Beowulf* or *Sir Gawain*. Some things are safer thought about than others.

And she'd ditched Tom by then. She had to. He was off at Art College in London, making a mess of things, quarrelling with his tutor, refusing to train for a career in advertising, too proud for this, too good for that, scratched and sore about the abortion, no matter that he understood the necessity, approved in theory, knew her body was her own, and so forth, knew there was lots of time for both of them – it had just been *that* baby, at *that* time – but he would keep reminding her, would keep upsetting her, and she needed a boyfriend on the spot, to save trouble and tantrums all around. Tom had to go.

Men pursued her, waylaid her, entreated her favours; yet when and if she looked in a mirror she could see only an ordinary, expected face, nothing special. Madge had never noticed how she looked, only what went on in her head. No one at home had told her she was pretty: Jeremy had seemed to notice her exam results more than herself, though responsive enough, it had seemed, to Laura. It was all a bother; too much to think about. She took up with a young man, a certain Stephen, a mathematician, good-looking, undemanding, as quiet and steady as Tom was noisy and wayward.

'You faithless bitch,' yelled Tom down the phone. 'You're never *here*,' she moaned, 'and when you are you're horrid.' 'I have to get my degree,' he shrieked, 'how can I be there?' 'I don't see why you can't be here,' she murmured. 'What do artists need with degrees?' 'You're cold, manipulative, selfish,' he said. 'You want to own me, control me. You treat me halfway between a little boy and a stud.' 'Then you're well rid of me,' she said. And he said, 'It's education has done this to you. It's changed you. Everything's in your head: there's nothing left in your heart. You don't know how to be natural any more: last time I was with you, you actually poured my coffee into a dirty mug. You've even forgotten how to wash up.'

'Good,' she said, and put the phone down. She stayed with Stephen for six years but wouldn't marry him, as he had hoped and expected, because of the problem of her needing to be in London – she had a good first job as a reader for MGM – and him having to begin his life as a chartered accountant in Newcastle, which was the only place he could get a job, so, coolly, she did without him. Well, fate was against her. If he'd been offered a job in London she would have stayed with him.

Madge and Jeremy were disappointed. When it came to it, it seemed they wanted her to be settled and ordinary, not independent and special. So much of it had been all talk.

And then Tom came back into her life, as they say in the magazines and, although it hardly seemed what she wanted, it was familiar, and would do. He filled her bed and sat opposite her in restaurants and they shared the bill, but he always had the feeling, did Tom, that she was looking over his naked shoulder – him on top of her, no variations considered – to see who was there, who had come to the party more important, more interesting, than he. And she would croon and stroke her little grey cat, sadly, even directly after they'd made love, as if it was his fault, as if he were the gatekeeper to some other, more richly sensuous world than this, but would not let her in. When actually it was the other way round.

———•◦•———

Julie Rainer's chosen parents were not academics and did not believe in girls taking examinations: on the contrary: they had a feeling, vague though it was, that too much thinking made girls undomesticated and argumentative. If Julie was seen with a book, her mother Katie would say, 'Don't mope about reading: why don't you go for a nice walk?' or 'Look, there's some washing-up to do,' and Julie would obligingly put the book away. Her father, Harold, worked in Sheffield for a firm of stockbrokers: Kate did voluntary work around and about: they lived in a pleasant house with a large garden.

Harold and Katie had tried to have children for eight years, unsuccessfully, before they agreed on the new and risky method suggested by Dr Holly, and Katie had the little female foetus implanted: but being pregnant, swelling up, did not bring the ease she'd hoped for, the sense of fulfilment she'd been promised. The fact that the baby was so close did not, when it came to it, make it feel less of a little foreigner, on the contrary: and Harold would not be present at the birth, which was just beginning to be fashionable, and in the end she'd have preferred to have adopted a baby in the usual way, actually *seeing* what she was going to have to live with for years and years, making much the same kind of choice as she had when she married Harry. 'Like that, want it.' Not a bad way, when it came to it. She was happy enough with Harry: they'd wanted a baby badly, so badly, because they wanted it, couldn't have it.

Nothing wrong with little Julie, on the contrary: the brightest, prettiest, easiest little thing, Harry's pet, too much Harry's pet at first, perhaps that was the trouble, always sitting on his knee, him fondling perhaps overmuch, but how could one say a thing like that, except the baby wasn't Harry's flesh and blood, was it, and he knew it. Dr Holly might have been right when he suggested Katie didn't tell Harry about the implantation, simply went home and said, 'We're pregnant! A miracle!' but she hadn't taken Dr Holly's advice though, had she? Then the miracle did happen; when Julie was five (and playing Mary in the school Nativity play, of course) Katie did become pregnant, in the ordinary marital way, with a boy, a son, a firstborn no matter what Harry said, a wonderfully easy, natural birth, and Harry was there to hold her hand, and they called him Adam, and after that, really, though she was always perfectly kind to Julie, of course, that went without question, Adam was her real child, her only child, and when Julie, by then trained as a secretary and working in a local estate agent's office, came home one day and said, 'Mummy, I've met this wonderful man, Alec: he's my boss, actually: I want to marry him,' Katie said, 'Of course, darling, if you really and truly love him' and Julie said, 'I love him with all my heart and soul,' and who knew enough about her to disbelieve her, and Harry, who was having a secret affair with his own secretary, a girl Julie's age, a serious affair, true love, and wondering whether he had the courage to leave Kate, and if he did would Julie and Adam ever forgive him, said, 'Her life, her choice: pity about his wall-eye, but I suppose it makes the one that works the more acute, and the fellow's got a good business future, that's the main thing. When the chips are down it's income that counts.'

And Julie married Alec, dressed appropriately in virginal white. (Neither believed in sex-before-marriage:
Julie: '*What would Daddy think of me? He'd die.*'
Alec: '*I think marriage should be a sacrament: should really mean something.*')

The wedding took place in the village church, and it was written up in the *Daily Telegraph*, and their first house was on an executive estate. And after Alec had had his wall-eye fixed, thanks to new laser surgical techniques, there was no stopping him: they moved to bigger and grander estates, and he was away most of the time, developing holiday resorts, flying the world Club Class British Airways with his computer on his knee: and she never worried about other women: Alec really wasn't interested, she knew that and she didn't think she was or why would she have married him? She would have loved children but Alec couldn't have them: and her father had left her mother and gone off with his secretary which had thoroughly upset Julie, but she had the cats and the dogs and the fish, and loved them, especially her little grey cat; she could run her hand over its soft fur and watch the light catch the grey and turn it into a hundred different changing shades and now suddenly she found herself in love with the vet, or rather he was in love with her, and it hadn't been sex, really, just closeness – but who in the world was there to talk to about these things? Not Alec. For Alec the past was over. Like his wall-eye, better not remembered.

And how could you talk to someone who wasn't there, but flying about the skies all the time? How could you talk to your husband about your lover?

There was no talking to her mother. Her mother had gone downhill since her father left. She ranted and raved and said odd things, which hurt. Julie thought she drank too much. 'You're no flesh of mine,' she'd say to Julie, and in the same breath complain that Harry hadn't been there at Julie's birth, and Julie had bitten her on the way out: she'd been born with one tooth already cut. So how could she talk to a mother who wanted only to hurt and confuse her? And how could she not go to bed with the vet, because it was bed first and talking after, with him. She'd have been faithful if she could, but fate was against her. If she'd had friends, it might not have happened. She could have talked to them. But friends where she lived came in couples, talked in couples; you could go out to dinner and talk non-stop and say nothing: and disloyalty over morning coffee was not allowed: and besides, the others had children, and she did not. She was an outsider, alone and lonely. Of course she went to bed with the vet. But she didn't want to. She would rather have been happily married.

———•••———

And Gina? Ah well, Gina. Gina lifted her skirt to show the boys her knickers when she was nine, and took off her knickers to show them more when she was ten, and at twelve was deflowered in the back seat of a cinema, and at thirteen was hitchhiking down the A1 for the fun of it, and at fourteen was declared beyond parental control, and by sixteen was back home again and quite reformed and at eighteen was pregnant and married to Cliff, a would-be pop singer, and garage mechanic, and by twenty-eight had three children by two different fathers, but she'd still have been monogamous if she could. She'd had sexual encounters with some thirty men by the time she was married, fate being against her, and had felt altogether happy and at ease for perhaps ninety minutes of her life till then: the minutes in which she exercised proper sexual power over men, became the magnet to which they were drawn which could never fail; the minutes, however brief, just before actual penetration. From then on the man's energies took over, she was neither here nor there, and it was no fun: sometimes, depending on circumstance, it was even horrific. The more of them, the less of her. She felt it.

Perhaps the seven-day-old Joanna-foetus that was to become Gina lacked some vital energy, or, if you look at it another way, perhaps some segment of the double helix of the DNA which so strongly and happily composed Joanna, Jane, Julie and Alice had become fused and blurred in Gina. These things do happen, chance intervenes, being no respecter of the wishes and intentions of geneticists, let alone microbiologists. Gina was implanted in the womb of an impetuous young woman, by name Annette, who'd come south from Scotland to start her life afresh, and had been swept off her feet by an earnest and intellectual bookseller named Douglas with exotic tastes and a wen on his almost bald head.

They were married within the week. She was a good cook and a fine bookkeeper and he needed both. She worked in the shop, typed the bills, learned the book trade, charmed the customers – and then she wanted a baby. Douglas didn't. Later, later, he said, standing over her every morning to make sure she took her contraceptive pill. He didn't trust her and was right not to. 'I'll do it another way,' thought Annette, and went to visit Dr Holly at the Bulstrode Clinic, whose fame had spread throughout London in the late fifties as the maker or taker away of babies, depending on which you wanted. She told Dr Holly what she hadn't told Douglas – that to date she'd had one stillborn baby, Down's Syndrome, and four abortions. And Dr Holly said, since her husband's sperm was unavailable, and her eggs not reliable, he could give her a baby of her own without either. And under local anaesthetic, there and then, he implanted little Gina.

Dr Holly wasn't sure how long he could keep the processes of cell division going outside the womb; he said time was running out for this particular foetus; he could feel it. Carl May said he saw no reason for or evidence of any such deterioration, but Carl May, Dr Holly said, thus offending his benefactor, had a layman's view of the material world – that is to say he thought there had to be a reason for things to go wrong. Things just happened, as any scientist could affirm. You knew by the pricking of your thumbs. Had Dr Holly not been in such a hurry, he might well have rejected Annette as a suitable birth parent: as it was, he trusted to luck. There were more than enough wombs to choose from; he had little excuse; they thronged the waiting room of the Bulstrode Clinic, brought there by rumour. There were women who wanted babies, and couldn't have them, or had babies and didn't want them, women trying to save babies, women trying to lose babies, and most of them weeping or on the verge of weeping. Dr Holly felt, and Carl felt with him, that an evolutionary process which caused so much grief could surely be improved upon by man: genetic engineering would hardly add to the sum of human misery, so great a sum that was, and might just possibly make matters a good deal better. No doubt in time the techniques of artificial reproduction would be further advanced and manipulation of DNA itself made possible so that improved and disease-resistant human beings could in the end be produced. In the meantime, Holly and May did what they could; May providing money and inspiration and Dr Holly surgical deftness and experience. It was just he was perhaps, this time, in rather too much of a hurry.

So there Annette was, pregnant with a diminutive Joanna, who seemed less and less likely to reach her potential as the pregnancy proceeded. Annette's husband, discovering her pregnant, threw her out of the house, claiming the baby was not his. She told him the truth, which made matters worse. (He'd tried to sue Dr Holly but lawyers would not take on his case: he was excitable and it sounded like sheer fantasy to them, a tale told by a guilty wife. In the end he gave up.) Annette, distressed, drank too much, smoked too much, went home to Scotland, had the baby six weeks early, failed to love it, left it with her parents, who, the more they feared their granddaughter would go the same way as their daughter, brought this fate upon her.

'Mum,' Annette would say, at the beginning, over the phone from as far away as possible, 'she can't inherit anything from me, because she isn't anything to do with me. Her genes are different. I know what you're going to say next. "We don't let her wear jeans. She always wears a dress." Christ, I could almost feel sorry for her.' Then Annette drifted away altogether. Grandfather had a stroke, grandmother's vision was impaired. Grandmother drank too much, mostly sherry. There were no books in the house. Gina learned to read from the back of the cornflake packet and the fronts of buses. She had a weak bladder and wet her knickers a lot which made her unpopular at school – a graffitied, run-down place – with both teacher and pupils. She was classified as disturbed, she was unhappy with herself, unhappy at home, beaten by teachers for answering back, frequently locked in her bedroom by her grandmother as a punishment for 'being dirty', frequently climbed out of the bedroom window, and on one occasion was helped by a passing alcoholic; as a result of which, being observed, she was taken to the police station as being out of control and put in a children's home from which Annette reluctantly rescued her.

Annette who by now kept a junk stall on the Portobello Road and lived with a Rastafarian drug dealer.

'You're not mine,' she'd keep telling Gina, 'but no one deserves my mum and dad,' and Gina would look down her straight disdainful nose and lower the lids of her bright blue eyes, in the sexy way she'd lately acquired, and wonder where she'd come from, if not out of Annette, and ate another chocolate bar to keep her somehow rooted, tied to the earth. The world outside kept changing, without apparent cause or reason, out of her control. She had a weight problem. If she didn't keep herself heavy she'd fly off and be lost, like a piece of scrap paper. She went round with boiled sweets in her pocket, and boys knew by just looking at her she was anyone's, which these days she wasn't: her stepdad Bilbo belted her if she was, though Annette jumped up and down and told him he was a savage.

Gina liked Bilbo: he seemed to care what happened to her, and actually stir himself to do something about it, however painful. They ate good food, hot and rich with chillies; they watched a lot of TV; the cat had kittens: Gina begged and pleaded to keep the fluffy grey one for herself, and was allowed. Life was almost good. She did OK in school, too: caught up, quickly: would have passed exams and even gone to college (she wanted to be a doctor: how her mother laughed) except she met Cliff, got pregnant, wouldn't have the abortion Annette suggested – 'But it's murder, Mum' – and married him, and there was young Cliff, son of a Portobello repairer of clocks, who wanted to be a pop singer, obliged to be a garage mechanic the better to support her and baby Ben. And Cliff drank too much, though he went into car sales and ended up selling second-hand old Rolls-Royces, which you can buy for a couple of hundred in the trade and sell for a couple of thousand to fools, so they lived OK, except Cliff began hitting her, and she knew somewhere she deserved it, and she could no longer look down her nose so well, if only because it had been broken a couple of times. He was always sorry afterwards, and she was sorry for him and bound to him, and loved him in a kind of way; but she was never quite sure Sue was his, though she hoped so – it had been an accident, a one-night stand when she was really miserable, between a black eye and an apology, right at the beginning – and Cliff certainly had no idea, he would *really* have killed her, and in a way she was killing herself, she knew it, but how did you stop, once you had begun? But she would have been faithful, if she could. One life, one man. But fate was against her.

———◦◦———

And Alice? Alice was implanted in the womb of Honeybell Lee Morthampton, a mother of four boys so anxious to have a girl she would not take the chance of another boy.

'Let's see,' said Dr Holly, 'we've only had frustrated wombs to date, eager and waiting. If we can make this one stick in an elderly multigravida with a history of rejecting females, we've really got it right.'

'I don't see,' said Carl May, 'why the womb history should make any difference; if hormone levels are sound, how can it? It's like believing that a pedigree bitch, once it's had pups by a mongrel, never breeds true again.'

'But it doesn't,' said Dr Holly. 'I have one and I know. The fleeting flavour of the brat about her last litter, purebred labrador though they are. Pure in theory, not in practice. There's more goes on inside the womb than meets the eye. Flavours are caught. Call it propensity, synchronicity, call it God, what you like: at the last fractional moment balances are tipped, this way and that. Interesting.'

'You mean we ought to *pray* this one sticks,' said Carl May derisively.

'I do,' said Dr Holly, and though neither of them prayed, little Alice stuck, and grew up, pretty little sister to four big brothers, alternately bullying and protective, resentful and admiring, lecherous and rejecting, mother's little helper, sweeping, cooking, wiping, serving, flirting, sulking, weeping, giggling, absurdly tender-hearted or else cruel beyond belief, valued for the sheer femaleness of her being, brought up with an amiable father and four big brothers no real kin to her.

Alice entered a beauty contest when she was fifteen, was 'discovered', won a holiday in Florida, kept the company of long-legged beach girls with millionaire boyfriends, came back, went to charm school, discovered the value of disdain, the power of active nonpleasing, failing to placate; she looked at her perfect self in a mirror one day and decided not to have children, not to get married. Who could she ever find to love better than she? Who better to be faithful to, than herself? Men were useful as admirers: sex kept them quiet: love was for suckers: when she felt the first pangs of love, lust, she went home to Honeybell Lee, the dogs, the cats, the nieces and nephews, love, muddle and mess abounding, and was cured.

'She's not like the rest of us,' said Honeybell Lee, puzzled. Honeybell Lee believed Alice to be her natural child: so far as she was aware the Bulstrode Clinic had carried out a simple investigation under local anaesthetic to change the acid/alkaline balance of her internal secretions in favour of the survival of sperm carrying female chromosomes when next it arrived. And it had worked to the great pleasure and satisfaction of all concerned.

And Alice would have been truly faithful to herself, if only fate had so allowed, and not pushed men into her bed, photographers and clients and so forth. Her infidelity brought her no pleasure. She really preferred to sleep alone, being of a nature that saw sex as a drain on her personal resources, not something that enriched them.

Jane, Julie, Gina and Alice.

18

So it was that the four clones, Jane, Julie, Gina and Alice, produced by the irritation of a single egg, were successfully implanted in waiting wombs. Beyond confirming that growth was normal and the infants were successfully born, Holly and May made no attempt to follow the fortunes of the children, or to do the personality studies that would, both agreed, be interesting, if only to make some contribution to the nature/nurture debate. But the complications of setting up such studies would be immense; their research would come under an ethical and legal scrutiny it could not for the time being afford; and it would, they told themselves, be difficult for the four little girls to live normal lives under scrutiny. Nor did they see any good reason to tell Joanna May herself what they had done. Joanna May, the calm, normal, healthy, beautiful and apparently well-balanced woman whom they had, out of love, respect and admiration so successfully reproduced, was still a woman, and therefore liable to extreme, hysterical and unhelpful reaction: she was a creature of the emotions, rather than reason. That was the female lot. And look at it this way: if the population of, say, Egypt increased by a million every nine months, why then, were four more Joannas dropped into the pool – rather than one each of a female Madge/Jeremy, Harold/Katie, Douglas/Annette, Honeybell/Patrick (unlikely in any case to come into existence because of nature's own inefficiency) – to be in any way abhorred? Holly and May had done no harm to anyone, so far as they could see, or anything: though Holly sometimes, when reviewing the past, did wonder a little about Carl May's motives: could a man brought up in a kennel, barking in his heart, baying at the moon, really ever know himself? Did anyone?

The Bulstrode Clinic experiments in parthenogenesis had long since ceased, becoming irrelevant as the whole field of genetic engineering and microbiology opened up. Dr Holly had moved on to run an enterprising and well-funded Research and Development unit at Martins Pharmaceuticals, an international conglomerate of which Carl May presently became a director. Here his field was at first the decoding of DNA; at which time the visits and special requests of Carl May became less frequent, rather to Dr Holly's relief. But later Holly moved on to the development of dehydration techniques in relation to egg-cell nuclei; there was much excitement and talk of Nobel Prizes – and all of a sudden Carl May was back again, having met up with Isaac King, requiring that Holly drop everything and search the gut of an ancient Egyptian body, dehydrated rather than mummified, which he just so happened to have in his possession, for cells with sufficient intact and living DNA for nuclei transference to be possible. Holly hinted, rather than protested, that he had better things to do than bring the past to life, since the present was surely difficult enough to cope with. He tried to keep the matter light in the interest of his funding, and in the attempt made matters worse than he had thought possible.

'If our motives are impure,' said Dr Holly blithely, 'we will suffer for it: we will be caught like birds in a trap.' The Curse of the Pharaohs was in his mind: Tutankhamen's curse which, according to Isaac King, pursued leading Egyptologists all over the world – tumours and heart attacks killing at an unusually early age, cancers and road accidents striking others down – so that the quality, forget the number, of professors in the subject fell as the best and brightest of them were removed from the human race. Dr Holly half-believed it, half did not, could joke about it.

Carl May did not consider it a joking matter. Carl May dismissed the matter of the Curse of the Pharaohs as the merest, most vulgar of superstitions; how could any scientist even half-believe such junk? Handling a lot of dusty, ancient, possibly carcinogenic material could well result in early death. Road accidents? Well, Egyptologists were by their nature impractical and vague. The myth of the absent-minded professor had its roots in truth. They just didn't look where they were going.

95

They got killed. Dr Holly, rashly, disagreed. He was a professor himself, he reminded Carl May. He was not absent-minded, not in the least.

The Curse of the Pharaohs, Carl May then pointed out, was no more than a warning, albeit engraved in stringent stone and in a prominent position. It was the Ancient Egyptian equivalent of a burglar alarm: 'If anyone enters my tomb with unworthy intentions, be warned. I will catch him like a bird in a trap and stand witness against him by the throne of the Lord of Eternity.' The Ancient Egyptians, Isaac King had explained to Carl May, who now took the trouble – and he was a busy man – to explain it to Dr Holly, caught their birds in clapnets, the two wooden sides of a net coming smartly and suddenly together, and that for the bird was that: kept trapped until it was time to be killed and eaten, or killed and embalmed by some patron who would gain credit in the afterlife for so doing. Absurd!

'You never know,' laughed Dr Holly, 'just when the past will catch up with you! You should always be prepared. Embalm a bird or two!'

Carl May did not laugh. Carl May took irrational offence. 'Gobbledygook!' he cried, and Dr Holly found his department's grant cut presently by many millions. For once too piqued to apologize or oblige, Dr Holly allowed his department to limp on as best it could, left the pursuit of Nobel Prizes to others, and diversified into the safe, cheap and interesting study of brain-cell activity in identical twins. Carl May did not take this side-stepping sitting down: no, he fretted, threatened and fumed – but shortly afterwards came the unfortunate matter of Isaac King's death, and the divorce of his wife, and he was quiet. Something seemed to have knocked the spirit out of him, at least for a time.

19

I, Joanna May.

Isaac King taught me many important things. Carl May taught me many boring things, mostly about how to keep him happy.

Isaac taught me that there need never be an end to seeing. Isaac insisted that I could look at the stubbed-out cigarettes in an ashtray and see beyond it to the meaning behind – know that everything has significance, even if it comes, for a time, to this trash. Those who grew the leaf and waited and prayed for the rain to come: those who profited by its processing and selling: those who smoked it, and defied death: those who stubbed it out, envisaging life – all are part of it. Even in that detritus of ash and grime was something to be marvelled at, something to make you quite giddy with delight. Isaac smoked, of course, and had no intention of stopping, and as it turned out, he was justified, his death by misadventure preceding any major damage to lungs or circulatory system. Carl did not smoke. Carl meant to live for ever in perfect health in a world he hated.

Isaac King taught me that patterns are being woven around us every minute of the day: if we have eyes to see them, they are there to see. When the stray cat miaowing on the doorstep one morning turns out to be the illegitimate grandchild of the grey Persian owned by your father's favourite patient, long deceased, there is no need for surprise. All things are interrelated: the cat was lost and found just to make sure all the cogs were locking properly; or some loose overlap, perhaps, needed to be sealed. The Egyptians knew how cats, who have their own strong familial links, interweave with ours, and our friendships and ventures. Fate offers us hints: shrugs if we don't take notice. No skin off its nose. Isaac taught me to accept mystery. Carl May believed in cause and effect, action and consequence, and nothing much else, except the laws of probability. He thought it was so obvious it didn't need teaching, or no doubt he would have. Brides get taught.

I once tried to explain to Carl what I meant by 'fate' but he didn't listen: he went on reading the *Financial Times*, fidgeting slightly to demonstrate his irritation. That was after Isaac and I had started sorting out exhibits together, but before our further intimacy.

The word 'fate', of course, did not help me, being inadequate to describe the sense of a multifarious, infinitely complex, dreamy yet purposeful universe which I had in mind – being altogether too singular a word, too single-purposed, like a chisel driven hard into the delicacy of experience. A single brain cell, one amongst millions, millions, were it self-conscious, might I suppose have just such an inkling of what was going on around it. The 'Fates' had it better, being at least plural, something capable of consensus, though separately driven.

Miss Watson taught me, I remember, that the concept of One God, Jehovah, was a great step forward for mankind – an end to all those piddly little Gods with brazen feet it thereafter became a capital offence to worship. I had done my best to believe her, but as Isaac and I unpacked and recorded from straw and sand the little artefacts, the various little deities of Ancient Egypt, our eyes melting from time to time and hastily looking away, I began to see the concept of a single God as a narrowing of our perception, not an expansion: the beginning of the long slow end of civilization and not its dawn at all – this cowardly insistence of ours on leaders, fuehrers, the someone who knows exactly what's going on and what's best for everyone; the One above All who demands our loyalty, our obeisance. Undemocratic. The truth is many, not one. Carl May was my Jehovah: it did me no good. I preferred Isaac. Now there's Oliver.

More, more! More and more Gods, each to be worshipped in a different way before lightning strikes us to death.

Isaac King nudged and nurtured my body into a capacity for orgasm, that stretching of the body until it meets the soul, with its astonishing shudder of recognition, elation. Proof, proof, cries the body, proof of my purpose, sinking back into languor, all passion spent: I knew it was there if only I looked hard enough. I perceived it, stretched for it, touched it, just with my fingertips encountered the infinite for an instant! I told you so! We're all in this together – we share it, one day we'll know this joy for ever, out of body. Those of us who can – which does not include those faithfully married to Carl May – must pass the message on to those who can't. It's OK. I told Carl May that day in the gallery just what pleasure Isaac gave me, and he seemed not to understand what I was talking about. Well, he wouldn't want to, would he?

Isaac King taught me about the Tarot pack and how it was possible to contain the world in just seventy-eight cards – shuffle the pack, deal them, and observe the pattern of the times: the Ancient Egyptians were great diviners. That there was a Major Arcana of twenty-two cards, which represented the great guiding passions of mankind; intellectual, moral, material. That there were four suits, Wands, Pentacles, Swords and Cups, from which our ordinary Diamonds, Clubs, Spades and Hearts derive. How, broadly, Wands stand for the power of the intellect, Pentacles the strength of the material world, Swords the capacity for endurance, Cups for aesthetic and sensual perception. Or so Isaac interpreted the cards; the power to interpret hieroglyphics at the tips of his fingers. Isaac was so *clever*: I was so proud of him: I felt I caught intelligence from him: and also, I daresay, something of his impracticality. It is wonderful to be taught: it is almost worth the years of ignorance to have it so suddenly, wonderfully stop. But I wanted my fortune told: I wanted to know the future. His future, my future. The cards are not for telling fortunes, Isaac said. They're for focusing the mind on the patterns which the world around you makes. But I wouldn't have it.

99

That was before we'd been to bed. Sex was in the air: it was inevitable: it was the best, the most powerful of times.

'Tell my fortune,' I repeated.

'What do you want to know?' he asked.

Will we go to bed, I wanted to know. When, where, how, what will happen next? Will you be the fulfilment of my life, will you take the cup of my emptiness and fill it to the brim, and so forth. But I didn't tell Isaac any of that. I wasn't quite such a fool.

'I just want to know,' I said, 'what's going to happen next.'

Isaac acquiesced. Isaac shuffled the pack, picked out the four queens: Wands, Pentacles, Swords and Cups. 'Pick the one that most represents you,' he said, but none seemed quite right to me. I reached for the Empress instead: a card from the Major Arcana. She held the world in her hands: it was what I felt like at that moment. 'Work with that,' I said.

So Isaac took out the Empress, put back the Queens. I shuffled the cards. He laid them face down:

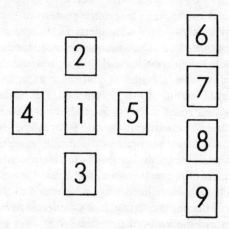

The Empress in the middle was at number one. Above me, two was what ruled me: beneath me, three was what underlay me. Four was what I was leaving. Five was what I was approaching. The significance of the positions of six, seven and eight I can't remember – it scarcely seemed important at the time. Nine was the final outcome: that was what I waited for.

Isaac King turned over the cards.

The four Queens surrounded me. Wands, Pentacles, Swords and Cups: above, below, to left and right. I cannot remember what stood at six and seven; but at eight there was the Hierophant; at nine, Death, a skeleton riding on horseback.

Isaac looked at the Hierophant and laughed.
'There's Carl,' he said.
I, Joanna May, looked at Death and moaned.
'Death means nothing,' said Isaac. 'The card's reversed. It means rebirth, new life; not what you think at all.'
'That's your story,' I said.
'But those four Queens,' said Isaac King, 'that's really something. I don't understand it.'
'I do,' I said. 'I didn't shuffle the pack properly, that's all that means.'
He laughed and swept the cards together and wouldn't say any more. I begged him to tell me more. I touched him in the begging, and though he wouldn't tell the cards for me, he kissed me and that was the beginning, and I forgot about the Tarot.

Except I told Carl that Isaac was teaching me about the Tarot pack: I couldn't resist it. I told Carl about the hand the Fates had dealt me, I tried to suggest to my husband that perhaps there was more to life than here and now, birth and death, that 'because' was a more complex word than he dreamt of – but he wouldn't have it, of course he wouldn't.
'I thought he was some kind of academic,' said Carl May, 'and he turns out to be a charlatan. Is the fellow weak-minded? Is his brain as limp as his shirt collar? Will I get a proper PR return on the gallery? Who does this fellow think he is?'

It did not occur to Carl May to be sexually jealous. How could the servant be preferred to the master? I was affronted. Pique made me guiltless. The more he spoke, poor blinkered Carl May, the

101

more I lost my respect for him, my fear of him. I felt justified in infidelity: it was a wonderful feeling: my spirit soared like a bird, circling, dancing, dizzy with sunlight: I was allowed to be happy. I was born to be happy. I remember sitting on my hands to weigh myself down, as though the very discovery would somehow waft me away. We were sitting, as I remember, in some riverside restaurant. It was night. Lights flickered over running water, and made patterns on the deep red silk of the dress I was wearing. There were only the two of us. It must have been our wedding anniversary, or we'd have been in company – some politician, or magnate, accompanied by boring wife. I've no doubt but that I appeared equally boring. Who is she? Oh, Carl May's wife. What does she do? Nothing. She is Carl May's wife. What does she think? Nothing. She is Carl May's wife. What does she feel? Nothing. She is Carl May's wife. My mother died on the fourth anniversary of my wedding to Carl May. I felt nothing. Carl May had somehow made my feelings for my own mother illicit – as if my life began with my marriage, and that nothing that went before was of any significance: not even the root of my very being, my mother. I went to the funeral alone. Carl May was in China. He did send a telegram and flowers: a wreath, too enormous for the coffin. My poor mother. Everyone should be mourned: remembered: somehow sustained in their journey through the afterlife, until the need for it is gone. Isaac taught me that as well: but I had never until that moment connected it to my mother.

'Superstitious nonsense,' Carl was saying. 'And by God I'll prove it nonsense.'

'How will you do that, Carl?' I asked, politely. 'People have been trying to prove or disprove magic, prophecy, ESP, since the beginning of time, and haven't succeeded.'

'I'll prove it,' he said, 'if it kills me.' And he started the Divination Department. I was glad to think the conversation had at least had some effect upon him. And in that original hand of cards – the first time the cards are dealt for someone the reading is always clear, always significant – was indeed my future. It was just that Isaac was to die, not me. No wonder he swept the cards up and reshuffled as quick as he could.

And I remember now what the cards at six and seven were. Six was the Star, kneeling by her pool beneath a sliver of moon; seven was the Fool, reversed. Treachery, one would imagine: self-delusion. I talked too much. I betrayed Carl, by finding sexual fulfilment with Isaac; and Isaac, because I couldn't resist telling Carl.

I, Joanna May. No longer 'Eye'. Acting; not observing. Doing, not looking. Dangerous, murderous, and not even knowing it.

20

Joanna May, impassioned at last by virtue of the blue-foldered report from the Maverick Enquiry Agency, which told of Bethany's existence, went straight to the heart of Carl May's evil empire, his glassy prison. She meant to tell him a thing or two. She rose by means of a pink and white escalator from the fountains and greenery, marble and glass of the reception levels, and smoothly ascended through layer upon layer of noise and tumult, panic and excitement, bells and clatter, of messengers running, girl clerks checking and pot plants wilting unattended. Then, audacious, was whisked up unchecked in a cage of green glass studded with yellow lights, right into the still centre of the storm, the quiet nexus of energy, the Executive Floor. She walked straight past secretaries on her expensive sensible heels and right into Carl May's office suite where all was silent, sparse and aesthetically correct. The nerve of it! There she found her husband, her ex-husband, flesh of her flesh, heart of her heart, with that tragic ruined girl, that Bethany, that almost beauty, with her sad brightness and her ersatz emerald eyes, his long pale tampering fingers tangled in her hennaed hair. And some might think it served Joanna May right, but she did not.

No. Joanna May spoke the truth to Carl May, or the only truth she knew: that once long ago she'd handed her life to him for keeps, as she was expected by all and sundry to do, being nothing but a girl, in truth, love, and hope, and what had Carl May done? Why, he had not only rendered these things sour for her forever, but drained her being dry as if it were an orange; with powerful lips sucked up the juice and the flesh through a hole in the skin the size of a sixpence, and then thrown the poor flabby thing away. And now look, now look, now look, Joanna May wept, self-pity overcoming rage. Look at me!

An orange, Carl May laughed, an orange. I thought women got thrown away like old gloves, not old oranges, and Joanna May screamed and shouted and banged her fists against his chest, and he didn't even catch hold of them to stop them, so distasteful did he find her flesh, or pretended to. And Bethany thought at last, at last, boredom is ending here, at last something's happening, not this quiet, this still, this nothingness, from which all things emanate but yet is nothing. So bored, she thought, I've been so bored. Ex-wives are better than nothing.

You have destroyed me, Joanna May said to her husband, in essence, used up my youth, my best years and thrown me out.

Carl May said to Joanna, men do not destroy women, some women destroy themselves, that's all; if Joanna May is indeed destroyed, why then he's glad for her sake since that was clearly what she wanted. Women choose the man they want, said Carl May, the man their calculating eye first falls upon; then, lacking the capacity and the will to stick by that decision, must chew away at their own loyalty – self-devourers all, rapacious of grievance, noisy in complaint – gossiping to neighbours and friends over fences and tables, round fires and out shopping, the yackety yak of the female affronted: first he did this and then he did that, can you imagine, and can you believe it, after all that she does for him how much she loves him the bastard, the brute! And how after all that complaint how can a woman expect to find in her own heart constancy, loyalty, truth or affection? Split a plain and single path into a thousand tracks of conversational interest and how can you expect to find yourself ever back upon the right one? In other words, Joanna May, in the course of our marriage, you talked about me to your friends, committed disloyalty with your mind and after that with your body which was how it was bound to end up. Your fault not mine, said Carl May, your fault, your fault, your fault, not mine. What's more, I just behaved as any man would behave, said Carl May.

What, murder? enquired Joanna May and Carl May said you're mad, you're insolent, my chauffeur knocked him down, that's all. An absent-minded Egyptologist, how could he ever bring the dead to life, and you were dead enough yourself by then. Old. A weak man, a *nebbitch*, a nothing, a better-dead, dead already so far as anyone had ever seen. Trust you to pick a zombie, Joanna May. Your fault for not finding a better man: how could you find a better man, a zombie the best that you could do, your fault that now he's dead, as dead as you, and you're alone. Lost him and lost me, lost us both, silly old you.

Oh phooey, she said, it's all men's fault, everyone knows it's all men's fault. Ask anyone.

Just a woman, only a woman, he said next. You should have died twenty years ago, what use to the world are you? A woman without youth, without children, without interest, a woman without a husband; old women have husbands by the skin of their teeth and there is no skin left to your teeth, Joanna May, your yellow discoloured teeth.

My teeth are not so yellow, said Joanna May, they're perfectly pearly white as ever. You're talking about your own miserable molars. And Carl May gnashed them and said he was a man, he was immortal, his immortality lay here in this building, this achievement – by his name on a hundred powerful letterheads he would outrun his death; but what was a woman such as Joanna May, a woman without children, here and now and gone with a puff, blown away like a withered leaf, just for an instant a stretch of limb, a flash of thigh, and gone, a flower that never left a seed, the merest annual, passing thing, a nothing. Here today, gone tomorrow.

I am so something, said Joanna May. Ask my lover, he'll tell you what a thing I am, how far from nothing, here today and here tomorrow. I have my lover, my young lover, I have a man a thousand times better than you, who makes me happy and satisfied, which is what you never did. Never, never, never, never.

106

Carl May was silent.

Oh ouch – thought Bethany, better she hadn't said that, better she'd kept quiet.

Then the fat was in the fire, oh yes it was. How it spat, how it sizzled and spat.

Carl May's eyes seemed to turn a kind of yellow red, as false a colour as Bethany's own emerald eyes, but the pupil went to slits through which a blackness showed, as her own would never do, or so Bethany hoped.

Then Carl May said in a voice as cold and clear as ice made from bottled water, let your poor old flabby legs be parted by whom you choose, it will be for money not love – Not true, not true, Joanna May began to say, but of course it was, it was perfectly true – so why then, she said, it's true for you too you poor old man; and he said no it's not, you poor Joanna May, you female, the music stops for women long before it stops for men, and pitiful and degraded are the ones who dance on when the silence falls; your dance is over, Joanna May, you thoroughly useless lonely person, and mine is not, why don't you go away and die?

Oh flesh of my flesh, love of my soul, husband of my heart, she weeps, to speak to me like this. How can you!

Because I am Lord of the Dance, he says, and I am man and you are only woman, and I am something indeed and you are nothing at all, in spite of your young lover. If he exists, which I take leave to doubt.

I am so something, she wept, I am, I am, and he does exist and I love him, but already she felt herself vanishing, though she still beat her hands against his neatly suited breast and Bethany yawned to hide her nerves and looked around for a door to leave by, but there seemed to be none, so perfectly, architecturally flush were they with the wall. You have to have good eyesight to detect those very expensive doors and Bethany's contact lenses had slipped and chafed and her eyes were watering and she couldn't see a way out at all.

You are nothing, said Carl May, quite bright and glittery all of a sudden as if the sun had come out to shine on a world of icebergs, hot in pursuit but chilly with it, and what's more I proved you nothing thirty years ago and I've known it ever since, and I swore I'd never tell you, but now I will. I proved then you were nothing so particular after all, and that, to be frank, is when I lost interest in you. I proved it by making more of you, and the more I made of you the less of you there was, so it hardly mattered when you betrayed me, because how can what does not exist betray. One a penny, two a penny, hot cross buns; more buns came out of that oven than ever went in.

What do you mean, she asked, quite soft and quiet all of a sudden, and listening hard, of course she did, so he told her – I cloned you, Carl May said, I cloned you, added another four of you to the world, and he told her how he did it, and Bethany put her oar in and said Carl only did it because he loved you really, did it as a compliment, take no notice of what he says today, he's bitter and twisted and furious because you've got a boyfriend, that's all, at which Carl May gave Bethany a push and a shove and would have sent her right through the window and windmilling to her death thirty floors below but the windows didn't open (and just as well, or how the bodies would have piled below, from hatred and self-hatred) so he didn't bother, just forgot.

Joanna May, shocked into calmness, paced and thought and considered herself split into five and her gorge rose into her throat.

Carl May smiled and it seemed to Bethany that his teeth were fangs and growing as long as the wolf's ever were in 'Red Riding Hood'.

There are many of you and many of you gloated Carl May and that means there are none of you because you amounted to so little in the first place. Now see how you like that.

Joanna May thought a little. All the more of us to hate and despise you, she said, flickering into defiance, and make wax models of you and stick pins into you. See how you like that!

Superstitious junk, he shouted, and I'm proving it, I'm proving it. Do you know who I am? I am master of mortality.

Bethany sighed: the children were squabbling again, that was all, perhaps that was all, perhaps it was nothing, could be sighed away, would vanish away like a thirties film disintegrating, unseen in its vault – the mad male cloning scientist crumbling into the dust of fantasy, Frankenstein dissolved, the monster only a dream, a fright, and the world return to normal. But no. It was real. It was true. It was the present – not the future. And it was all Carl May's fault. It was his fault.

You're the devil, said Joanna May, you're the devil. Your mother was right to chain you up with the beasts, she knew the truth about you. I wish they'd gnawed you to death, eaten you up, why have you done this terrible thing to me, imprisoned me forever in a bad bad dream?

You did a terrible thing to me, he said, you made your bed and didn't lie on it, chose a man and wouldn't stick with him; you're a piece of drifting slime in a murky female pool. You're all alike, you women.

Carl May, said Joanna May, I'm sorry for you. You look out of the dark prison of your soul which is your body, and the only windows you have are your eyes, your ears, your nose, your touch, and what can you know but what those windows look upon and it isn't up to much, never has been: a little tent of sky outside a kennel. What a pity you slipped your leash, you should have stayed forever, baying at the moon. I see a different world, said Joanna May, I see one which is perfectible without your tampering.

I don't, said Carl May, and my view is the true one, however disagreeable. I see a world of accident and not design, never perfectible left to itself. Besides, I want to amuse myself. I can make a thousand thousand of you if I choose, fragment all living things and re-create them. I can splice a gene or two, can make you walk with a monkey's head or run on a bitch's legs or see through the eyes of a newt: I can entertain myself by making you whatever I feel like, and as I feel like so shall I do. Whatever I choose from now on for ever.

I don't believe you, said Joanna May.

Believe what you like, said Carl May. Chernobyl has exploded and now all things impossible are possible, from now on in.

And then Joanna May just laughed and said do what you like but you can't catch me, you'll never catch me, I am myself. Nail me and alter me, fix me and distort me, I'll still have windows on the world to make of it what I decide. I'll be myself. Multiply me and multiply my soul: divide me, split me; you just make more of me, not less. I will look out from more and different windows, that's all you will have done, and I will watch the world go by in all its multifarious forms, and there will be no end to my seeing. I will lift up my heart to the hills, that's all, to glorify a maker who is not you. I should carry on if I were you, cloning and meddling, you might end up doing more good than harm, in spite of yourself, if only by mistake.

Carl May snarled and his eyes grew redder still for this was the heart of the evil empire and he was its lord, or so it seemed to Bethany, and he dug his yellow fangs into Joanna's neck just above her genteel string of pearls and he scraped up a piece of her skin with those disgusting teeth and went to the little designer fridge where he kept his whisky (for guests) and his Perrier (for him) and he took out a little box and with a spatula scraped the flesh, the living tissue, of Joanna May off the teeth and shook it into the box with a short sharp shake and put it back in the fridge and said now I'll grow you into what I want, he said, I can and will, see how you like that, I'll make you live in pain and shame for ever more, I have brought hell to earth.

Joanna May just laughed and said Carl May you've really flipped, wait till I tell Oliver about this, Oliver loves my soul not my body he loves my mind, my hope, my courage, me: he loves about me what you loved, Carl May, and still do, you silly spiteful thing, judging from how you behave. I was made in heaven not hell, as you were. You're not king of the Dark Domains, that's all in your mind, you're just head of Britnuc and in a state because of Chernobyl and the guilt and responsibility you feel and the whole world nagging on.

Carl May said if you'd loved me properly, Joanna May, if you had kept your word, I would make roses without thorns, I would make dogs who didn't want to bite, I would make all men kind and good and wonderful, and women too, I would create a sinless race, I would perfect nature's universe, because nature is blind, and obsessive, and absurd – consider the ostrich – and has no judgement, only insists on our survival, somehow, any old how: nature is only chance, not good or bad. All I want is the any old how properly under control, directed, working better: I, man, want to teach nature a thing or two, in particular the difference between good and bad; for who else is there to do it? But how can I, because woman makes man bad, I know it, I feel it. Joanna May, you nearly saved me once, you nearly made me good, and then you failed me, that is why I can't forgive you. You have made me bad, Joanna May: if I'm the devil that's your fault: if I create monsters, you've no one to blame but yourself.

Oh phooey, she said. So I'm Eve to your Adam, am I, that old thing. Take your own apple, bite its flesh, give me a break. All I wanted was a little conversation, for once: all I was doing was discussing the apple: if you chose to see that as temptation, God help you.

And Bethany saw them both standing in the Garden of Eden, Carl and Joanna May, or thought that was what she saw – Carl May long-limbed, tall, ruddy and eager, as he ought to have been, if everything had gone right, and Joanna May young again and looking down her perfect nose, as ever, just a sniff of disdain about her and in the sniff of that disdain the root of much trouble to come, perhaps even all of it, and between them they stared at the apple, red one side, green the other. Carl May bit first, choosing the red half, the better half, the riper half, and that made Joanna really spiteful. But Bethany had taken pills that morning, to get her through the day, as people will these days, and the pills were tiny and the pillbox in a muddle and as her lenses had scraped her eyes were blurred and she could easily mistake the yellow and the red, so who knows what she saw.

111

Thank you, Carl, for the gift you have given me, said Joanna May, cheerfully, and now I'm off to find my sisters, and I bet I find them different every one, different as sin and yet the same.

And with no apparent trouble at all she found a door in the perfect wall and was out of it and gone but on her way down in the lift she wept, and she nearly stumbled getting off the escalator, she trembled so. What woman of sixty would want to meet herself at thirty: rerun of some dreary old film, in which she gave a bad performance, like as not, and split-screen technique at that.

21

Bethany said to Carl May, 'That was a perfectly horrid thing to do, scraping her neck like that. You're nothing but a Dracula.'

And he said, still in a bad mood, 'Be careful or I'll do it to you too. You might be helped by a little sorting and a proper upbringing, so I should shut up if I were you, or you'll have a very sore neck indeed.'

So she did shut up, for a time. But unlike Joanna she could see the advantage of being more than one: the thought did not horrify her at all, not one bit. The more of her the better. She would sit back while the other clones did the shopping, yes she would; after all she could rely on them bringing back what she wanted, choosing what she would choose – until, thinking about it, she realized that was like believing you were Marie Antoinette in another incarnation, and not one of her maids, which was more likely statistically (one of Carl May's favourite words) there being so many more ordinary people than queens in the world. One of the other clones might seize command, and Bethany would be doing the shopping while the Queen clone was the one just sitting – and Bethany wouldn't know what was going on in the Queen's head, really, except she'd know it was pretty much what was going on in her own, which might or might not be a help. But somehow Bethany felt she would indeed have the benefit of extra strawberries and cream upon the tongue, not to mention all the lovemaking multiplied, because she'd know what the others would be tasting, feeling, doing, not just having to guess.

And, then again, though Bethany loved her parents, she could see they had not brought her up in a safe or sensible kind of way. Reared in another fashion, encouraged in different directions, Bethany might be a fashion designer, or fly an aircraft, not be just a girl who lived by her looks. Or would she? How could one tell? Except by trying.

Bethany said to Carl May later that evening, when he had calmed down and lost his satanic overtones, and she and he were in the bath – it was too small for their cavortings (she knocked her elbow quite painfully) and white, which she thought boring and old-fashioned – 'What happened to Joanna's clones? Didn't you want to find out?' and he said, 'Good heavens, you didn't really believe that tale did you? I was annoyed with Joanna, that's all.'

This time Bethany didn't believe him. Bethany said, 'You did so do it. You just frightened yourself with what you'd done. You realized, and stopped, the way people do. You set things marching you couldn't control, so you just shut your eyes, and left it to the other people to clear up the mess! Like the waste from your power plants. What's going to happen to that?'

Twenty-four going on forty-two. He got out of the bath. Either she annoyed him with her perspicacity, or irritated him with her stupidity. She confused him. He would be filled with tenderness and gratitude towards her, when she had rendered him some peculiar sexual favour – though in theory that was when he should most despise her – and yet wish to push her out of the window if she failed to read his mind properly, or was insensitive to his feelings. Carl May did not like being confused.

'Oh,' said Bethany, 'now what have I said? Why did you get out of the bath?'

'Because I banged my knee,' he said, wrapping himself in a towel, which smelt of Bethany, sweet and warm and agreeably cheap, 'and bed is more comfortable. Let's go to bed.'

In bed she said, 'If you were making it up about the clones – and you told me about them yourself once before; did you forget? – why did you take that piece from her neck?'

And he said, 'To frighten her off. Who wants ex-wives dropping in at any time of day or night, making scenes?'

'Well,' said Bethany, 'if you ask me, it was a bit drastic. Most

114

men don't behave like that when they find their ex-wife has a lover. And after all, it's only natural that she should. You have me, after all. And there can't be one law for men and another for women.'

'Oh yes, there can,' said he.

'Well, don't have him run over too,' said Bethany, 'or there'll be more talk. Punish him some other way. Have a thousand of him made, each one with a high sex drive but impotent. That should pay him out.'

'I'll pay him out the simple old-fashioned way,' he said, and looked at his watch and laughed aloud.

'Why are you looking at your watch?' she asked.

'Because it's the most expensive watch in the world,' he said.

He wondered how Dr Holly was doing; how long he would hold out, when he would give in and return to the fold. Men within a whisper of a Nobel Prize do not easily turn their backs on glory, renown and the plaudits of their peers. If Holly didn't, there were younger, smarter, more ambitious men in Holly's own department upon whom Carl May had his eye, more than ready to do a favour or two. But Holly was the best, the most creative, the most imaginative: the younger generation of scientists were more concerned with their careers than the marvels of the universe. You had to pay them to get them to think. He would confront Holly with hard evidence on the absent-mindedness of professors of Egyptology: how they did indeed step out in front of cars: how they died young for reasons which were nothing to do with the Curse of the Pharaohs. Dr Holly would admit Carl May was right, would agree to put at least a section of his department to searching the gut cells of the ancients for living DNA, and get his grant back, and off they'd go again, Holly and May, May and Holly!

Unless of course Joanna was herself the Curse of the Pharaohs. The thought made Carl May laugh aloud.

'Why are you laughing?' Bethany asked.

'Because you're such an idiot,' said Carl May, 'and that's the way I like it. I want you bright, I don't want you clever.'

'I may be cleverer than you suppose,' said Bethany.

115

'What great big teeth you have, Grandmama,' he said, which was silly, she thought, because she had very little white even teeth of which she was very proud, having spent many years wearing a brace, about which her parents had been very particular, allowing her to take it off only when being kind to their lame ducks, their lonely sea-captains, their newly widowed majors. 'One day you'll be pleased,' her father would say, when she moaned and groaned about the brace, and so she was.

Carl May looked at his watch again, and this time she didn't ask him why. He had the bright eyes and flushed cheeks of a delinquent child; he was up to something; she knew it, and she thought it might be better, safer, not to know exactly what it was, and she was right.

The next day Carl May took part in a TV programme about the Chernobyl disaster and the question of the threat or otherwise of radiation, which seemed to so absorb the nation. He took an aggressive and positive line, as suited both his whim, his business interests and the future of the nuclear industry; all of these being pretty much the same.

He said he doubted very much the story of 2000 dead and large areas laid waste and desolate, never to grow a blade of grass again. He deplored the scare stories in the media that death was raining down from skies all over the world. He drank a glass of milk front of camera, and said there was more to fear from cholesterol than radioactivity. He said he thought the death toll would be more like thirty-five – very modest for a major industrial accident (though of course tragic for those concerned: families, etc.) and naturally there would be a statistically calculable increase in cancers in those countries subject to fallout but certainly no more than would be produced by atmospheric pollution consequent upon the continued burning off of fossil fuels. These things had to be balanced.

Look, Carl May said, this argument that we should all live as long as we possibly can is barmy: who wants to live an extra five years in a walking frame anyway? Better an earlier death, be it cancer or heart attack, than a later one. It was an old-fashioned sentiment which favoured length of life over way of life, quantity over quality. You found it the other end of the spectrum, when it came to how societies regarded birth: the old school, emotional, religious, said no contraception, no abortions, let the disabled live: the more life the better, regardless of quality of life. A younger, more reasonable, generation said no, let's have quality not quantity. Freely available birth control, worldwide family planning, sterilizations, vasectomies on demand, termin- ations all but compulsory for those diagnosed before birth as handicapped, every child a wanted child – and so forth, Carl May said, while Friends of the Earth, a Bishop and the Minister of Energy tried to get a word in edgeways.

Friends of the Earth managed 'What about childhood cancer? Leukaemia?' and Carl May replied briskly if this nation really cares about the lives of its children it will stop driving about in cars – how many get killed a year on the roads! – and in- crease family allowances: if it cares about cancers in the old it will ban cigarette smoking and free hospitals for the potentially healthy and those who have not brought their troubles on themselves.

Now look, said Carl May, people will work themselves up into a state about anything, especially if it's new. They thought the building of railway lines would destroy the nation, they thought TV would destroy its culture, they thought vaccination killed. ('They were right, they were right,' muttered the Bishop.) Nothing much to fear from radiation, compared to other dangers, compared to crossing the road, compared to smoking. A burst of intense radiation could kill you, sure. So could an overdose of aspirin. Nuclear power stations were, if you asked him, even more crippled by safety regulations than they were by the unions, and that was saying something. The un- thinking and uninformed always fear an unseen enemy. From reds under the bed to radiation in the head, the public gets the wrong end of the stick, is ignorant and hysterical and impossible.

He stopped. Everyone in the studio was startled; even the camera crews were listening.

117

Next day Gerald Coustain called from the Department and said he thought Carl May had gone a little far in insulting the public so; it might not be a wise move considering the state of near-panic it appeared to be in. Let him at least appear to take the Chernobyl fallout seriously.

'OK, OK,' said Carl May. 'I'll bleat away in public if that's what you want.'

'We've now pulled together some very fine and modern instrumentation,' said Gerald, 'so we won't be calling on Britnuc any more. I have to tell you that in some parts of Cumbria, it now seems, the needles had been going once round the dials and back again, and our technicians simply hadn't noticed: they weren't expecting it. Human error's the real problem.'

'It certainly is,' said Carl May.

'Still, we've got the problem solved now, I think. We may have to take lamb off the market, though.'

'That'll just panic people more,' said Carl May. 'If Cumbrian lamb is twice as radioactive as Sussex lamb, why don't you ask people just to eat one Cumbrian lamb chop instead of their usual two? Or if they're *really* hungry, buy Sussex.'

'Because people's minds don't work like that,' said Gerald.

'I know,' said Carl May. 'That's the trouble with them.'

22

The world turned upside down. I went to Carl's office to have it out with him, but he had it out with me, and took some living cells from my neck, what's more: the kind of good fresh bloodless tissue that's rich in DNA: he could grow all kinds of me from that – he's right. Ugly, headless, always miserable, always in pain: five-legged, three-headed, double-spined: every leg with perpetual cramp, all heads schizophrenic, and spina bifida twice over. If he wanted, if he could persuade them to do it, that is – and he is a Director of Martins Pharmaceuticals, isn't he, and benefactor of this and that: an interesting experiment, he'd say, a favour. You do this for me and I'll do that for you. Would they? Snip and snap, create a monster? Not if Carl May put it like that, probably not, but if he said, humbly, in the cause of knowledge, just let's see if we *can*, just let's see. Only the once, then never again. (For once is ethical, twice is not.) Then you never know. They might. But what should *I* care; what is it to do with me? 'I' wouldn't suffer. The 'you's' might. Poor distorted things.

I saw my husband run his hands through her hennaed hair, that's what I remember, that's what makes the 'I' suffer, become well and truly me, with a shock which got to my solar plexus. I know he despises her. I could tell. Yet still he ran his fingers through her hair. Patronizing little bitch, little whore: in my home, bathing in my bath, her hairs blocking my plughole. I know. It was all in the blue-foldered report of the Maverick Enquiry Agency: there it stuck, a hennaed hair, long and silky, catching soap scum. Disgusting. Bethany! To be supplanted by a slut called Bethany: me, Joanna May. It would be easier if she was called Doris, or Betty, a name so ordinary it was deprived of resonance: became what I wanted it to be.

The world turned upside down: inside out, round and about; fire burn and cauldron bubble: bubbling vats of human cells, recombinant DNA surging and swelling, pulsing and heaving, multiplying by the million, the more the merrier: all the better, the more efficiently for biologists and their computers to work upon the structure of the living cell, the blueprints of our lives, decoding the DNA which is our inheritance. A snip here, a section there, excise this, insert that, slice and shuffle, find a marker, see what happens, what it grows: record it, collate it, work back and try again. Link up by computer to labs all over the world. Bang, goes Mr Nobel's gun, and off they go, false starts and fouling, panting and straining, proud hearts bursting, to understand and so control, to know what marks what and which – and better it. This DNA, this double helix, this bare substance of our chromosomal being, source of our sameness, root of our difference – this section gives us eyes, that segment of this section blue eyes, take it away and presto, no eyes – laid bare the better to cure us and heal us, change us and help us, deliver us from AIDS and give us two heads. And all of it glugging and growing in a culture of E.Coli – the bacteria of the human colon, tough, fecund, welcoming, just waiting around all that time to do its stuff at our behest – toss it, turn it, warm it, start it; nothing stops it. Well why not? Let the brave new world be based upon E.Coli – the stuff that gives us healthy shit. If our purpose on this earth is to salvage goodness from a material universe gone somehow wrong (which was what Oliver maintained) how more appropriately should it be done than by starting with shit and building up: creating not out of nothing, where's the glory in that, but forging miracles from debris, detritus. Now there's an accomplishment!

The vats are filled with pale, thin, milky translucent fluid, life itself, remarkably reflective of colour; slip, slop, plop. If the lab ceiling's green, then the culture shines green. Change the colour at will. Violet most impresses the visitors, but who wants a violet ceiling?

If you've got a good cow, don't breed from it, just repeat it: two by two, out of the ark. Take out the nucleus, cow-and-bull, mix in a newly fertilized cell, reintroduce an all-cow nucleus and what do you get, with any luck? Little twin clones, cow plus repetitions! I, Joanna May, beautiful and intelligent in my prime, now past it, am a woman plus repetitions, taken at my prime. Carl's fault, Carl's doing.

I am horrified, I am terrified, I don't know what to do with myself at all, whatever myself means now. I don't want to meet myself, I'm sure. I would look at myself with critical eyes, confound myself. I would see what I don't want to see, myself when young. I would see not immortality, but the inevitability of age and death. As I am, so they will become. Why bother? Why bother with them, why bother with me? What's the point? I can't bear it. I have to bear it. I can't even kill myself – they will go on. Now night will never fall.

I have never felt so old: I am all but paralysed. The back of my neck hurts where the vampire bit it. My heart aches where he struck at it.

I should have stayed home, as Oliver suggested.

23

Gerald Coustain said to his wife Angela, 'I don't know what's got into that fellow Carl May.'

Angela said, 'Is he any worse than he usually is?' They were eating fish and chips in a Chinese chippie with an eat-here section. With the meal, which included slices of white bread and butter, they drank sweet tea. This was their favourite food. They resented spending good money on food they liked less at expensive restaurants.

'Yes he is,' said Gerald. 'He's saying what he thinks on television. He's usually much too discreet for that. There'll be a public outcry. People can hear the sound of jackboots marching, the minute he opens his mouth.'

'I expect it's his new girlfriend,' said Angela. 'People who're foolish in one direction become foolish in them all.'

'What makes you think he has one?'

'Joanna rang me up in a state. Something had set her off.'

'That's not very reasonable of her,' he said, 'if what you say is true, that she's having it off with the gardener. What's sauce for the goose is sauce for the gander.'

'Yes,' said Angela, 'but neither likes the other having any.'

'Is he a good gardener?' asked Gerald, when he had absorbed this.

'She didn't say. I expect so. She's very fussy about that kind of thing. Always having her curtains cleaned and her wallpaper changed, and her kitchen units brought up to date.'

'I'm a good gardener,' said Gerald.

'I know you are, my dear,' she said. They each took a chip from the other's plate, in a gesture of continuing love and trust.

'Now she has a lover,' said Gerald, hopefully, 'we won't have to ask her to the lido again, will we? We won't have to be sorry for her.'

'I rather liked her coming to the lido with us. I think she enjoyed it. She looks very good in a cossie, I must say. Didn't you think so?'

'I didn't notice. She looked down her nose at me,' said Gerald. 'I had to stay wrapped in my towel. I didn't want her to see my paunch. There was nothing I could do about my varicose leg. She stared at that. No wonder Carl May got rid of her.'

'It would be a better idea,' said Angela, 'if you got rid of your paunch and your varicose veins. Eating here won't help. If only something healthier was our favourite food. Do you think the fish is radioactive?'

'Pretty well everything is,' said Gerald, sadly, 'if we're to go by our new monitoring equipment. But I'm not sure if it's been calibrated correctly. We'll just have to hope for the best. You don't mean to go round and see Joanna, I hope? You know my feelings about getting too close. All of us at the lido is obviously a good deed: you and her together smacks of a conspiracy.'

'She's my friend,' said Angela. 'I really do like her. She keeps saying things I don't expect!'

'If being her friend makes him your enemy, it isn't safe. I've told you that. I always take care to be very polite to him.'

'I think,' said Angela, 'they ought to get back together again. I think they still love each other in their hearts.'

He was pleased she thought so; a professor of Modern History both so wrong-headed and so romantic at heart; his wife, sharer of his chips.

24

Joanna May did not get back for many hours to her house on the banks of the Thames, where once a monarch had kept his vulgar mistress, and when she did she found Oliver dead. She'd wasted time talking to Angela, and then walking around Richmond Park to calm down. She found Oliver hanging by a rope around his ankles from a beam in the barn which was now a garage, swinging gently first this way, then that, his arms fastened gently across his chest as if he were an Egyptian mummy. His face was calm and not distressed, his eyes were open and everything he saw, if only the dead could see, was upside down. His bare young feet were smooth on top and rough-skinned underneath, but that was no surprise to Joanna May: she'd felt them often enough, and the nails were tough and horny and had earth beneath them as usual – the boots he liked the most to wear were not watertight. They stood neatly together in a corner of the garage, placed as if on guard. Who in the world would want them now, poor battered useless things? This way, that way, he swung. She sat down to adapt to a world deprived of this especial goodness, to recover from the shock. She grieved for his mother, and his friends, and the girl in Scotland he would never marry and the seedlings in the greenhouse which no one now would get round to planting out. She grieved for herself, of course she did. Who now would fill her bed? She was old. She was old: surely the old could be spared the shock of losing a lover, of understanding that the body that inspires you, fills you, is frail, mortal, corruptible, as liable to stop on the instant as anything else. This way that way. Through the grief and shock ran a thread of relief: it was over, finished: sharply, quickly: now he would never decide it wouldn't work: wouldn't one day see her wrinkling skin in a clear light, or some aspect

124

of her nature she could no longer hide and decide she wasn't the one for him, and be off (in the fallow season, of course) to some other garden in need, some other divorced lady with excellent alimony and a waiting bed. The back of her neck hurt when she moved it. The graze smarted.

Her fault, of course, her fault: she wailed aloud, and a bird fluttered down from the eaves and out the open door. (She thought it carried Oliver's soul with it, and now she was truly alone and he was truly gone.) His eyes had shut now, the lower eyelids drooping, as the flesh gave up its residual resilience. She was glad of that: he had seen more than enough upside down.

On the floor, beneath the hanging body, brushed by Oliver's hair, lay a single card from the Tarot pack. It was the Hanged Man, from the Minor Arcana, that benign and peaceful fellow suspended by his feet. Above, below, to right and left were four more cards, the Queens of Wands, Pentacles, Swords and Cups.

She should never, as a wife, have tried to discuss the nature of reality with Carl: her fault. She should never have told him about the Fates, about there being more gods than one God, about the Tarot pack: fidget as he might over the *Financial Times*, he heard, he heard: he did not forgive and he did not forget. As an ex-wife she should have faded away, ceased to exist: not quite murdered, not quite unmurdered. Her fault. She should never have told Carl May about Oliver, boasting, denying the inevitability of her desolation, her non-existence; her fault: she should never have answered back: her fault. She should never have gone in the first place, but listened to Oliver. She should have come straight home to warn him: her fault: she should never have allowed him into her bed: her fault. She had, she had, and now Oliver was dead. Her fault. A little niggle of anger arose, swelled; she screamed and screamed. Not her fault, not her fault at all. Carl May's fault. Carl May the murderer.

She went into the kitchen and found Trevor the butler, with his soft hands and soft round face, sitting at the scrubbed-elm table shaking and weeping; and the expensive wall-to-ceiling kitchen units, which he so loved and Oliver found claustrophobic, rising like the walls of a mausoleum around him, and a dozen hanging copper pans caught the reflection of his shock and grief and threw it back and forth across the room, one to another. Well, it was his world: it was fitting.

'What happened?' asked Joanna, and Trevor told her.

25

Why was Joanna so late home? Should not her instinct have been, having betrayed Oliver, to go straight back home and warn him? Of course, but her neck hurt, she was confused and upset; she was not convinced, even if she tried to persuade him of it, that Oliver would appreciate the danger he was in. He would say she was imagining it, and go on shaking off dahlia tubers, or whatever he was doing. It was difficult to convey the extraordinary and drastic nature of Carl's world to a young man whose concerns were so very horticultural, with a dash of rock guitar thrown in. He would be positive about the matter of the clones, which she was not sure she wanted him to be. He would say, 'Well, you always wanted a family: now you have them. Sisters and daughters both,' and if she complained that it was altogether too sudden, and done against her will besides, and Carl May's behaviour outrageous, he would have told her not to be so negative, or the peas wouldn't swell in the pods or the bees wouldn't fertilize the pears – some threat, at any rate, to hold over her head – and remind her that the reason she was no longer married to Carl May was because he was outrageous, so why act so surprised?

In the end she called Angela from a phone box and confided in her, and Angela was gratifyingly startled.
'You mean you didn't even know, Joanna?'
'No.'
'Cloned, and not known it?'
'That's right.'
'Well, I wouldn't like that.'
'Neither do I, Angela. That's why I'm calling.'
'Poor Joanna.'

'Because you know how all this time I've been complaining about having nothing – no children, no career, no family, no husband, nothing I've earned or worked for myself: a whole life wasted –'

'Yes, I do, Joanna –'

'Well, there was a kind of pride in that, Angela. It was my singularity. He has taken away my singularity. He has shovelled all these bits and pieces at me, and I hate it.'

'It would make me feel better, I think.'

'It made me feel like just nothing, Angela; and this makes me feel perfectly dreadful, I can tell you. All I can do is just wander about. I'm calling from a phone box, I'm not even home.'

'Why did he save it till now, do you think?'

'Because he was angry, I suppose.'

'I expect he was. Men don't much like their ex-wives bursting into their offices. Good old Carl, always has to be in the forefront of everything, even test-tube babies. Tinker tinker with the universe.'

'I don't know how you can say that: "Good old Carl."'

'I was being ironic, Joanna.'

'Oh. I see.'

'Joanna, would you say Carl was mad? Answer frankly.'

'No,' said Joanna, 'I'm afraid he isn't. I think he just likes to have his own way, and get his own back. He's childish.'

'I see,' said Angela. 'Can I tell Gerald about the clones?'

'If you feel you have to,' said Joanna, a little tearfully.

'Are you going to try and find these creatures?'

'I don't think so. I don't suppose they know. It might be an even worse shock for them than it has been for me.'

'I can see that. A kind of extra mother, dreadfully like oneself. Seeing what one would grow into. Thirty years ago, you say.'

'Yes.'

'What it amounts to is you've got four identical twins half your age walking round unclaimed.'

'I suppose so, yes.'

'Well, don't tell your Oliver or he might go after them.'

'You mean to kill them? Because they upset me? Like slugs, snails and greenfly?'

128

'No I don't mean that, Joanna. I mean he might fancy them.'

'Why should he?'

'Because they're half your age. You, but more so, Joanna.'

And Angela thought, but was too kind to say, even though she was jealous – how could she not be jealous with Joanna still beautiful, still pulling them in, at sixty – 'You'd be the first taste of a drug on his tongue, Joanna, and they the real stuff, the full flavour.' Instead, she said, 'I hope you didn't tell Carl about your gardener lover. I hope that wasn't why he was so angry?'

'Well yes, I did.'

'Oh dear,' said Angela. 'Wasn't that rather stupid?'

'Yes,' said Joanna.

'I hope your clones are more prudent than you,' said Angela, 'or their nearest and dearest will be having a terrible time. I think you should go straight back home and warn this gardener of yours. Gerald takes Carl quite seriously, you know.'

'I should hope so,' said Joanna.

Joanna went and walked about Richmond Park, in totally impractical shoes. When she was thirty she had imagined all her troubles would be over by forty, there would be nothing left to go wrong: at forty she had imagined the same about fifty, and at fifty she had given up: she still found herself walking about distracted and alone, carefully refraining from crying, just as she had when she was a child.

She remembered coming home from the Bulstrode Clinic and that time she had really wept, from physical weakness more than anything else, or so she had supposed. She remembered that the doctor's name had been Dr Holly. Holly and May, she'd thought at the time, berries and flowers. Red berries, white flowers, and nothing coming out of either.

Well, she'd been wrong about that. Too much had come out of it. She would go back to Oliver and tell him everything, everything, no matter what Angela said; they would go off for six months to some secret destination. New Zealand, perhaps. The soil was good, she believed, and the gardens were wonderful.

If he loved her, he would believe her; they would go. Or she would apologize to Carl; tell him she'd been making it all up. Something. Her head ached, her neck hurt: she had to sleep.

26

Angela went straight up to Gerald's office after she'd talked to Joanna; she took the car to the station, the train up to London, a taxi to the Department, and Gerald came straight out of a meeting to see her. She hadn't been to his office for eight years, he reminded her, not since the time their eldest son had made a passing girlfriend pregnant and she'd been upset.

It was Joanna May, she told him. Joanna had phoned her from a callbox on Reading station to tell her the most extraordinary story. Gerald said perhaps he'd better get back to his meeting, since it wasn't family, and the less he knew about the Mays the better and the same went for Angela, and the news from Chernobyl was not good, it was still belching peculiar things into the atmosphere, and there was more trouble with the monitoring equipment. He might have to go back to Britnuc for help. But he didn't return to the meeting, of course. They went to the canteen instead, for tea. Not liking the look of the pastries, he had the steak and kidney pie: she took the braised beef and mushrooms. Both had roast potatoes, boiled potatoes and buttered parsnips as well. It would keep them going until supper-time.

'It probably isn't the equipment's fault; it's just the technicians don't know how to use it,' said Angela, which hadn't occurred to Gerald. He admitted they were barely trained. The truth was, the nation was totally unprepared for such an emergency. If emergency it was – radiation was still pretty much an unknown quantity. The danger was not critical or immediate – damage would show up in the morbidity statistics of the future when a different government altogether would be in power.

'I hope you were careful,' said Gerald. 'I wouldn't put it past Carl May to have our phone tapped.'

131

'Neither would I,' said Angela. 'Is cloning someone without their knowledge illegal?'

'I have no idea,' said Gerald. 'I hope so.'

'The other thing that bothers me,' said Angela, 'is will Carl try and get rid of the gardener?'

'You mean fire him?'

'I mean kill him, like he did the professor. What Joanna calls "that thing with Isaac".'

'I shouldn't think so,' said Gerald. 'There was more to that than met the eye. I nipped over to the Home Office and had a look at the files.'

'Why did you do that?'

'Always useful to have a hold over a fellow like Carl May,' said Gerald, and there was a gleam in his eye she seldom saw but liked to see. Not for nothing had he risen through the ranks of public service; she used to know the reason well: these days, as his face grew softer and pudgier, she tended to forget. All round them people drank herbal tisanes and ate muesli bars. No one took tea seriously any more. She cleared their plates, and went to fetch spotted dick. Custard was off.

'I hope you like foam cream,' she said when she came back. 'There's no custard and it's kind of stiff without any lubrication at all. What did the files say?'

'Just that prosecution was against the public interest,' said Gerald. 'That fellow King had a pretty dicey record, anyway. He was collecting brain tissue from Egyptian mummies and taking it to some lab somewhere and trying to grow an ancient Egyptian. Garden Enterprises was funding the lab.'

'What a peculiar thing to want to do,' said Angela, 'considering how the population of Egypt grows of its own accord. By a million every nine months, I believe.'

'I don't know about peculiar,' said Gerald. 'It might have been rather interesting, if it had worked. Anyway the Home Office didn't seem too upset the professor was out of the way. So I don't reckon he was got rid of just because Carl was jealous. Something else was going on.'

'Poor Joanna,' said Angela, 'she won't like that at all. But at least it means the gardener is safe. Well, safe-ish.'

'So long as he keeps out of the rain,' said Gerald. 'That seems to be the main danger, these days. Personally, I hope he stays out in it, and his balls fall off. Are you sure there's no custard?'

'One wonders a little,' said Angela, 'about the wisdom of having a man such as Carl May in charge of quite so many nuclear power stations.'

'They're very old ones,' said Gerald.

'I should have thought that made matters worse.'

'Not really,' said Gerald. 'They're like old cars. You can patch them and repair them and keep them on the road; and they give you due warning when something bad is going to happen. They knock and clank a bit: in time for you to do something about it. It's the new ones that are the problem: all built-in, fail-safe factors, and non-labour-intensive, because human error is always the non-calculable hiccough, ergonomically speaking: nothing at all to go wrong in the new ones, but if it does, pow!'

'All the same,' said Angela.

'We'd never have him in charge of the new ones,' said Gerald, reassuringly. 'Don't you worry. As it is, he's a popular fellow and a public hero and good for the image of the nuclear power industry.'

'But he's a murderer,' said Angela.

'Hush,' said Gerald, 'that's a very strong way of putting it. All these fellows tend to dispose of their enemies one way or another: if governments can do it, they think, why can't they, quite ignoring the electoral mandate. One can't condone it but it does happen. At least Carl May confines his activities to the personal sphere.'

'Think about it, Gerald,' said Angela.

'He isn't mad,' said Gerald. 'One draws the line at people who're mad, in charge of anything.'

'I'm not so sure about that,' said Angela. 'I'm not so sure about him being sane.'

'We'll see what transpires,' said Gerald. 'We'll keep a careful eye on things. Are you really sure there's no proper custard?'

'Quite sure,' said Angela, brushing away a flake of suet pudding which stuck to her hairy chin.

'Pity,' said Gerald. 'This cream is rather much.'

133

27

Had Joanna bitten back her anger, jealousy and resentment, and not visited Carl, her life would have gone calmly on: as it was, she was saved. Without the assault of these passionate saving graces she would have aged slowly and gracefully, developed a touch of arthritis here, a backache there: Oliver would have drifted off – men with guitars seldom stay, as she knew in her heart; a few languorous, heart-strumming chords, and they're off – and her fate would have indeed been that of the elderly woman who has never been employed, has no husband, no children, no former colleagues or particular interests, a handful of friends still around, with any luck (though their particular loyalties stretched by distance, exhaustion, their own problems) but who is fortunate enough to have a lot of money.

She would have given up the King's House in time. It would have come to seem, as her body shrunk, too big, too echoey, too frightening, too empty. Most women end their lives in bedsitting rooms, one way or another; possessions exhaust; they get discarded. Even pets become too much of a responsibility. The walls close in as the years pass: rooms get smaller. Joanna might have joined, for a time, those groups of women who go from good hotel to good hotel, up and down the coasts in winter – in to the cathedral cities in summer – filling up the vacant rooms of hoteliers, who smile to see their income coming through the door, but whose hearts sink at the very sight of them, boredom and grievance incarnate. And how can these old ladies, these outlivers of men, not be boring, being so bored themselves? And how can they not complain, whose very life is a reproach to the young and vigorous? Joanna May's mind would have narrowed with her life: she would have stopped contemplating the nature of existence, stopped worrying about the constituents of identity, thought only of whether Tuesday's lamb chop and mint sauce was any more or less digestible than Wednesday's escalope and mushrooms. These terrible things she knew in her head: they lurked on the edge of her consciousness. And with that instinct for the preservation not just of life but of aliveness, not just the body but the soul, Joanna acted; driven by indignation, whipped-up emotion, frothed up to twice its proper size like a dollop of cream in a fast-food restaurant, she was moved to confront Carl in his lair, knowing perfectly well that he'd snarl and scratch, that his snarls and scratches were dangerous, and she was glad of it.

Why else had she married Carl May, in the first place, but to be saved from boredom? The boredom, the depression, of childhood, of home? Why had she brought about the divorce, but because boredom hadn't been routed, no: it had been creeping behind her for thirty years, waiting to pounce, and it had almost caught up with her again, peering out from behind soup tureens at official dinners, perching on the white ties of elderly gents at functions, waving; nothing to talk to Carl about any more: or anything he was prepared to listen to, his life so divorced from hers, yet she so used to him, he to her, they could hardly tell each other apart.

Something had to *happen*.

Isaac happened. Isaac talked, talked, everything interested him; more, he listened. Illicit excitement sent boredom running, far far away, over distant hills: but excitement, danger, was like a drug, you got used to it, you needed more. At first, sex in his bedsitting room was enough, more than enough, mad enough, with the strange smells of toothpowder, and undone laundry, and disorder, books and papers everywhere, bits of old pottery, half a mummy's head; dead flowers in a vase, from 4000 BC for all she knew, the old sometimes looked so new, the colours so bright, the shapes so distinct. And Isaac's voice wonderfully on and on, including her in his universe, and the universe seemed to have a history, a purpose, a meaning, which started in the past, collecting as it went, arriving at *now*. Carl's universe started in the future and came back to today – it collected nothing. Well, that was understandable. Carl May's experience of the past was not pleasant, so he looked to the future, of course he did. But then Isaac's bedsitting room was not enough: she got used to it: it seemed too ordinary for something as extraordinary as Isaac and Joanna May, wife of Carl: boredom crept back, nearer, began to wave, sitting on mummy cases, on the edge of the chipped bath, sooty from an ancient gas-fired geyser, which puffed out black dust if you wanted hot water to wash. In the end the gallery was the only place he wouldn't come, this ghost of her own past, outdone at its own game by the half-haunted gloom, the watching eyes of history, which seemed to approve – or Isaac said they did; sex was just fine with the Ancient Egyptians, according to him – and of course in the gallery it was perfectly possible for Carl to come in at any time. They must have been mad. She must have been. But again, she was angry. A woman without children, now wanting children, too late to have children. Carl's fault. She loved Isaac, let Carl know it. He deserved it. Something had to happen. And one day it did: Carl pushed the door open.

And that stopped Carl being bored, for a time. He'd got too cosy anyway: he was the media's darling, the Government's blue-eyed boy. Garden Enterprises was under way. Britnuc was belching clean air into a threatened atmosphere – with only the occasional release of unscheduled radioactivity, which was in any case the least of many polluting evils. Something had to *happen*.

Carl May, before his wife's infidelity, was beginning to get pains in his chest. His was the kind of boredom which destroys life, like a slowly creeping fungus on a pear tree, causing leaves to wither and fruit to fall, unripened. Let him lose his wife, then, thought Joanna: that'll cure him: a swift blast of fungicide in the form of jealousy, outrage, anger. She'd been right. Carl shook himself and thrived. Only in the shaking he'd shaken her off too. She hadn't done it for his sake, had she, but for her own.

28

If thine eye offend thee, pluck it out! Now there's a desperate doctrine, a right dollop of lateral thinking, a fine biblical recipe for preserving thy view of thyself as a fine and upright person. Kill the bearer of the bad news, would you; much good may it do you. The enemy still advances over the hill. If thine eye lusts, sever the optical nerves; chop off your hand if it strays where it shouldn't: destroy your ears to keep out the seducing voice: eyeless, earless, legless, armless, roll around in the mire: you will still be in the valley of desire. Just unable to function. After the inquest, after I, Joanna May, had perjured myself and betrayed the memory and love of Isaac King, the better to protect the interests of my husband Carl, I walked back to Eton Square, to the big pillared house which was Carl's and my home. I walked up the steps, put my key in the lock, and found it would not turn. The key was the right key – it was the lock that had changed. I banged the knocker and rattled the handle but no one came. Yet I'd seen Anna's pudgy face at the window, just a glimpse of it, or thought I had.

I believed that by perjuring myself I would win Carl's forgiveness, that it would be over: it could be forgotten. That Isaac's death was sufficient punishment for me. I stamped and shouted and banged upon the step, and I expect I screamed and cried, I can't remember. The solid door stood between me and my marriage, my home, my friends, my clothes, my possessions, my past, my future, my life. Those strong upright houses of Pimlico are built to keep the poor out; to keep the rich secure, the noise of riot at a distance. Carl had cast me out of his life; I had become a supplicant: I belonged the wrong side of the door. I knew it was no accident. It bore the hallmark of Carl's vengeance. The sudden shock of horrid surprise which he knew so well how to deliver, the lightning stroke out of an apparently clear sky. First he lured you into complacency; then, clap, snap, he got you.

I went to the phone box on the corner and rang my own number but no one answered. I wondered what Anna was thinking as it rang and rang, and she knew it was me: poor Anna, straight from the Philippines, witnessing this cruelty, obliged to be part of it. Carl paid her wages. Would she be horrified, or would she just think this is what happens, always happens, always will happen, to women when they cease to please or, worse, step out of line. A plain girl herself, stocky and puffy-eyed, bad-complexioned, hesitant in English, used and abused, fleeing one set of harshnesses to run into another, still thinking herself lucky, allowed to pick up the crumbs of Carl's and my life. Poor Anna. She'd know whose side she was on: whichever hand had the power, held the food, would be the one she licked. I went back and stood on the step: it began to rain a little: I didn't know what to do: to go to friends would be to start a scandal: I was still Carl's wife.

And then the garage door whirred and opened, and the big Volvo backed out, black and shiny and somehow ordinary, with the dent still in the wing which had been the death of Isaac, and in the back was Poudry the solicitor, and in the front was Philip the murderer. And Poudry held the door open for me, and I got inside, because I didn't know what else to do. And while we drove to a small and rather grimy hotel in Paddington – where someone or other who needed their wages no doubt, and knew which side their bread was buttered, and that it wasn't my side, had unkindly booked me a room – Poudry told me Carl was divorcing me, that I would be bought a house and given an income, that I was not to set foot in Eton Square again, that I was to think myself lucky.

That my clothes had been destroyed, my papers and my books and my family photographs shredded, and my parents' marriage certificate and my father's death certificate too; and no sign of me was to be left in the house, all trace of me was to be destroyed. I was free to begin life again as he would be, without evidence of the past, and I should think myself lucky.

138

'Do you think I'm lucky?' I asked Mr Poudry.

'Yes, I do,' he said, after thinking about it for a little. We were, I think, both very conscious of the dent in the Volvo's back wing, and of Philip the chauffeur in the front. Mr Poudry hummed a little in a nonchalant way that reminded me of Pooh, in *The House at Pooh Corner*, singing a little song the better to sound at ease: 'How nice to be a cloud, floating in the blue. It makes me very proud, to be a little cloud.'

As it happened my husband was generous. Not that 'as it happened' is a phrase that was much bandied about in Carl May's life. It suited him, for reasons of his own not immediately plain to others, to be generous, or appear to be.

I moved out of the Suffolk Ease hotel only when the decorators finished in the King's House. I could have left at any time, but the hotel was a desperate place and suited me. I had a room to myself: others, immigrants, lived twenty-five to a room, in a stench of urine and cooking, refugees from one horror or another – flood, famine, persecution, torture, war. Carl, booking me in here, meant to tell me something. So I sat it out, recovering from my own desolation, my own sudden loss of home. I had no one. The other lodgers had each other. Night after night I sat alone in a room, sitting on a bed – damp stains on the wall, the murmur of human grief around, crying children – staring at television: a woman of more than fifty, whom even money couldn't save. And I wanted to see Carl, and he wouldn't: I wanted to talk to Carl, and he wouldn't. How could he do it? How could he wrench us apart? If it hurt me, surely it hurt him? I mourned Isaac but I mourned for my marriage more.

And all Mr Poudry would say, when I visited him in his office, was, 'You are very lucky, Mrs May,' and one day he added, 'It might be a good idea to move out of the Suffolk Ease: you'll forgive me for saying so, but there is beginning to be about you the pong of the underprivileged.' And I looked at him closely for the first time and saw he was not more than thirty: it was the weight of authority had aged him in my eyes. I wouldn't go. The hotel was where Carl wanted me to be. I was obedient. Only when I moved into the King's House did I begin to find my will again, or some of it. I washed, I dressed, I looked after myself: I became accustomed to life without Carl. Sometimes I even enjoyed it. I began to like the vision of myself, the drama of a woman lonely and alone, living in isolation, rejecting the world which rejected her.

Then I employed Oliver as a gardener: and one day he took out his guitar and sang some folk song to me, some wispy song of lust and longing, and asked me if I'd like to play the guitar, and I said yes, and he put the guitar in my arms, and stood behind me and put his arms round my arms, and that was that. I no longer thought about Carl. I was cured. I assumed he was cured too. I thought I was safe from Carl.

I thought all would be well if I did not love Oliver: I could not let myself love him. I knew quite well what would happen if I did. That if I cared when it ended – and it must, it must, I knew in my heart it must though my head pretended otherwise – the pain this time would kill me. A lump in my breast, a swollen lymph gland under the arm and that would be that. And who would there be to come to my funeral? Gerald (reluctantly) and Angela (weeping: if only for the loss of a good gossip) and Mr Poudry and the accountant, and a nurse from the hospital if I'd remembered to smile while dying; and Carl would not come, or if he did, it would be so the press didn't pick up the fact that he had not. The funeral was not worth the dying for: let Oliver be a nightly visitor to my bed, let him return me, little by little, to the fullness of the world, but that must be all. It should not be difficult. I had loved Carl May: having loved Carl May, I could not easily fall in love with, become emotionally dependent upon, sexually infatuated with, addicted to, a gardener who played rock guitar.

Oliver died and I found it was true. I had not loved him. You only know what you've got once it's gone, and it wasn't much. Trevor the butler gave an account of Oliver's death, his murder – and how could it be anything but murder: a man doesn't easily hang himself by his feet – and I heard the account with equanimity. I winced, for it was a horrid thought that a life which could bring me to life, purply-red, strong and pulsing, had changed suddenly and permanently into limp white rotting tissue. I wept a little, because Oliver had been cut down in the spring of his life, and of the year, with the whole blossoming, blooming, fruiting season yet to go. I was saddened because now my evenings would have to be spent alone, the forbidden pleasure, the companionable calming marijuana joints no more. I was shocked, pale and shaking – a physical reaction, I imagined – but the roots of my being were untouched, steady, compacted in dry earth. I surprised even myself.

If thy love offend thee, pluck it out.

29

The gardens of the King's House ran down to the river Thames, gently sloping, occasionally terraced. The river split to form an island, shared by a little group of houses, of which Joanna's was the biggest and best. The jetty, however, was seldom used. Oliver did not like the water, and Joanna mistrusted it. The garden was old; first established in the eighteenth century, used originally as an overflow for Kew Gardens, neglected and cosseted by turns. 'What a pity you don't like gardening,' Oliver would say to Joanna. 'Looking after a garden is like looking after children. Feed plants and they grow, neglect them and they suffer. It's all rewards and punishments – with more than a dash of chance thrown in, in the form of weather. I'm sure you'd be good at it.'

But what Joanna liked was to sit out on a sunny morning, and breakfast at leisure, dressed in white as often as not, watching Oliver work: the garden and herself presently drifting into one: she the prize lily, a little past peak flowering perhaps, but still what the garden was all about: the culture and cultivation of beauty.

She liked to sit in the spring and summer and watch the pleasure boats go by, music approaching, passing, fading – while those who had the gift of life, the understanding of enjoyment, the privilege of friendship, went sailing by. Or so it seemed. Joanna did not doubt that on closer acquaintance the crews and guests aboard the yachts, steamers and launches were as vulgar and foolish as anyone else, as prone to anxiety, misery and jealousies as she: that the music masked a thousand discontents, and that the champagne moved to mock exhilaration, not necessarily the real thing: nevertheless the illusion was pleasant, there was no need to get too near. She did not grudge these river people the possibility of happiness, at least, and certainly admired their ambition to achieve it. 'Such a lovely day! Let's go on the river . . .' Still, she had managed the lido, with Gerald and Angela: that was water and outing enough.

On the afternoon of that day, the day Joanna, her own resentments finally focused, had gone to Reading to have it out with Carl, Oliver, having finished with the rhododendrons, was weeding out the herbaceous borders. He worked with a hoe, standing to unsettle the shallow roots of the clover which crept up from the river bank in spite of all efforts to prevent it; or, occasionally, kneeling, with fork and trowel, to dig out plantains, patiently easing out the long, stubborn root, loosening soil and levering back and forth until they gave up, apologizing as he did so for thus putting paid to their best endeavours. His habit of talking to plants of all sorts, including weeds, and especially weeds he meant to destroy, quite irritated Joanna.

'If you're going to kill them, kill them,' she'd say. Oliver would droop his lids over his soft brown eyes to mask his displeasure, giving him what she called his 'I meant to please but now look' spaniel look; his hippy look, of reverence to all things, gentle, kind and understanding; his Age of Aquarius look. Then she'd say, 'I don't know why you don't just use weedkiller, like anyone else,' just to incense him, to watch the pallor of determined sweetness give way to the pink of indignation, and then she'd laugh and he'd know she was teasing.

But these pleasures were over now. An expensive-looking pleasure launch of the kind Oliver least liked, being moulded in some kind of new fashion to give it rounded, bulbous lines, and in a colour Oliver knew to be called Whisper Pink, trimmed with Whisper Cream, its CD playing Elgar's 'Pomp and Circumstance', cut its engine, its music, on the stretch of river which ran by the King's House, slid slowly into the jetty and tied up. There were five young men on board, strangely dressed.

Oliver straightened up, and watched the five young men disembark and come towards him, up the garden path where the tiger tulips bloomed on either side. They smiled, but he knew they were not friendly: something about the tense way they held their necks; he knew at once that retreat would be more dangerous than standing ground, that to placate would be safer than to challenge. They were, he thought, in their mid-twenties. They talked and joked amongst themselves, halfway between yobbo and yuppy: yobbo down below, layers of ragged and chain-strewn trouser; up above, collar, tie and suit jacket. Their heads were apparently shaven, and they wore bowler hats.

'Nice place you've got here,' the leader said. His name was Jacko. He was blond and beautiful. 'You the gardener?'

'Yes,' said Oliver, 'that's my trade.'

'Got quite a bit of age to it,' said the second in command. His name was Petie. He was dark and sulky. 'This garden has.'

'That is certainly so,' said Oliver. 'It was old when George Three bought it and renovated it for his mistress.'

'Did he now?' said Elwood, who was black and beautiful. 'Those old geezers weren't half naughty boys.'

And Haggie and Dougie, who were pale, thin and spotty, and didn't fill their trousers or their suit jackets nearly as well as the other three, kicked a tulip or two out of the ground.

'Pity to do that,' said Oliver, mildly. 'That's quite a rare flower. A black tulip. Not my favourite, as flowers go, a black flower being unnatural, if you ask me, but some people like them.'

In answer, Dougie and Haggie tore up handfuls of daffodils, and Oliver didn't mind that so much. They were more or less over and he'd been going to move them, in any case, to some less-overlooked patch of ground where they could deteriorate in peace and wait for their replanting in the autumn. But he pretended dismay, since that was what they wanted.

'Can I help you fellows?' he asked, wondering where Trevor was. Trevor would sometimes come out in the mornings with a cup of coffee, and sit on a stone wall in the sunshine and talk about the minutiae of his life with his lover – he was having an up-and-down relationship with a masseur at a nearby health farm – and Oliver would listen patiently and respond construc-tively. If Trevor looked out of the window and saw the young men he might, with any luck, call the police.

'Is the missus out?' asked Jacko.

'The missus is out,' said Oliver, 'but the master's in,' half a truth being in his book better than no truth at all, albeit in the circumstances any lie might have been justifiable. Those capable of knocking off the heads of black tulips, in passing, were in Oliver's eyes quite capable of knocking off human heads.

'That's a lie and a half,' said Jacko. 'The mistress is out as we very well know – and what a naughty boy you are, Oliver, young enough to be the lady's son – and the master ain't here neither.'

'If you know,' said Oliver, brightly, 'then why ask me?' and was quite pleased with his own courage. He'd said the same thing, at the age of four – according to his proud mother – to his teacher when asked what three and two made. 'If you know, why ask me?'

Jacko took out his fob watch and looked at it, and took off his hat to reveal a topknot of golden curls, and nodded to Elwood, who opened his briefcase and took out a length of bamboo pipe. Petie took out a dart from the yellow child's lunch box he carried, and Petie carefully handed the dart to Elwood who put it in the hollow tube and blew the other end, hard and sharp, and it landed in the back of Oliver's hand, the one that was carrying the trowel.

'Ouch!' he said, and dropped it, and Jacko, Petie, Elwood, Dougie and Haggie counted to five in unison and Oliver felt numbness running up his arm and down to his heart. He noticed the sudden quietness of his whole body, as it stopped beating. He thought, this is what it must be like for a fuchsia killed by frost; when water turns to ice, and that was all he thought.

Trevor was coming out to meet the lads. He had seen the gleam of yellow hair when Jacko took off his hat, and the flash of handsome male profiles, and wanted to know what was going on. He feared no evil on his own home ground.

But they were bending over Oliver, whoever they were, and turned their smiling faces towards him, and one said, 'It can only be Trevor, the man's man,' and he detected in their smiles something which made him shiver. 'Better get in the house, Trevor, before it's you as well,' so he did. He walked smartly back into the house and locked the back door and slammed shut the stainless steel mesh shutters on the windows from the security console. He watched through the mesh but they did not come after him, and he was affronted, as well as relieved. It seemed he was no business of theirs. Instead, they picked up Oliver and carried him shoulder high into the garage, which had once been a barn. Trevor thought they were singing something.

He did not call the police. He had enough trouble with the police. They followed him when he went out shopping, just waiting for him to go where they assumed he was going, to the public convenience that is, the better to pounce and get him for some disgusting act or other, which he would never perform, but they quite happily invent.

After five minutes Haggie reappeared and looked over the garden in a puzzled kind of way. He called to his friends, 'What's a shitty rose look like anyway?' and Petie came out and wrenched a branch off a rose bush, and went back into the garage, Haggie following.

After ten minutes or so all five men appeared again, without Oliver; marched down to the launch moored at the jetty, boarded it, and left in the direction of Reading. Trevor went out to the garage and found Oliver hanging as Joanna was later to find him. The back of his hand had been scratched by, presumably, thorns from the rose branch. A few petals lay on the floor. Oliver's boots had been pulled off and tossed aside. Out of custom, Trevor put them neatly together. On the floor, beneath the hanging body, brushed by Oliver's hair, lay a single card from the Tarot pack. Trevor recognized it as the Hanged Man. Trevor had had his fortune told often enough to know that the card was supposed to signify innocence and the overcoming of difficulties by sheer good luck, but he had always taken leave to doubt it; the Tarot pack in his opinion was more sinister than its diviners would often allow. In this case he could see the card signified what he had always suspected: death by hanging because you didn't look out. And above, below, and to the left and right of the signifier, the Hanged Man in person, were the four Queens. Oh, kinky, thought Trevor: what is going on?

He said goodbye to Oliver in the same spirit as Oliver would say goodbye to doomed weeds and went to sit in the kitchen. He opened the shutters. There seemed no point in keeping them closed. He would wait until Joanna came home and let her decide whether or not to call the police. If she did, he could explain the delay as the general inefficiency and stupidity of the man they insulted him by supposing him to be. He tried to call his friend Jamie but the line was dead. That did not surprise him.

He assumed Joanna would understand the significance of the four cards, and he was right.

30

'On either side the river lie,' quoted Carl May, from Tennyson,

   'Long fields of clover and of rye –'

'Barley,' said Bethany, and Carl May chose to ignore her. Once.

   'That clothe the wold
   And meet the sky
   And through the fields
   The road runs by
   To many-towered Camelot.'

   'That's where my ex-wife lives,' said Carl May, 'in Camelot.'
'I thought she lived at the King's House, Maidenhead,' said
Bethany. They lay in bed together. The sheets were white. There
were blankets, not a quilt. How quaint, had thought Bethany
once, how like him, how pure, but now she thought, how
old-fashioned, how uncomfortable, how like death. He ignored
her. Twice.

   'And up and down
   The people go
   Gazing where the lilies blow
   Round an island there below
   The island of Shalott –'

'Shallots, onions,' said Bethany.
Thrice.

   'Four grey walls
   And four grey towers
   Overlook a space of flowers,
   And the silent isle embowers
   The Lady of Shalott.'

'Yes, I know,' said Bethany, '"She left the web, she left the loom, she made three paces through the room" – we did it for diction – "the mirror cracked from side to side, the curse is come upon me, cried the Lady of Shalott." Then she mooned about for a bit and topped herself from sheer boredom. Which reminds me that the curse has not come upon me. What are we to do, Carl?'

Carl was silent.

'I know you said you had a vasectomy, Carl, but it can't have worked because I'm pregnant and I've been with no one but you, Carl.'

Still Carl was silent.

'There, I've said it,' she said. 'I'd been getting really nervous.'

Carl sat up in bed, looked down at her bare breasts, her smooth narrow arms, her blue eyes – she took out her contact lenses at night – and rested his hand upon her throat. Then he moved it down over her body, on the whole quite gently, though tweaking her nipples rather sharply, to which she was not averse.

'You be careful,' said Carl, 'or you'll end up like Squirrel Nutkin,' but she didn't understand the reference. Nor did she have time to puzzle it out, as the whole of Carl May advanced upon her.

'You were only joking about being pregnant, I suppose,' he said, presently, disentangling his legs from hers reluctantly, but he felt the first twinge of cramp, to which he was prone.

'Of course,' said Bethany. 'Twice in one night. Wow! What a man!' She was tired. She used the language of porno films. She did not have the energy for finesse. He did not seem to notice. There was no real reason for her to be tired. She thought it might well be the effect of boredom.

'I had a man killed today,' said Carl, pleased with himself. 'Perhaps that's it.'

Bethany blinked, but was careful not to let her body tauten against Carl's. She no longer felt tired. Then she thought, well, one pregnancy joke deserves a murder joke. A death for a life. Silly old you.

'He didn't suffer,' said Carl.

'If you're going to kill a man,' said Bethany, 'why bother if he suffers or not?'

'One does bother,' he said. 'For some reason. I don't wish to inflict pain, or terror. Some lives simply need to stop. Have you ever had a termination, my dear?'

'Once.'

'Well, there you are. You understand.'

Bethany put on her contact lenses and turned her eyes green, and fluffed out her red hair, and pranced about the room. It could do no harm.

'Who was Squirrel Nutkin?' she asked.

'Squirrel Nutkin danced about in front of a wise old owl,' he said from the bed, 'taunting him and teasing him, asking riddles and telling jokes.'

'What sort of riddles?'

'Riddle me, riddle me, riddle me, ree,
How many strawberries swim in the sea?
I answered him as I thought good,
As many red herrings as grow in the wood,'

said Carl May, 'for example.'

'What happened?'

'Nothing happened.'

'Then what was the point?'

'Nothing happened and nothing happened.'

'Then what?'

'Something happened. The old owl pounced and ate Squirrel Nutkin up and there was peace in the wood again.'

'Oh,' said Bethany, and put on her clothes rather quickly. Sometimes he did give her the creeps. But presently her spirits were restored, for she was indeed young and she found herself singing her favourite song:

'For a young man he is young
And an old man he is grey,
And a young man's back is good and strong,
Get away, old man, get away.'

150

'I haven't finished yet,' said Carl May. 'Indeed I have only just started,' so she had to get back into bed again, but that was not really what he was talking about.

31

Thus thought Joanna May, missing Isaac King badly (for he *knew* what the cards meant, and she could only guess): now, if the four Queens of the Tarot pack, or, as some would have it, the long-lost Egyptian Book of Toth, are seen together, they denote nothing worse than arguments. If reversed, however, the argument might become excessive; fatal, even. In conjunction with the Hanged Man, a card from the Major Arcana, which when reversed denotes selfishness and sacrifice, rootlessness and riot, things don't look too good. If you laid all at the head of an actual hanging man, murdered, they might begin to look very bad indeed. And, as the Queens of Wands, Pentacles, Swords and Cups could be seen to represent all the women in the world – excepting only the few from the Major Arcana, the High Priestess and the Empress (positions Joanna May and Angela might contend for) or the female half of the Lovers (which might well suit Bethany), these great cards having in their own peculiar way dominion over all the humble folk of the four suits – why then, things might be looking quite appalling for all the women in the world.

Prudently, Joanna spoke none of this aloud. She merely said to Trevor, 'Gobbledygook. The police will not be interested in what they say is gobbledygook: they will not understand the insult and the threat involved: go and fetch those cards and put them in the kitchen drawer, and don't even mention them.'

Joanna May called the police. Of course she did. What else could she do? The duty sergeant she spoke to said they would send a police car the moment one was available. He was soothing and competent. He said if she was certain her gardener was dead, leave him where he was and touch nothing. It sounded, from her description, like some kind of inadvertent death by way of sexual perversion, and was at least less messy than a crucifixion. They'd had quite a lot of those lately: a lot of nuts in the homosexual community: they were sending an ambulance, but that might take even longer than the police car. Emergency services were stretched.

'I don't think he was gay,' said Joanna May.

'Gay, bi, hetero,' said the duty officer, 'makes no difference to us. We are not prejudiced. Where did you say? The King's House? The big place on the island? Wait, that's come up on the computer recently . . . yes, here we are . . . knew I'd seen it. Trevor Hopkins, occupation butler: indecent behaviour. And this one was the gardener, you say?'

'The charge against Mr Hopkins was not proven,' said Joanna May. 'In fact the charge was dropped. What's it doing on your computer?'

'You're quite right,' said the duty officer amiably. 'It shouldn't be there. No doubt it's on its way to wiping.'

It was an hour before they arrived, and an hour and a half before the ambulance came to take the body to a morgue. The police doctor said there'd be an autopsy but it looked to him as if the young man had had a heart attack while engaging in some kind of kinky sexual activity – there was no evidence of foul play. No end to the things that people got up to: a pity: from the look of his garden he was good at his job. The world was short of gardeners.

'And of police officers, too,' said the plainclothes man, hurrying him on. They had another suspicious death waiting. Four men had arrived. They questioned Trevor, but kindly, to his surprise. He told them nothing about the boat, about the bully boys: just that he'd gone out to the barn to take Oliver his coffee: had found him swinging, dead and upside down, and gone inside and just sat, till Joanna came home. If they thought there was more to it, they didn't say. It would only take everyone into the complex and miserable area of sexual deviance, and Mrs May's butler had, from the look of him, suffered enough.

'What we don't want', said the police officer, by way of

153

explanation, 'is copycatting. If it gets into the papers, before we know it everyone's hanging from their ankles trying to get heart attacks. We have enough to do –' and they left. The body had already gone, by ambulance.

Joanna May called Angela and told her all about it. Angela offered to come over but Joanna said she was OK. Only quite some time later did she begin to weep.

32

God flew off in three stages, if you ask me, Joanna May, the childless and the cloned, and none of them anything, I have now decided, to do with nuclear bombs or Logie Baird.

God the Father flew off on the day mankind first interfered with his plans for the procreation of the species: that was the day the first woman made a connection between semen and pregnancy and took pains to stop the passage by shoving some pounded, mud-steeped, leaf up inside her. He flew off in a pet. 'But this is *contraception*,' he cried, 'this is not what I meant. How can I work out my plan for your perfection and ultimate union with me if you start doing this kind of thing?'

God the Son flew off the day the first pregnant woman made the next connection and shoved a sharpened stick up inside her to put an end to morning sickness and whatever else was happening inside. 'But this is *abortion*,' he cried, 'it's revolting, and no place for a pro-lifer like me to be.'

And God the Holy Ghost flew off the day Dr Holly of the Bulstrode Clinic, back in the fifties, took one of my ripe eggs out and warmed it, and jiggled it, and irritated it in an amniotic brew until the nucleus split, and split again, and split again, and then started growing, each with matching chromosomes, with identical DNA, that is to say faults and propensities, physical and social, all included, blueprint for four more individuals, and only one soul between them.

Call me egocentric if you like, but that's when the Holy Ghost flew off, muttering, 'Christ, where is this going to end?' for it's been trouble ever since, hasn't it, all downhill; war, and riots, and crime, and drugs, and decadence, and dereliction, and delinquency, because there's no God. Well, there's no bringing him back; it's up to man to step in and take over. (I say 'man' advisedly; I don't think women will have the heart, the courage.) He gave us minds, didn't he, and the aspiration to do things right, as well as the tendency to do them wrong.

Carl may be wicked, but Carl's right. Takes a wicked man to be prepared to think like Carl, that's the trouble. I know how Carl May thinks: though not always what he thinks. I know what he was doing; I know why his teeth did not draw blood. Carl is not interested in my blood: blood cells do not contain DNA. A good place for obtaining DNA, from the tissue at the back of the neck. What Carl does with it depends upon what he feels like. So many things are possible. He could take a fertilized egg from, say, Bethany, give it the blueprint for my growth, put it back inside her, and she'd give birth to a little me. Would she like that? Perhaps she would. Perhaps mothering a man's first wife might make you feel altogether better about her. All these relationships are about incorporation, if you ask me, everyone in one big bed together – me, Carl, Oliver, Bethany, Isaac – all rolling around, warm and safe and companionable: we only get upset when we're left out in the cold. If I had a cell from Isaac I would ask Bethany to re-create him, in penance for taking Carl from me. And death would not divide us any more. If he were dug up from his grave, there'd still be enough residual DNA there, even now, to do it. But I won't do that: it seems forbidden, as forbidden as abortion ever was. I don't think Carl will do it: to impersonate God is a terrifying thing. Even for Carl, who as a child bayed at the moon. Microbiologists get so far, then lay down their tools, put aside their electron microscopes: take up gardening instead: they frighten even themselves. These days scientists talk a great deal more about God than does the rest of the world: they acknowledge magic – though they call it 'propensity', or 'something intervenes'. 'Something intervenes,' they say – as they break matter down to its smallest definable particles, the merest flicker in and out of existence of the most fragmented electric charge – 'or else our observation alters it.'

156

What is that but obeisance to the shadow of the God who ran off, the God they drove off, when bold and young and frightened of nothing!

What Carl could do, what Carl might well do, for Carl controls the scientists, since Carl has the money, is mix up some of my chromosomes with those of some other creature and set it growing, and know more or less what would get born, forget a fingernail or two. He could snip out the section that decrees I will have long and elegant legs, and snip in a section from someone else's DNA, someone with short piano legs, the kind without ankles. He could give me a dog's back legs. If he wanted, he could do horrible things. He could do good things: sometimes he wants to do good things. Just as man can use nuclear weapons to make war or keep peace, to destroy or build, Carl could make me live with arthritis for ever or keep me disease free, never to catch cold again. He could interfere with my mind: make me nicer, more gregarious, kinder, happier, more socially conscious: he couldn't control the environment I grew up in, not in the short term, but if everyone was kinder, happier, loved their children better, didn't shut them in kennels – why then presently the environment of the growing child would indeed change, improve, step by step, little by little. Look at it this way, Carl would say, every time a woman uses contraception or has an abortion, she interferes with natural selection. Not this baby, the next baby, says the mother, bold as brass, standing in nature's way. Let's go for a better father, or a better environment: let's hang on a bit. That's what it's about: that's what's important. Not the first baby that comes along but the best baby, the one that'll have a decent chance in life. And let's do better by the ones we have, stop at two, not six. Quality, not quantity. Choice, not randomness, and there being no God, why not? That's what Carl thinks.

In the meantime, being unreconstructed himself, and cured of the notion that death is final – for it isn't, not if he can keep the genetic line running – Carl May has killed Oliver, and now he means to kill the clones. He has told me so, by way of the cards. He thinks this will hurt me. He offered me a family: now he

157

snatches it away again. But I'm not at all sure that I recognize their right to life, these thefts from me, these depletings of my 'I', these early symptoms of the way the world is going. I might myself be rather in favour of termination. I must think about it.

Time to consult the Maverick Agency once again. I like the Maverick Agency. They make me feel the world is real, that the boats on the river, the cars on the road, are truly there. That a debt could affect you, a bullet kill you. Everything in this house is so still and quiet. The weather is warm. The windows are open. The watered-silk curtains, palest green, stir just a little. In the garden the weeds are growing, that's all, with no Oliver to clear them. And the caesium falls, and the strontium, and God knows what, silent, minute, invisible, as Carl makes his deadening presence felt.

33

Jane, Julie, Gina, Alice.

In the lives of the clones of Joanna May something stirred, some instinct of self-preservation was awakened, and not in that fact itself (for what woman does not wake in the morning once or twice in her life saying 'this can't go on a moment longer') but in the timing of that fact, lay whatever strangeness there might be to find. As Joanna May, Empress of inner space, fought for once to control her life, so too did the four Queens – Wands, Pentacles, Swords and Cups (rulers of the provinces, as it were), fight to control theirs, not quite sure what had moved them to action, groping for understanding of their own behaviour, and not quite finding it, so looking for justification instead.

———❖———

Jane received three letters by the same post. One was from her employers to announce the appointment of the new head of the London office: and it was not Jane but a snip of a girl of twenty-three, without a degree to her name, who got it. Too old at thirty! If you hadn't made it by thirty in the film world, you'd had it. The next was from someone she'd never heard of, a woman called Anne, written on thin blue paper in what looked like a drunken scrawl, saying she, Jane, should take her claws out of Tom and let him get on with his life, or she, Anne, would come round and personally strangle her, and the third was from the ground rent landlords, asking her for her £8000 contribution towards repairing the roof, a matter she'd never heard of until that moment.

She rang HBO and offered her resignation, which was accepted with an alacrity she found humiliating. She rang Tom and asked him who Anne was, or rather screamed at him about her, and Tom said she was just a friend: he'd come round. She rang the landlords and said it was monstrous, and they agreed, but nevertheless, there it was. If she did not hand over £8000 forthwith they could, if it came to it, foreclose on her mortgage and resell to raise the necessary funds. She rang her father, Jeremy, who said he feared she hadn't read the small print of her tenancy, and she said, 'Why couldn't you read it for me? Why have you never helped me?' and he said, 'Jane, you were always so self-sufficient, even from a baby: it came more easily to admire you than help you,' and for some reason this made her weep and weep more than did any of the other sudden and unexpected blows from fate.

Tom came round and showed her photographs of Anne, who was blowsy and uneducated and had a daughter called Roma, aged eleven. Anne was his landlady. Yes, he spent nights with Anne sometimes. Why not? Why had he never told her? It didn't seem anything to do with her, that was why: Jane only wanted half of him, so she could have half. She couldn't own him: they didn't have a child. Jane knew he wanted a child. Little Roma needed him. She didn't have a father of her own.

'You're not fair, you're not fair,' wept Jane. Once men, according to Madge, said if you don't sleep with me I'll find someone who will. Now the threat had changed, gotten worse: now it was if you don't have my baby other women will be only too glad.

Anne didn't have a degree: she worked down the council baths: she had a council house: she acted as his model: yes, he was painting nudes. No, he didn't want Jane as a model, she was too twitchy. She couldn't relax. He thought he would have an exhibition soon. He was sorry about her job, her roof, her father. But her job made her hard and smart and cynical; it was a good thing she'd lost it: if she sold her car she could pay for the roof: and she'd always been hopelessly in love with her father and how could he, Tom, compete: and yes of course he loved her, what was all this talk about love all of a sudden; if he moved in with her and she settled down and they had a baby he would finish with Anne though of course he'd have to go on seeing Roma, she was only a child.

'You go back to Anne,' said Jane. 'That's the end, I don't need you, I don't want you, I don't want to see you ever again.'

So he went, and she wondered why it all felt so familiar. She began talking to friends and colleagues about possible openings not just in films, but in journalism, put her solicitors on to the matter of the roof, went round to the doctor and demanded a sterilization, which was refused. She did not argue, however.

For it seemed to her, as she advanced reasons, both laudable and derisory, in favour of her sterilization – her career, her freedom, her revulsion, her dislike of baby mess and smells, her figure, her need of sleep – that there was another one she was only just now beginning to put her finger on. She didn't want a boy; but who would understand that? If she had a boy it would be homosexual. It would have to be. Because how could she, being female, give birth to something male? Her little twelve-week foetus, which they'd said was male, had looked a real mess to her, and she wasn't surprised. She could understand how her body could somehow spit out a daughter, a replica: but the female was less than the male: how could the lesser give birth to the greater? How could she tell Tom a thing like that? Better forget the whole thing: just not have babies: just be in some other more rational arena, where life was for living not passing on. Nevertheless, when refused, she was remotely, somewhere, somehow, pleased. She had a coil put in, instead.

So much for the Queen of Wands.

<hr />

As for the Queen of Pentacles, Julie, well, her husband Alec flew in, ate supper without tasting it, went to bed without noticing her new provocative nightgown, let alone her determined serious sweetness – she had parted for ever (or so she really and truly believed) with her lover, for the sake of the marriage – was too tired to make love, rose in the morning, grumbled at the state

161

of his shirts – though they were perfect – and flew straight off to West Berlin.

'This can't go on,' she said, and made an appointment to see a solicitor. Yet Alec had flown in and out, just so, a hundred times before.

Julie, Queen of Pentacles.

———◆◆———

Gina, Queen of Swords, woke up to a usual kind of day and limped to the doctor's, as she often did. But while she was sitting in his waiting room – and she had to wait for a full hour with coughing young women and spluttering old ones all around, trying to reassure Ben (who had stayed off school to help her) and pacify little Anthony, who sat grizzling on the floor dealing harshly with the few old toys brought in by passing benefactors – she said something strange, to no one in particular. 'This can't go on,' she said.

'What, Mum?' asked Ben. 'What did you say?'

Ben always listened out anxiously as if his life's duty was to be on guard, waiting for something he could do nothing about, except watch for its coming.

'Never you mind,' she said. 'But don't worry. Things will get better,' and she'd said that to him a hundred times before, and it hadn't got better. But this time when she limped into the surgery – her knee stiffened and swelled with every hour that passed – and the doctor said grimly, 'I suppose you fell downstairs again,' she actually said, 'No, I was pushed. Will you write it down, please. I'll need some kind of record.'

The doctor wrote it down, with alacrity. The clones of Joanna May always found protectors: though it must be said that this particular clone seldom looked her best.

Gina, Queen of Swords.

———◆◆———

And as for Alice, Queen of Cups, that morning Alice woke from a terrible dream in which she had been split into five from the waist up and four of them were eating alive, with fanged teeth, the one which was her, and when only one of her eyes was left and half her mouth, Alice woke screaming. She told the essence of her dream to the photographer who happened to be with her and he said well that's you struggling for survival with your four big brothers, and having understood it, or thought she understood it, she felt better. Except that the one-eyed image continued to bother her, and instead of going back to sleep, she thought about it. One eyed, cock-eyed; something was wrong. She, usually so restrained, too controlled even to smile if she could possibly help it, suddenly kicked the sleeping photographer (his name was Radish; an absurd name) with a smooth, round muscular foot and shrieked, 'I can't stand it a moment longer. Go back to your wife' – for of course Radish was married: her relationships usually were with married men, who could be relied upon to go away – so he did go back to her, poor man, startled, surprised and upset. That is to say, he walked the streets until ten the next morning, when he was due back home, believing Alice had thrown him out because he was married, and had the evening before explained how he couldn't leave his wife, she being pregnant and relying upon him, and so forth. He could see it was all for the best: but it hurt, it hurt.

Alice had to take four sleeping pills before she could get back to sleep and as a consequence failed, for the first time in her life, to turn up for a 7.00 a.m. call. The studio had to send a taxi for her, and she arrived without her make-up box, and was, in fact, so thoroughly unprofessional all round they decided not to use her again. She was clearly paranoic. She claimed she was being followed by a young man carrying a child's lunch box, that he was standing outside the studio even now, and if they looked out they'd see him – and they looked to placate her – but there was nothing unusual to be seen, just people standing about on street corners waiting for taxis, and workmen waiting for other workmen and so forth, but no one looking out for Alice. Who did she think she was? Really beautiful women are admired and loved but seldom liked. She could not afford to step out of line, and she had. Alice, Queen of Cups.

34

Carl May did not believe in divinatory magic, of course he did not. To tell the cards, the stars, the lines of the palm, tea-leaves and so forth was to divine what was in the fortune-teller's heart, and that was all. How could it be otherwise, the clues to interpretation being so numerous and to reach that interpretation so many contradictory clues having to be taken into account? Moreover, the wisdom behind that interpretation – that is to say the sum of the experience of long-dead seers and necromancers – had always been so sloppily recorded and translated from one language to another, one culture to another, as to add up in the end to sheer gobbledygook.

Gobbledygook, and he would prove it.

To this end Carl May had started Britnuc's Divination Department, housed on the eighth floor, a floor which had heating and ventilation problems. Divination was made up of cartomancers, astrologers, crystal gazers and so on, and the greater part of its work involved participation in research, funded jointly by Britnuc and the University of Edinburgh, into the comparative validity or otherwise of the various occult disciplines. So far, as Carl May had expected, the balance was tipping otherwise. To justify the existence of the department in the eyes of his fellow directors and the shareholders its reports and prophecies were registered along with those of other sections: forward planning now included propitiousness of time in relation to event in its computerized forecasts. All other things being equal, which seldom happened, recommendations from the eighth floor would be allowed to tip the balance on minor decisions this way or that. Carl May reckoned it would be no worse than tossing a coin, which on occasion he had been known to do – though sitting alone at the head of the great board table as he did who was to say whether he reported its fall correctly?

Carl May was interested and displeased to observe how quickly the staff came to take the existence of the department for granted: how it had become common practice for Garden Developments to plant according to phases of the moon in spite of the virtual impossibility of controlled testing – variables in the rearing of plants being almost as numerous as they were for humans; how at lunchtimes the lifts to the eighth floor would be busy with not only female clerical staff (which he would have expected) on their way to have their fortunes told, but with middle and senior management as well. He wondered if there were a marker gene for gullibility: he waited impatiently for Holly to repent and come back on line. He would not wait for ever.

Since the Chernobyl event Carl May had had Divination, in conjunction with the University, working on maps of the British Isles, predicting regional variations of wind patterns and subsequent fallout. Now came a phone call through to his office from Edinburgh. A former music-hall entertainer, Wee Willie Bradley, who had the apparent gift, or talent, or capacity – call it what you like – of shutting his eyes and projecting imagined pictures on to ordinary black and white film, was proving successful in producing accurate maps two days in advance.
'How successful?' demanded Carl May, who was putting on his shirt.
'One hundred per cent,' said Edinburgh, smugly.
'Impossible,' said Carl May, 'because no one's maps are accurate. As well say today's instrumentation readings are influenced by Wee Willie's maps two days ago.' Which stumped Edinburgh, for a time.

'What's your star sign?' Carl May asked Bethany, who, dreamy and languid, still lay on the palely carpeted office floor, since she found the designer chairs too uncomfortable to sit upon. Since bits of carpet came off on her yellow cashmere sweater she hadn't bothered to put that back on. It was an idle kind of day.

'I can't remember,' said Bethany, prudently, for all Carl May was in a good mood. 'I don't really believe in all that junk.'

He wondered whether there might be a gene for the propensity to tell lies, and whether it would be desirable or undesirable to shuffle it out. Would Bethany honest be less or more desirable? He tickled her chest with his bare toes. The red light on the telephone blinked.

'What a busy day,' said Bethany.

It was Gerald Coustain. He had come back to Carl May, reluctantly, to ask if Britnuc could possibly make available to the Government one or two technicians properly trained in radiation diagnostic techniques, in the urgent national interest. Carl May was pleased to put at his disposal Britnuc's entire Divination Department.

'I don't quite understand,' said Gerald. 'What use are astrologers and palm-readers in this particular situation?'

'Our research shows,' said Carl May merrily, 'that they're as good at anticipating fallout as our technicians and they certainly cost less.'

'That may be,' said Gerald cautiously, 'because your diagnostic equipment is out of date. You have the technicians, the Department has the equipment; couldn't we just get them together?'

'I'll think about it,' said Carl May cheerfully. 'How's the family?'

'Just fine, thank you.'

'I hear you've been seeing something of my ex-wife.'

'We all had a jaunt to the lido, one day,' said Gerald, after only a second's pause.

'Joanna must have really liked that,' said Carl May. 'I'm glad to hear she's taken up swimming. Women need to look after themselves as they get older. Poor old thing, did you hear about her gardener?'

'I think she called Angela, just to say. Quite a shock.'

'Good domestic staff is always hard to find,' said Carl May, 'even more difficult than trained technicians and accurate, up-to-the-minute equipment in this ever-changing field of ours. Perhaps the Department of Energy will see its way to some form of co-funding when this Chernobyl lark has calmed down. That way we could ensure Britnuc was always in a position to help you lot out.'

'I'll put it to my Department,' said Gerald.

'And I'll put your requirements to mine,' said Carl May. 'You're quite sure you can't make use of my Divination Department?'

'No thank you,' said Gerald.

'Pity,' said Carl May. 'What a lot of old stick-in-the-muds you civil servants are!' He was in a talkative mood. 'Reminds me of someone I used to have working for me. What was his name? King? That's it. Curator of the gallery – you know my gallery? The May Gallery? Egyptologist fellow. Well, never mind, it's a long story – he was interested in the Tarot pack. Hieroglyphics, and so forth. Poor fellow, he got knocked down in a road accident, killed.'

'I seem to remember that,' said Gerald, cautiously.

'That's the problem for stick-in-the-muds,' said Carl May. 'So stuck they can't even look where they're going!'

'Well,' said Gerald, 'it's been an interesting conversation, Carl. I'll come back to you when I've spoken to my Department.'

As Gerald Coustain put the phone down he heard Carl May laughing, and the sound of agreeable female giggles. He wondered if it were mad laughter and decided probably not: just that Carl May had discovered the answer to executive stress. You murdered the people who angered you, tormented those you despised, teased those who depended upon you, and kept bimbos in the office. He was about to pick up the phone and discuss these suppositions with Angela, but thought better of it. If Carl May knew about the trip to the lido, someone's phone was probably tapped: possibly even his own. It could wait till he got home.

35

The Queen of Swords and the Queen of Pentacles.

———•••———

The Queen of Swords left the doctor's surgery with one child in a pushchair and the other walking just a little behind her, as was his practice, and had been for years. She walked away from home, not towards it, she wasn't sure why.

'Where are we going?' Ben asked.

'I don't know,' she said, 'but I don't want to go home.'

'Where else is there to go?' he asked, which was of course the point. But he moved up to keep pace with her, and actually took charge of the pushchair, since she was limping, and it was the first time he'd done that – as if admitting their common interest, mother and son, in what was going on in the family, and encouraging this new train of thought in her: namely that things could not go on as they were, but would, unless she did something. At least for once she was walking away from home, away from Cliff, and not back towards him. They kept walking in the wrong direction until it was lunchtime – although Ben should have gone straight to school, and she would have been more prudent to have just sat down and rested her leg, as the doctor had instructed. Then they went to McDonald's, which was a luxury, and bad for them, but she had lost faith in a future in which care taken meant benefit returned. Ben ordered at the counter while she, her whole leg now painful and throbbing, unstrapped Anthony and heaved him out of the pushchair and into the high chair provided by McDonald's. He enjoyed sitting in it, which was something. She should never have had him, of course.

168

'These children that we should never have had,' she said aloud, 'still have to eat.'

———••———

The Queen of Pentacles heard. Julie was sitting at the table next to Gina's. She had gone to visit her solicitor: he had not given her good news: she had no children and the house was in her husband's name: she was young and able-bodied: if she divorced she would be expected to shift for herself. At the same time she did not, as her solicitor pointed out, have the capacity, let alone the training, to earn a decent living. His advice, offered to her unasked, was to stay home and make the best of things. And so she had driven not home but in the wrong direction, not sure why or where, alone and lonely, childless and more than ever conscious of it, but also let it be said without the exhausting responsibilities that went with the company, the pleasure of children. This Julie recognized, and now tried not to stare curiously at Gina; this messy, overweight, distracted, sloppy woman of too many responsibilities who had said aloud something so remarkable. 'I might have been like that,' she thought, 'if I'd had too many children too young,' and envied the other woman but at the same time pitied her, and felt, if not grateful for her own lot, at least a little more reconciled to it. Her heart was breaking, but she would not, would not, see the vet again. He was married, so was she. Supposing Alec found out? A woman could lose everything, so easily.

Gina saw Julie watching and thought who does that woman think she is, staring, and why is she so familiar: do I know her from somewhere? And what was a woman like that doing, sitting in a McDonald's, in a pale cashmere jumper, trying to get her pearly teeth into a Big Mac when everyone knew you didn't bite but somehow drew the layered substance into your mouth. Prettier than me, thought Gina; taller, thinner, younger, certainly richer: dressed so you hardly noticed, but you could tell expensively, and looking miserable but down her nose. If things had gone differently for me, thought Gina, if I'd been given a chance in life, if I hadn't had these bloody children, if someone, anyone, had had the heart to stop me, got me to school, let alone college – but they hadn't, had they. No one had cared. She felt herself beginning to cry. She was stuck here in McDonald's, marooned. Now she'd stopped walking and taken her foot off the ground she didn't think she could put it back down again. It would hurt too much. Moreover, she had set things in motion at the doctor's she could not control, and wished she hadn't: there would be more violence ahead: how was she going to collect Sue at four o'clock: she could send Ben, she supposed, but Ben would resent it, Ben had never wanted Sue to be born any more than Sue had wanted Ben to exist; and worse, she, Gina, wouldn't be there to stand between the two children and their father when they got home: and they were as likely to be met by blows, insult and humiliation, as chips and a video: you could never be sure with Cliff. Sue could walk home on her own, and would if no one turned up, but she would sulk for days and that would feed back tension into the whole family and make matters worse. Ben always wanted things to get better: Sue somehow wanted them to get worse, so whatever awful thing it was would be over quicker. Only, one row was just like another. When Cliff was sorry, and making amends, he was the best person in the world, but these days his being sorry was turning into a memory: a hope. She had failed her marriage, herself, her children.

Gina caught sight of her face in a mirror, and the tears running down it, and thought she didn't look so bad after all, almost glamorous, and then realized she wasn't looking at a reflection of herself but at the woman opposite, who was also in tears.

'Well,' said Gina, startled into friendliness, 'I suppose all women look the same when they're crying.'

'I don't cry,' said Julie, 'I never cry,' stopping on the instant, though the same thought had crossed her own mind: that looking at Gina she was looking at a reflection of herself. What a terrible thought! She gave up battling with the Big Mac and sipped a little black coffee and dabbed her eyes with a lace handkerchief. ('A lace handkerchief!' thought Gina, astounded, blowing her own nose on a McDonald's serviette.)

170

When Ben came back with the two Big Macs, one Chicken McNuggets, three large fries and two milk shakes, Julie gave up altogether and joined Gina at her table. Julie said, 'You're so lucky to have children; we can't have any,' and began to cry again. Gina wished she wouldn't cry in front of the children, but Ben seemed impervious to this extra distress, just stared stoically into space over his hamburger. He was a handsome child; but he did, she acknowledged, look pale and nervous. How would he grow up? 'You could have mine,' said Gina, joking, but Julie said, quite seriously, 'It's not the same. And I have this great house with no one to fill it, and somehow it makes things worse to have so much of what you don't want. I am never going back into that house again. I'm not. I don't care what anyone says.' Even as she spoke she realized she was, in her own mind, peopling her world with concerned observers, who of course in reality didn't exist. Lonely so lonely!

'Aren't you lucky,' said Gina. 'I have a house with too much to fill it, and I reckon I've got to go back into mine, I've no option.'

Gina looked across at Julie and again had a sense of familiarity. Had they known each other as children? At school? She couldn't put her finger on it. Julie looked at Gina and thought this woman is like the sister I never had, and doesn't she just need cheering up, cleaning up, and taking over. I could do some good here, for once in my life.

Ben said, 'Mum, there's a man following us. He was behind us when we left the doctor's and there he is, sitting over there –' and he pointed to where a young man in a suit sat behind a copy of the *Sun*, hiding his face. He had chosen a coffee and an apple tart. There was a briefcase on the empty chair beside him.

Gina said, 'Well, I haven't lost all my charms, then,' and Ben, who didn't seem to take to Julie but kept looking at her curiously all the same, went into a real sulk at being made, as he felt, to look a fool. Sometimes, when in a mood, he was so like his father, Gina quite disliked him. One of the problems about bringing yourself to divorce point, deciding this was the man you hated and not the man you loved, as you had rashly thought at the beginning, was not just the practical one of how you went

171

and where you went, or the emotional one of how you lived on your own, coped on your own and put up with loneliness, but how, if you hated the man, you went on loving the children, who were after all half his. You saw the father looking out of the eyes of the son. The whole business of it taking two to make one, Gina had long ago decided, made being a mother and doing it right all but impossible. She found her daughter easier. She just told her what to do and she did it. But that irritated her, too. Where was the girl's spirit? And she would snuggle up to Cliff, too, as if she was taking Cliff's side, as if she'd just move in with him the moment Cliff had battered her mother to death, and that drove Gina mad. It was all horrible; everything all went right or it all went wrong.

Julie said to Gina, 'Why don't you come home with me until you sort things out?'

Gina said to Julie, 'What about your husband? What would he say? He wouldn't like it.'

Julie said, 'He's never there, and if he does turn up, so what? The house may be in his name legally but it's mine morally, and it needs filling up with people. I do what I want with my own house.'

'Well,' said Gina, 'in that case, yes, OK,' and that took Julie aback, but she was not the kind of person to go back on her word.

'What a day of surprises,' Julie said, as she helped Gina limp to the car. Ben pushed Anthony.

'Yes, isn't it,' said Gina. 'But my motto is, something always turns up at the last moment!'

This had not been Julie's experience but she supposed that if you were consistently afflicted by misfortune, as Gina appeared to be, you would develop, as antidote to it, the art of optimism. Julie had never had the opportunity of so doing. The misfortunes that afflicted Julie masqueraded as good fortune, and so were the more difficult to locate, comprehend and deal with. If your husband blacked your eye and threw you downstairs, you at least knew there was something wrong. If your husband was away most of the time, but paid large cheques into your bank account, how could you tell what was going on?

172

'There is another child,' said Gina. 'A girl. We have to collect her from school.'

'Oh Good Lord,' said Julie, startled. 'Well, never mind. The more the merrier.'

If that husband came home to a house suddenly full of women and sticky, sulky, noisy children, none of them his own, it might force things to some kind of issue.

As the two women left the restaurant, two young men got up from separate tables and followed them. They met at the door, engaged in a brief conversation, and strolled down the street together. They got into the car parked behind Julie's, and when Julie pulled out, so did they. All this Ben noticed but did not say. His mother had laughed at him, now she would have to take the consequences. It was the same kind of drastic, horrid, nourishing feeling his father often had about his mother, and Ben knew it, and though he didn't like it there wasn't much he could do about it. You could stop how you acted, but hardly how you felt. This new friend of his mother's, picked up at random in a McDonald's, seemed to have something of the same quality. He didn't like it. And where were they all going? It seemed that their lives were about to change, and no one had the courtesy to explain it to him, let alone consult him. But he could see that simply to be away from home for a time, without the fear of bangs, crashes and screams in the night, not having to put up his own defences against his mother's terror or hurt, not to have to watch anxiously for the turns and changes in his father's mood, not to have to listen out for his mother's putting of her foot in it, which he sometimes thought she did on purpose, not to feel so confused about Sue, whom he felt obliged to protect but didn't want to, would be a great relief.

'You OK, darling?' asked Gina.

'I'm fine,' he said. He'd missed another day at school, and no one seemed to bother about that, either.

'Do you often go to McDonald's?' Gina asked Julie.

'No,' said Julie. 'Hardly ever. Only when I'm upset; then I like it. It's as if you were more like other people than you thought, and you might as well accept it. We're all in the same boat together.'

173

'That's what I feel too,' said Gina, feeling quite uneasy, that there was more to all this than met the eye. She wished there wasn't. In better times, she would have got out of the car there and then. But like so much else, once you had children, it became a matter of necessity, not choice. Where you were was where you stayed.

The car that followed them was white, all white, from its white-painted hubcaps to its white-coated aerial; a vehicle fit for angels from some phantasmagorical heaven and on the front seats, grey-suited, prosperous and clean, two young men who might have been God's accountants. The boot of the car was slightly open: part of a bicycle stuck out of it. People stared at them and forgot them.

Petie said to Elwood, 'Well, fancy you.'
Elwood said to Petie, 'Fancy you. Wheels within wheels. Just as well, my calves are aching.'
Petie said, 'That wasn't a coincidence, was it, that was drugs. That was the McDonald's connection.'
Elwood said, 'It was, and was I glad to see it. I'd begun to think that was no lady but a wild goose set up by Carl May to get his money's worth out of us.'
Petie said Carl May knows what he's doing and Elwood said you mean Jacko says Carl May knows what he's doing and Petie said it's the kids I'm sorry for and Elwood said we were all kids once even Carl May, especially Carl May, and Petie tuned the radio to rock but Elwood wanted classical so they had an argument about that, and Elwood drove rather hard around a corner just as Petie was feeling the sharpness of a knife against his thumb, so they ended up outside Julie's house with rather a lot of blood on the white upholstery. 'Serve you right,' said Petie, child at heart.

36

The Queen of Wands and the Queen of Cups.

———◆◆———

The Queen of Wands tossed and turned in her penthouse bed and the moon shone in. 'I want, I want,' she said aloud, but she wasn't sure what it was she wanted, except perhaps what she couldn't have, that is to say Tom. And him she could have, if she would, which she wouldn't. Some barrier stood in her way: some wall of glass. She could not allow herself to be happy.

The attic was now a penthouse. Thus the landlords advertised it, threatening to call in her mortgage if she didn't cough up for the roof: they had put it on the market just to frighten her: they didn't have a legal leg to stand on: she'd put her solicitors on to them. It would be all right in the end, it would, it would, if only the moon didn't seem to rock so in the sky, if only her limbs didn't twitch with longing, the feel of Tom's body beside her so lacking, if only her savings would last for ever, if only she had the energy and will to go out and find another, better, less blackmailing lover than Tom, but she didn't, she couldn't.

All you had to do, she supposed, if you wanted sex, was to get dressed and go out in the night street and walk about, and see what happened next, and something would. Only such an act was unthinkable. Why? What did other people do? Did they have possible partners lined up, waiting? The longer she lived in the world the less she knew about it. It baffled her.

Other people had the gift of peopling their lives with friends and colleagues; went to outings, parties, reunions, but she remained solitary, distant, voices sounded from the other side of the glass wall, muffled: people's smiles were distorted. She waited for some kind of matching private intimacy to happen, but it didn't. She'd known Tom for so long he'd gotten through the wall, but perhaps he was the wrong one: how could the only one be the right one? Was that the trouble? Perhaps she just couldn't believe her luck?

She would go home for the weekend: she would retreat and lick her wounds a little: she would try and feel close to her parents. Difficult to look her father in the face since his strange adventure with Laura: difficult to feel close to her mother since she'd been so wounded: no matter how unaffected Madge seemed to be, how bright her intelligent eyes still shone behind her pebble glasses, she now sapped the energy of Jane's youth: she no longer fed it, nourished it. Madge had been mortally wounded, and that was the truth of it and there was no strength left in her.

'I'm depressed, that's all,' thought Jane, no longer wanting anything, and remembered standing as a small child in the hall of the big, pleasant house, and seeing through the glass door of the study her father working at his desk: and the other side of the study window the dim stumpy form of her mother, working in the garden. She'd begun to cry, for a reason she didn't then understand, from the sense of not-belonging, sense of having herself received some mortal wound, and knowing, with the clear prescience of a child, that she would thereafter limp through life: there was no healing this. Yet nothing had happened — just the sight of an ungainly woman through glass, and the understanding that beauty of spirit and beauty of body were not the same, and that the knowledge itself could maim for life.

She was grown-up now: she had controlled her life: she had remained free of emotional and domestic commitments for just such an eventuality as had now happened – she was free to move to Los Angeles where the obvious career opportunities were: the English were popular: their special talents appreciated. And now she didn't want to go. Nor did she want to lie where she was, in an empty bed, staring at a moon tossed by clouds. Where did clouds come from? She scarcely knew what clouds were, let alone why they were. It was all intolerable. The thing to do, obviously, was to let 'I want' get the better of 'I don't want'. Desire must triumph over reluctance. But how?

The Queen of Wands felt like the kitchen maid. She gave up sleep, got out of bed and switched on the light, and a sensor peeped gently in a van parked outside, and Haggie, who had been sleeping therein, woke and yawned and took out his notebook.

Jane got on with her work, her diversionary activity. She went through files and cuttings. She was writing a series of articles for *Film International* on 'Images of women: the changing generations'. She could not get excited about it, but it was work, it would keep her name up there in front of those who mattered. In the morning she could try and contact Alice Morthampton, who had the reputation of being a smart-arsed bitch. A year back she'd turned down a film part – typecasting, playing the lead, a model. She'd turned it down on moral grounds, the screen view of the model's life being so far from reality, she said, it was intolerable, and the producers refusing to change the script. Well, you were as moral as you could afford to be, supposed Jane. Alice Morthampton must be pretty rich. Pretty rich. She could not understand why Alice Morthampton was considered so beautiful. A face was just a face. The features were regular, it was true. There were two kinds of women, Jane supposed, the ones who looked like herself, and this Alice, and the others, the majority, who looked like Madge. Jane took out a ruler and measured the proportion of eyes to nose, to ears, to jaw on a fashion shot of Alice, and then did the same for herself, in the mirror. As she thought, pretty much the same. It proved something, she wasn't sure what. She was suddenly very tired.

Morthampton – house of death. She hoped not. Jane went back to bed and fell promptly asleep, forgetting to turn off the light, so Haggie was up pretty much all night.

The Queen of Cups.

Alice lay in bed with eyepads over her eyes and considered the emptiness of her life, and wondered why nobody liked her and decided it was because she didn't like them. She could see the justice in it. She thought if she called her agent and instructed him to double her fees she would then halve her work and be just as rich. If she priced herself out of the market altogether, why then she would have forced an issue: she would have no option but to change her life. She might have to anyway. She had a feeling sour looks were going out of fashion and smiles were coming back and she wasn't going to start smiling for anyone; before you knew where you were they'd have you doing idiot shots, up telegraph wires and under water on your head.

The phone rang. It was some woman journalist without an appointment; freelance, too, not even an assignment. Alice thought perhaps she'd better try to be pleasant. When it came to it, self-destruction was a frightening thing.

'So long as there's none of that crappy feminist junk about sexism in fashion,' said Alice, 'you can come on round now. This minute, before I change my mind.'

Jane came, within five minutes. She only lived around the corner it seemed, in Harley Street. Alice lived in Wigmore Street. Alice opened the door. Jane and Alice stared at each other. Alice's eyebrows were plucked and her hairline had been taken back to give her a high medieval forehead. Jane's frizzy hair fell down to her eyebrows and beyond. Alice thought she might be looking at herself on a bad day, when she was feeling particularly short and squat. Jane thought, 'I could look like that if I wanted to. Which I don't.'

Jane went inside and sat on a sofa covered in the same Liberty fabric as covered her own sofa, only hers was green and this was brown. Still, it was a fairly common fabric. But there was the same Picasso print on the wall. She said as much.

'Someone gave it to me,' said Alice. 'I don't know anything

about art. But there's a damp stain on the wall so I put it up –
the roof's leaking. What's it meant to be?'

'Children playing,' said Jane.

'What, those splashes and dots? Well, write down I know
nothing about art, and hate children. That should be a start.
Who's it for?'

'*Film International*,' said Jane.

'Add I hate films too,' said Alice. 'I know nothing about them
and don't want to.'

'But you did once turn down a part. It was that I wanted to
talk to you about.'

'That old thing,' said Alice. 'I'm not an actress. I'm a model.
I couldn't remember the lines.'

'I thought you turned the part down for moral reasons.'

'That's what my agent said. I was fired.'

Jane's pen stayed poised.

'People aren't going to want to hear that,' she said.

'You talk like me too,' said Alice. 'Only I try not to. This is
going to be a crappy interview. So let's forget it.'

A little grey cat jumped up on to Jane's lap. Jane squealed.

'Don't tell me,' said Alice, 'you have a little grey cat just like
that one and *Candid Camera* is hiding somewhere in the room.
I warn you, I'll sue.'

'Would it be watching you or watching me?' asked Jane.

'Me, of course,' said Alice.

'Bloody egocentric,' said Jane, but both looked for signs of
Candid Camera. There was no sign of hoax or hoaxer. They
looked at each other.

'You should do something about your hair,' said Alice. 'It's
an insult.'

'I like it as it is,' said Jane. 'I don't believe in artifice.'

'Then you're a fool,' said Alice, and both fell silent.

Presently Alice asked Jane when her birthday was and Jane
replied September first, and Alice said, well, I was born on
September thirteenth, so that's something, but Jane said not
enough. Twins could be born as much as three weeks apart,
even identical twins.

'Who's talking about twins?' said Alice.

179

'I am,' said Jane. Then she said, 'But I'm sure if I'd been a twin, someone would have told me. Besides, it's not in my parents' nature to give children away. If my mother Madge had had twins she'd have reared them both, and made a good job of it, at least in her terms.'

Alice said, 'You might have been the one given away. You're the one who's egocentric. My mother never did anything she didn't want. She'd have given away anyone.'

Jane said, 'I'm certainly not adopted, if that's what you're suggesting.'

Though when she came to think about it, she could see that not to be Madge's natural daughter would relieve her of a great deal of guilt. The wonder had always been that so pretty a child as she had come from a pair so rigorously plain as Jeremy and Madge: friends, both hers and theirs, had remarked on it: she'd hated it: she saw herself as the source of her parents' discomfiture. If you had no friends, you didn't have to put up with the pain they caused: she'd learned that early.

'My mind's going so fast,' she complained, 'I think I'm going to be sick.'

She was, in Alice's mirror-lined bathroom, so full of creams, unguents, oils and lotions she could only marvel. She kept books in hers. When she came out she said, 'I can't possibly be your twin; we're completely different,' but Alice was standing in front of yet another mirror and had combed her hair down over her eyes and there was no doubting it.

'My experience is,' said Alice, 'it's not that people tell you lies, so much as they forget to tell you the truth. Personally, I trust no one. But then I was brought up with four brothers. All the same, I can see we're going to have to face up to this. Who's going to see whose parents first?'

In the street outside, Haggie found himself double parked next to a manhole in which none other than Dougie was working on telephone wires, yanking them out and then plugging them in. Dougie wore bright-yellow Telecom overalls.

'Well, fancy that,' said Dougie. 'Looks like yours has gone to visit mine. What's the connection?'

'Drugs?' said Haggie. 'Do you reckon?'

'More than likely,' said Dougie. 'Or prostitution. Women living alone.'

'It's too bad,' said Haggie, 'what goes on these days.'

'The world would be a cleaner place without their likes,' said Dougie, as Haggie joined him in the snugness of the manhole. 'Spreading disease with needles and sex.'

'This isn't a snuff mission,' said Haggie. 'It's a sniff mission.'

'One drifts into another, in my experience,' said Dougie.

'Mine's a tough cookie: no doubt about it,' said Haggie. 'No husband, no boyfriend, no children. Send a scrap of foreskin, or more, through the post, but if it's a stranger's what does she care?'

'You could slash my girl's face,' said Dougie, 'and all she'd do is call round the photographers, and there'd be even more of them in and out of her bed. Oh yes, they're tough. You have to admire them.'

'You don't,' said Haggie. 'You just have to stop them before they spoil the world for everyone else,' and Dougie said, 'I'm sure that yellow lead matched up to that yellow socket a moment ago,' and Haggie said, 'What the hell, Dougie, what the hell. At least Carl May knows what he's doing.'

'I suppose,' said Haggie.

37

'This Holly fellow has got nothing to hide,' Mavis of Maverick told Joanna, seeming disappointed, 'or if he has, he knows how to act innocent. Easy-peasy to trace.' Young Mavis strode into the house with muddy boots, reminding Joanna of Oliver, bringing the world with her.

The Bulstrode Clinic, according to Mavis, who – or so it said in the Maverick prospectus – had a First Class Honours Degree in Classics from Cambridge, was one of the first fertility clinics in the country, part NHS funded, part private, properly registered, licensed and inspected: it did legitimate terminations, blew fallopian tubes and stuff (said Mavis, with distaste) and carried out a few properly authorized tests on artificial insemination and ex-utero fertilization (makes you puke, doesn't it, said Mavis. Why do women *want* babies?). They also did vasectomies (more like it, said Mavis). When it closed there were letters to the papers saying what were women to do now? (What they did, said Mavis, was to come out as lesbians and sod the men.)

Holly had moved on to the Genetics Research Department of Martins Pharmaceuticals, where he'd been ever since: some files he left, a few he took with him: a common enough practice, in research. He was married, had grown children, lived within a comfortable income, contributed to the odd learned paper: apart from dabbling about in women's insides, said Mavis, he seemed OK. He wasn't making an illegal fortune, so far as anyone could see. Of course your ex is a director of Martins, said Mavis, but then he's on the board of most things, isn't he, so it probably doesn't mean much.

Martins Pharmaceuticals, said Mavis, specialized in the manufacture of synthetic hormones and made a particularly popular brand of birth-control pill with good sales in Third World countries, and drugs for hormone-replacement therapy in the West for, said Mavis, spoilt old women who wouldn't give in. Martins had a good reputation, compared to other pharmaceutical companies, for responsibility and reliability – which wasn't difficult. They had been known to take drugs off the market as soon as dangerous side effects were notified, and not fight through the courts for years to keep them on: they had been known to pay damages voluntarily to people whom their products had blinded and maimed, and their gifts to the medical profession could not be said to amount to bribes. Martins maintained large biotechnology departments in their various divisions, and their latest claim to reputation was the development of a certain Factor 10, which almost amounted to altruism, inasmuch as it offered hope of treatment to sufferers from sickle cell anaemia and everyone knew genetic engineering would eventually breed the disease out of the human race so Factor 10 was not even a long-term money spinner. They've cost-accounted integrity, said Mavis, and found it pays.

'Why do you want to know all this?' Mavis asked Joanna May.

Joanna May told her.

'Bloody men,' said Mavis, 'so competitive, always muscling in on women's wombs. I hope you're not going to barge into the lives of these wretched young women and stir everything up.'

'I don't know,' said Joanna.

'Well, think about it,' said Mavis. 'Thirty years on! How would you like it if your ninety-year-old self came walking through the door?'

'I wouldn't mind,' said Joanna, but she wasn't sure.

'Unless you have another reason,' said Mavis, booted feet up on the sofa, 'you're not being straight with me. What else is your ex-husband up to?'

Joanna May told her.

'I don't know anything about Tarot cards,' said Mavis, 'or all that gobbledygook, but that's a nasty wound you have there on the back of your neck, and you should get it seen to. A man who can do that to a woman, forget what he can do to other

183

men – which is really of no interest to me, murder-schmurder, call it what you like, it's a man's gotta do what a man's gotta do affair, and boring with it – but I don't think he should be let loose on your young versions. God knows what he'll do, vindictive bastard, since no doubt he thinks he owns them, typical male, taking claim for their creation.'

'He had a very hard childhood,' said Joanna May.

'Childhood-schmildhood,' said Mavis, 'reclaim your sisters! I speak both in the political and the family sense.' She sat on the sofa where Oliver had been accustomed to sit, and, like him, she smoked; and like him she coughed. Her skin was tough, her hair was frizzy, her T-shirt none too clean, but she brought with her energy, common sense and determination. The world was not too much for her: it was for action, not contemplation.

'Well,' said Joanna. 'Perhaps.'

'Perhaps is not enough,' said Mavis. 'You must go to Dr Holly straight away. You must insist that he opens his records to you, the ones he took with him.'

'Can't you see him for me?'

'No,' said Mavis, crossly. 'There isn't time. You do it. What are you frightened of? What did men do to you that has made your generation so timid? I accept that Carl May is a special case, he scares even me, but an old fruit like Dr Holly?'

'He wore such a white coat,' said Joanna, remembering. 'He was so kind, he was so clever; and I, I was doing something so very wrong, something I didn't want to do. I was getting rid of a baby; I was having my husband's abortion, not his child. I put the Bulstrode Clinic out of my mind and tried not to think about it again. What I did was so very wrong.'

'It wasn't,' said Mavis. 'You weren't pregnant. Two psychiatrists certified it as an hysterical pregnancy.'

Joanna May's hands moved to her small waist, her flat belly, no longer young; she felt her belly swell – she knew it could still. She understood her body's desire to do just that – its capacity to think wilfully, to deceive itself. She felt herself widen and grow, and then she felt herself shrink again, defeated. Tumescence and detumescence.

'Oh,' said Joanna May, cheated all her life.

'Your husband had a vasectomy early on,' said Mavis.
'I see,' said Joanna May.

Joanna May saw. Joanna May saw back into the pattern of
her life, black and white, greys and duns. There are no colours
in the inner landscape. She saw a dull web of non-response,
picked out by miseries and misconceptions, disappointments
and remorse, sparkling away with courage where no courage
was needed, glittering with hope where no hope was; of trials
overcome where no trials were; a false web, not her own, woven
by Carl May: and she was the wretched fly and he the whimsical,
scuttling spider.

'I'm pregnant,' she had said to Carl May. Where had they
been? The States. Boston. She remembered a hotel suite, and a
big white boxed-in bath, and taps out of which water gushed
with terrifying power. She had been afraid to say it: fear where
no fear should be. He did not want children. The day before the
wedding he'd told her so – a walk in the park, a moon, a lake,
romance, as the world knew it – he'd said, 'Just you and me,
forever, no one else, no children, I don't want children, to be a
child is to suffer . . .'
'Not my child, my child wouldn't suffer, I'd protect it.'
'Yes, your child too, anyone's child – to be helpless is to
suffer: there's no escape. Let the human race end here, with
us, its triumph, love complete and final, whole.' And in that
understanding she had agreed – only you, Carl, you and me:
our no-children and our perfect love thus linked: and the stars,
the treacherous messengers of fate, looked down and smiled.
Carl and Joanna May, hand in hand.
Yet there she was in New York, ten, eleven years later, with
her breasts heavy and sore, like the breasts of her friend Nancy,
and feeling sick, as her friend Helen had been, and all her being
focused in on this one wonderful fact: a baby, a baby! Treachery
to Carl, but he'd understand, he'd forgive; surely their meshing
was not so tight now, not so complete, as to forbid a little
budding-off to come between; his past must seem a little further
off, the remembrance of it not so desperate. Surely! What was
her love worth if it hadn't healed him, hadn't undone the past

185

sufficiently to make the future possible? Carl May had been kind. But he had said no.

And now, see! The kindness a lie: the no unnecessary. No living baby there: a notional baby in the head, not a real one in the womb. She'd had a spaniel once, whose nipples grew, whose sides heaved – nothing there, said the vet: an hysterical pregnancy. Animals do it a lot, said the vet, if you stand between them and their purposes. The bitch, Carl May had said; I've half a mind to have the thing put down. He'd laughed. A joke. Kick it and that will cure it. Later the animal had simply disappeared: it and its labrador companion. Dog thieves, people said. Now she wondered. A lifetime believing Carl May was sane, seeing black where white was, white where black was; if you practised too long you could no longer tell. You just saw what was convenient, what sounded best, what kept you out of trouble. Perhaps he'd envied even her dogs.

'Just you and me,' Carl May had said. 'Just you and me.' So back from Boston to England, off to the Bulstrode, to meet charming Dr Holly. Really nice, when it came to it, understanding so much, interested in everything. After the termination she'd felt he owned her body. She would have run off with him if she could, if she'd known how to go about it. But she never knew how; she'd had no practice. It was a trick you learned: as a kitten learns to scratch earth to cover its mess. If there's no one to teach it, it never learns. Tales of Joanna May, the deceived, the self-deceiver.

No baby, no abortion. No pleasure in the sadness, no delight in the grief, no soaring knowledge of I can, I can, I have, I am real, a woman, a grown woman, here's proof of it at last – likewise no regret, no shame, no sense of courage failed, of having thrown a child away, because that child's life was not worth hers. Selective breeding, Carl May had said. Come now, Joanna, if you make a fuss, if you weep and wail, I'll think you don't love me wholly, totally, as you promised you would, for ever and ever, in the park, with the moon, the most perfect moment of my life. Was it yours? Oh yes, Carl, yes. A sacrifice on the altar of Joanna's love for Carl, Carl's love for Joanna.

All lies, all lies. What was a mountain was in fact a chasm: what looked a chasm had been a mountain. Falling when you thought you were climbing. What a fool she'd been. What fools women were: they didn't need mothers to teach them folly.

Lonely and alone these last few years; used to it: liking it. I alone, Joanna May, in the perfection of my childlessness, the tragedy of this single drama: content here in the centre of the web of my life, what's left of it, repairing it as Carl May tears it: only not my web, it now turns out, a borrowed web, too late now, to build my own.

These clones, these sisters, these daughters, what are they to me? I know nothing about them. Let them die. Carl was perfectly right: to live is to suffer. And not just the child, but the adult too. It never stops. The clones, like their original, are better dead. I don't have the courage to die, to kill myself, to put an end to the shame, the rage, the desire, the fear that is Joanna May. But let them die, those other versions. No action is required by me. Leave it to Carl May to act. That at least is familiar, true, comforting.

'It must be upsetting,' said Mavis. 'All this kind of lovey-dovey complication.'
'It is a little,' said Joanna May, politely, vaguely.

Joanna May saw herself at the centre of a web: what did it matter who built it? It was no one's responsibility but her own. She perceived that she was held suspended, harmless and impotent, by the equal forces of the passions which stretched the web, one at each corner. Shame, outrage, fear and desire, the four saving and refining passions of the universe, holding her suspended, centring in her in exactly equal proportions, cancelled themselves, nullified Joanna May. The shame which should purify, the outrage which should move to action, the fear which should quieten, the desire which should sanctify, brought to nothing.

'Are you all right?' asked Mavis.
'I'm just fine,' said Joanna May.

And the greatest of these is desire, and the second greatest outrage, through which we recognize evil and sweep it away because it has no business hanging around, spoiling things. Joanna May willed: it was like using a muscle forgotten for years: you searched, focused, used – it hurt, but it worked. Enough.

'I want my life back,' said Joanna May, petulant and passionate as a child of five. 'The murdering bastard! He took Isaac, he took Oliver, but he shan't have the clones. I want them. I need them. They're *mine*.'
'That's better,' said Mavis.

38

'Hey ho, the holly,' said Carl May, bouncing into Dr Holly's office, 'this life is so jolly.'

Perhaps he's been taking rejuvenating hormones, thought Dr Holly, or is it just those old things, amphetamines, or perhaps youth is indeed in some measure infectious and he's caught a rather hefty dose of it from the young woman who keeps him company, but this is the third time in a week he's been to see me, and I wish he wouldn't. I don't like it. What does he want?

'Hey ho, the holly,' corrected Dr Holly, 'this life is most jolly.' Carl May is a powerful and wealthy man, why doesn't he get his secretary to call me on the phone, why doesn't he send his chauffeur, what is going on that he needs to see me in person? Does he have nobody to talk to? Or does he just want to show off his young companion? That was most likely.

'He's always getting things wrong,' said the young companion, and then, rather quickly, 'don't you, darling?' and she moved over to plant a kiss just above Carl May's eyes where the white hairs grew sparsely in stretched skin.

She seemed nervous. Just a two-a-penny scrubber, thought Dr Holly; an old man's toy, equivalent of a young man's Porsche, and then thought, no, that's just defensive, if she were mine I'd take her everywhere too, for all the world to see — could you breed from the emerald eyes? She wouldn't age well: the bone structure of the face was blurred — she had a look about the mouth: how was it you could tell the whore from other women, just by looking? Psychosomatic damage affected growth, as surely as did hunger: the failure to reach emotional potential left its evidence in the face: the outcome of the psycho-genetic battle was there for all to read. Poor thing. Poor damaged thing. As for Carl May, it was pathetic: a humiliation. Dr Holly did

189

not like to see it. The girl was so clearly bought. He wondered if there would be any point in trying to find the marker for the propensity to use younger members of the opposite sex as symbols of status – it might not be too difficult; some variant in the reproductive organs might well prove to have just such a behavioural link – but decided there were far more urgent matters to attend to. Future generations might locate and shuffle the marker out, if it existed. If they had a mind to. Certainly his own department, after his disagreement with Carl May over the absent-mindedness or otherwise of university professors, could not even begin to take it on board.

'Did you hear what I was saying, Holly?'

Dr Holly hadn't. Bad mark, Holly.

'When do they make you retire, Holly? Got to make way for the young ones, isn't that so, Bethany?'

'Young men are boring,' said Bethany. Then quickly, 'Anyway, Carl, you're not old.' Whew!

'I'm ageing better than he is,' said Carl May. 'I've pickled my bones in radioactivity, that's what it is!' He poked Bethany's young flesh with a bony finger. 'Isn't that so, Squirrel Nutkin?'

'Martins don't enforce a retirement age in their R & D departments,' said Dr Holly, whose beard was white but whose eyes were bright, alert, even kind. 'Good men are hard to find. There's a surplus of competence in the young, but not much imagination.'

'Is that so?' said Carl May. 'No fixed retirement age! I must have a word about that with my friend Henry.' Henry White, chief executive, Martins International, subsidiary of Britnuc. And Dr Holly wondered exactly what kind of task Carl May had in store for him and how he would get out of it. Certainly Carl May was building up to something.

Dr Holly had read about Carl May's divorce in the newspapers and had appreciated the silence which followed it. The man, he had hoped, was permanently subdued. But then he had turned up again, Bethany on his arm, bouncing about like a newly-inflated balloon.

On the first visit Carl May, on his way to a board meeting,

had talked amiably about the possibility of injecting more funds into Martins R & D. He had then left two specimens for dry-storage, which Dr Holly could see no reason to refuse. Carl May did not volunteer information about the nature of the specimens. Dr Holly did not ask. Bethany had worn white boots, black stockings, a scarlet miniskirt and an old grey-white torn T-shirt.

On the second visit they'd talked about the quest for the new non-addictive painkiller the world was looking for, and how after the expense of Factor 10 Martins deserved to be the ones to find it. Bethany had worn a grey suit, a white blouse and pearls and would have looked like a businesswoman only her hair kept falling out of its combs. On that occasion Carl May had been called away abruptly, back to Britnuc. Chernobyl was causing an uproar, apologized Carl May; the world had gone mad; and the thought came into Dr Holly's head that Carl May believed he was the world and was trying to tell him something. Carl May certainly had delusions of omnipotence.

On this occasion Bethany wore a long flowered skirt and an ethnic blouse, which kept falling open at the front where a buttonhole was too large for its button, and Carl May said, 'Tell me more about what you're doing,' and Dr Holly, who thought Carl May knew very well, told him more. He was studying brain-cell function in addiction, said Dr Holly, using identical twins as subject and control, stimulating the pleasure centres of the inner brain, rather than the pain centres – which would hardly be ethical –

'Impractical, shall we say,' said Carl May, 'since I daresay you're dependent upon volunteers, and only masochists would turn up, and then you'd have a biased sample.'

'Quite so,' said Dr Holly, calmly. 'How well you put it. Fortunately, you get much the same kind of hormonal excretion from the brain cells whether they're excited by pain or pleasure.'

'Much the same!' scorned Carl May. 'Time was when you wouldn't be satisfied with "much the same". Time was when you could have got a Nobel Prize, if only you'd pressed ahead, not backed out, sold out, let me down.'

'Well,' said Dr Holly, 'chance would have been a fine thing.

It just so happened that Martins halved my funding one fine day for no reason that I could see.'

'Perhaps they halved it,' said Carl May, 'because you, being a professor, were such an absent-minded old fart and only half there most of the time.'

Bethany stirred uneasily. Language! Another button popped open.

'Perhaps they did,' said Dr Holly, 'perhaps I am,' and Carl May smiled. He always won, in the end.

'Time was,' said Carl May, 'when you'd have bubbled the vats and brewed the broth and grown a million million brain cells and not have had the bother of asking in living twins and parking electrodes into their brains, and perhaps the time will come again, sooner than you think.'

'Do you think so?' asked Dr Holly. 'At least stimulating the pleasure centres of consenting twins, triplets, quads if we're very lucky, is ethical.'

'Ethical smethical,' said Carl May. 'What do you think Martins are doing in the other labs, or don't you ask? Pushing ahead with what you began but didn't have the guts to see through. The transfer of nuclei, perfect and whole, dried not frozen, from the frog right up to the mammal – and by mammal I mean human, you bet I do.'

'So much is interesting,' said Dr Holly. 'There is more to science than genetic engineering. Perhaps, as you say, the field should be left to younger men.'

'Potter on, potter on,' sang Carl May sweetly, which meant he was taken aback, 'to the end of the road, and you'll never walk again,' and he pinched Bethany so that she squealed and leant forward and the next button came undone.

'Walk on, walk on,' corrected Dr Holly, 'to the end of the road, and you'll never walk alone.'

'How's the wife?' asked Carl May kindly. 'She must be getting on.'

'She's very well,' said Dr Holly.

'No arthritis, no spondylitis? A fluttering of Alzheimer's in the brain?'

'A little,' admitted Dr Holly.

'Pottering on to the end of the road,' said Carl May. 'I really

must take young Bethany home. Look at her! I'll be back for
your answer within the week. A plague on your living twins, I
say. I need you back in the field. Money no object.'

Dr Holly nodded and smiled vaguely as if he hadn't quite
understood, but Carl May seemed satisfied and left with a cheery
'Hey ho, the holly', and when he was gone, in spite of the relief
that he was gone, Dr Holly's office seemed oddly dull and quiet,
as if Carl May had sucked out all the energy through the door,
like juice from a hole in the skin of an orange, leaving nothing
but pith and fibre behind. He wondered what would happen
next and he hadn't wondered that for quite a while.

39

Dr Isadore Holly looked up from his desk and said, as Joanna May came into his office, 'Why, Mrs May,' he said, 'you've hardly changed at all.'

'Don't begin by telling lies,' she said. 'You haven't seen me for thirty years. You can't possibly remember me.'

'I'm not telling lies,' he protested. 'It's not in my habit to tell lies. I remember you very well. Naturally, you look older; time has passed: I merely remarked that you hadn't changed, and you may think of that as a compliment, or otherwise. You were the most beautiful of all my patients; your husband claimed you were perfection itself, and I had to agree. The mixture of Scandinavian, Celtic and Norman stock we call typically English sometimes turns out very well indeed. And you have aged well. That too is in the genes; of course. Like mother, like daughter, we find.'

'And you could say the same of identical twins, I daresay. Like this one, that one. No credit in it.'

'Truly identical twins are rare in nature,' he said. 'When the single fertilized ovum splits, it seems the division of the chromosomes is not necessarily exact. It is possible to get identical twins with different-coloured eyes, did you know that? And eye colour is known to influence behaviour, and therefore personality. But I don't suppose you've come here for idle chitchat. One must not suppose that one's life's passion is even remotely interesting to other folk.'

'Your life's passion, Dr Holly,' said Joanna May, 'has had quite an effect on me. Tell me, if someone came to you and asked you to grow a human with frog's legs, would you do it?'

'It wouldn't be a very practical proposition, Mrs May,' said Dr Holly, his shrewd eyes crinkling with artificial mirth. 'We have to respect the laws of physics. Such a creature wouldn't jump – it would be top heavy. And it wouldn't look very nice.'

'I was not talking about practicalities, Dr Holly, nor aesthetics.'

'You mean the ethical considerations? Rest assured we would not. We are not in the business, Mrs May, of creating monstrosities, but of removing disease and, in the fullness of time, and with all possible ethical and legal safeguards, mental illness – a tricky area, mind you, because what is defined as mental illness differs, as we know, from society to society, culture to culture: what seems insane to one nation is mere dissent in another – but no doubt we'll come to terms with it. And eventually we will have to tackle the genetic basis of behavioural problems, and that too will be ethically and politically tricky. But nowhere does anyone wish to create monstrosities, Mrs May. Do I look like a mad scientist to you? No, of course not! Don't you go believing what you read in the gutter press.'

Dr Holly smiled benignly. Joanna May did not smile back.

'But you *could* do it.'

'Of course.'

'And no one would do it just for money, say.'

'Good lord, no.' Dr Holly looked quite shocked.

'People do all kinds of things for money,' remarked Joanna May, 'they make instruments of torture and poison gas, for example. Why not me with frog's legs, for money: or worse, just for fun, to see just how far I jumped, or couldn't jump? Fun is a great incentive. There's always a shortage of it.'

'Mrs May,' said Dr Holly, 'this is very interesting, but I'm a busy man. Can I help you in any way?'

'I just wanted to know what kind of person I was dealing with,' said Joanna May. 'What kind of person you'd turned into since, under cover of performing an illegal abortion thirty years ago, you stole what was rightfully mine, one of my eggs, you and my husband between you. A lot can happen in thirty years. I have come for the names and addresses of the women in whose wombs you implanted my babies.'

Dr Holly was silent for a second or so.

'I think "my babies" is an unfortunate misnomer, Mrs May. I don't think ownership comes into it. Does a woman's egg, once fertilized, belong to her, or to the next generation?'

'Mine wasn't fertilized,' said Joanna May, 'that was the point. It was jiggled into life. So, yes, I reckon it was mine.'

'I should point out,' said Dr Holly, 'that there was no question of illegality, since as I remember there was no actual pregnancy. But these are interesting points; for lawyers to decide, not us. And, as I say, I am no longer personally engaged in genetic engineering. It's a young man's field, these days.'

He felt discouraged and resolved that he would stay with the study of brain cells. They at least would not turn up years later to pester and reproach him.

'The files,' said Joanna May. Mavis waited in the car outside, to make sure she persisted. 'Or has my husband been to see you already? Is that it?'

'Your husband?' Dr Holly seemed surprised. 'I haven't seen him for a couple of years, since he had this idea about cloning a mummy.'

'Cloning a mummy? An Egyptian mummy?'

'The idea was, if we could get enough tissue with at least some segments of DNA intact, we could shuffle it together, insert what we had into a growing egg cell, and the resulting child would have the same genetic make-up as an ancient Egyptian. What a lot we'd learn! Of course, the child's privacy would have to be respected. Just because someone dates from the past doesn't mean they don't have present rights.'

'How far did you get?' asked Joanna May. If Dr Holly was playing for time, she had enough of that and more to spare. This was the advantage of being useless. He was a busy man, she was not a busy woman.

'Well,' said Dr Holly, 'not very far, as it happened. Dead's dead, so far as I'm concerned, and in nature this turns out to be pretty much the case, though your husband finds it difficult to accept. On the whole such scraps of DNA as we managed to retrieve weren't sufficient for our purposes. We had such a deal of patching and joining to do, whatever we grew might well have had the odd toenail missing. Of course these days we can dehydrate the cell before freezing; every year brings new developments, and indeed, more promising ancient bodies to light. We reckon, eventually, to find a few gut cells inadvertently dehydrated. There's one fungus which will do it – before death –

196

which would help a lot. Your husband doesn't give in easily, does he?'

'No,' said Joanna.

'Unhappy childhood; to the point of trauma. Your husband represents the victory of nurture over nature: he is a great encouragement to us all. A source of inspiration. Interesting to reproduce him, wouldn't it be, and rear him in more benign circumstances, see just how it turned out.'

'It must have been fun,' said Joanna May, 'to clone me and see how that turned out.'

'Our major concern at the time,' said Dr Holly benignly, 'was in the successful implanting of fertilized eggs in stranger wombs, and testing the efficacy of certain immuno-suppressive drugs, rather than in personality studies, or making any contribution to the nurture-nature debate.'

'The records, Dr Holly.'

'I must say here and now, Mrs May, I would be happier if the request for information came from the child, rather than the natural parent.'

'I am not a parent, I am a twin.'

'You could look at it like that,' said Dr Holly. 'These personal and ethical ramifications do keep emerging – one hardly thought about them at the time. But, as I say, in ordinary adoption cases, the natural mother and child are brought together by the relevant agency only at the request of the child. The mother gave up certain rights, knowingly and willingly, when she gave up the child to adoption.'

'I neither knowingly nor willingly consented to anything at all,' said Joanna May, 'wriggle as you want, and I want those records now or I'll blow the whole disgraceful thing wide open.' She felt the pressure of Mavis waiting, filling the car with cigarette smoke, thicker and thicker as the minutes passed. She felt the dependence of the Queens of Wands, Pentacles, Swords and Cups: her sisters, her children, her family. They needed her.

'There is nothing to blow open,' said Dr Holly. 'Nothing that was not approved by the district medical ethics council at the time.' But he allowed her access to his records just the same.

40

I, Joanna May; not so young as I was, not so strong as I was, but braver: finding courage. My bed is empty again, but I dream it is filled, with lovers real and unreal, lovers I remember and men I never knew I wanted. I wake to find Joanna May sleeps alone, to face a day now peopled with the ghosts of the past: they throng around me, reminding me, instructing me. This, they say, relates to that. How simple! Why did you never see it before? But still the nights are stronger than the days. When the days triumph, I will act.

How the feelings of childhood haunt us. We think we forget, but we don't. Those initial pains grow stronger with the years: instead of fading, as one might expect, they merely afflict the present more and more. One image now torments me. I remember standing on the wide polished staircase in the big house in Harley Street. A scarlet carpet runner ran down the centre of the stairs. The pattern was both boring and complicated. I must have been very small. The front door bell rang and the receptionist walked through the hall. She wore a white coat, and was not friendly to me, or anyone. She opened the door to the patient. On the step stood an old woman. She had on a black coat with a fur collar and brought with her an air of what I can now see was genteel despair mingled with anxiety: the sense of a life misspent, of opportunities missed, of knights in white armour who never came, of husbands, children who were never grateful. So many of the patients were defeated women. Women, I perceived at that moment, were by their very nature supplicants. The outside world knocked on our front door and yielded up its goodies, and its goodies were nothing but female desolation, decay and disappointment. My father's voice sounded from

198

behind closed doors in one direction: my mother's from another. My mama played bridge, and I was not supposed to disturb her. I ate in the kitchen, with the receptionist: rationing was in force. There was a war on. Food was simple and boring: so was conversation. My mother and I were not evacuated from London: she said we must defy Mr Hitler but I thought it was because she did not want to miss her bridge. My father said the same about Hitler and I thought that was because he did not want to miss his patients. Even fear was a deceit. Sometimes bombs fell and the outside world trembled and crashed and the door knocker banged of its own volition, but the house didn't fall down, which was what I wanted to happen.

I remember standing on the stair as my father's patient was let into the house, and voices sounded, muffled by closed doors, and I knew I was cut off from the real world; that I was alone: that other people would never quite touch me, or me them: that I was only acting this child upon the stair: there was no real and undeceitful me: therefore the voices that came would always be muffled. The prescience was true: children fall into uncontrollable grief when they realize, small as they are, certain truths about the world, and about themselves. 'I just feel like crying,' the small child will explain. Don't believe it. The future is seen: the grief is real and profound.

Only Carl could I hear loud and clear; his voice came through to me not muted, but somehow at first hand. I didn't like what he said or did: that didn't matter, it wasn't the point. When I met him I thought he was rude and plain and rather short, but his edges were somehow defined; quivery, like a real person superimposed against a fake background in an old film. And that was that. I don't suppose it was love I felt; I think I just recognized an opportunity for being healed, for becoming real, breaking through the shrouding veils and mists, and that for me was all, at the time, I needed. I somehow knew what Carl knew, though I had come to the knowledge in a different way than he. Carl had suffered cruelty and hardship and I had not. Carl's early world had been small, black, wretched, terrified, until suddenly the clouds had parted and revealed a new bright world, full of privilege, animation, possibility: and with the last drop of strength he had leapt out of the one world into the other. And myself, female, given everything yet nothing, in my grey, muffled, lonely world, bred to serve, to be a supplicant, knew a different kind of cruelty, but the same kind of terror – the inevitability of illness, age, death: the impotence of love. When I lifted my eyes to Carl's I thought how peculiar, how bright and naked they are – and then realized that was how eyes ought to be. It was other people's which were out of order, clouded by wishful thinking and self-deception. There were just the two of us, in all the world, who knew what the truth was, and how terrible it is. 'You have my kind of eyes,' he said.

It took little to persuade me that I didn't want children. How had it happened to me that I knew what Carl knew? The thought frightened me. How could you protect your own children from that one dreadful moment on the stair, the prescience of defeat and death? You could feed your children, love them, nurture them, act the good mother, do all you could to be close to them, and still it might happen. On that one occasion when I thought I was pregnant I was afraid. When I had what at the time I thought was a termination I was relieved, as well as angry. Let me not deny it.

When Isaac said of the card 'Death' that it meant rebirth too, I took leave to doubt it. But then Isaac's eyes did not have the naked brightness of Carl's. I liked Isaac because he talked to me. Even good wives get bored. What are stay-at-home wives, executive wives, determinedly childless, supposed to do, even if, like me, they are wives of captains of industry not the mere foot soldiers? It is all performance in the real executive estate. She must be like the others, or he will know the reason why, and so will they. She must act, in the first few years, as if she waited for a child: she must hold the babies of other women, and sigh with longing, although the little wriggling thing appals and upsets her. Is this the sum of woman then – to be the instrument of reproduction, a walking womb; the pulsing, gurgling, bloody redness inside the whole point of her being? Never, but let her dissemble! Later she must act out the emptiness of not having children; lament her inability to conceive: it is expected of her:

though she glories in the leisure of her mornings, the flatness of her belly, her peace of mind in a world where the lot of women appears to be worry, grief, toil and anxiety, as their children, their hostages to fortune, sap their cheerfulness, will and energy. Only later, when it's too late to change her mind, when the cyclical messiness has stopped, does a kind of truthful desolation set in, as the world around her empties; and she understands that of her own volition she has become one of nature's dead ends: an experiment set aside, because it didn't work. Then she may well blame whoever's around (as I do Carl), whoever, however unreasonably, she holds responsible for her initial decision, the tying of the knot that severs her from the future. She curses fate, instead of herself. Her executive husband has not got quite where he wanted, what he wanted: whoever does? She has seen him through an affair or so: smiled bravely and grimly through this or the other dinner party, when his mistress picked at her avocado and crab salad; worried through his threatened heart attack, put up with the bad temper and depression of his mid-life crisis; and at last she says what about me, me? Where is this promised life, this happiness, this fulfilment? It must be somewhere!

Perhaps, she says, she could be of service to the community. But how? She has learned something about the world, for all the comfort and security of her life: enough to know there's nothing she could tell the poor and oppressed that they didn't know already. That what the poor want is not advice but money. She knows above all the value of money: how it keeps people quiet and good. Put a hundred thousand pounds in the hands of a child abuser and he'd stop abusing. She can't even give all she has to the needy, because she has nothing of her own to give. It is his. The outside world knocks upon her door: she goes to open it, softly on deep carpets, and outside in the storm, begging for shelter, stands a crone, a beggar woman, and it is her future self. She slams the door, she closes her ears: calls up her bridge partner. If it's not too late, if she's kept her looks – and why shouldn't she? – she 'takes' a lover. Well, one just happens to come along, even if she's married to Carl May. Forget takes. A woman gets taken.

I, Joanna May! See how easily it comes to me to turn from 'I' to 'she' – joining my lot with other women, universalizing an experience, as if the better to justify myself. As if I, a woman who never gave birth but has four daughters, an only child with four sisters, could ever be quite like anyone else. Perhaps what Dr Holly took away from me at the Bulstrode Clinic was not so much my identity, as my universality. He made me particular, different from other women: he turned me into someone of scientific interest. Worse, he stole my soul, the thing that threads me through and back to the human race, and never mind that in my heart I'd tied a knot in it, it wasn't too late at thirty to change my mind, give it a sharp tug, untie it, take my chances along with everyone else, not let the moment on the stair last a whole life, but send my children and my children's children on down through the centuries, mingling and mixing with the others, sharing and partaking, into the future. I think when they took that part of me, the singular me, away, and interfered, they stopped me in my tracks. It isn't reasonable to think so, but when Dr Holly says to me, 'You haven't changed,' I think he's right, and I think it's his fault I haven't changed. He has stolen thirty years of life from me. And now it's too late. For me, but not for them. I have my four more chances, and that's how I must see it.

How had it been for the Queens of Wands, Pentacles, Swords and Cups? If Dr Holly was not interested, I was. I would ask them. I wondered if they lived their lives, or acted them. I wondered if they had their equivalent for the moment on the stairs, and if they had overcome it, as I, their master copy, had not. I felt what it was to be Dr Holly, to want to *find out*: I felt the pleasure of it. I felt what it was to be Carl, and want to change the world: I felt the power of it. But most of all, I wanted to see what I would be, born into a newer, more understanding world: one which allowed women choice, freedom and success. Perhaps I had merely been born thirty years too early and that was the only trouble. The young Queens of Wands, Pentacles, Swords and Cups: myself the ageing Empress: not devastating, frightening, shocking any more – just how very *interesting* to see how it all turned out. What fun it would be – that rare commodity.

202

It was with pleasure, animation and excitement that I waited impatiently for Mavis to come to me with the names and whereabouts of my sisters, my daughters, my twins, myself.

41

Angela called Joanna May.

'Darling, how are you?' asked Angela. 'I wondered if you had any clues as to your ex-husband's current mental health.'

'One or two,' said Joanna. 'Why?'

'Well,' said Angela, 'Gerald is getting quite alarmed. I tell him there's no need. I tell him that for a man to wipe out his wife's lovers may not be legal, or nice, but it doesn't mean he's insane.'

'Angela, I know you're only joking but I think this telephone may be tapped.'

'Ah. Well, listeners hear no good of themselves. My husband says your husband wants him to employ the entire staff of the Divination Department over this fallout business.'

'Then perhaps he should, Angela. I'm very fond of Gerald.'

'But then everyone will think *my* husband is insane.'

'He will at least be around to refute the view, Angela.'

'I see. You mean, on the whole, it's best to do what Carl May wants.'

'For the moment,' said Joanna May, 'yes.'

'In that case,' said Angela, 'Gerald is right. Gerald says it's quite alarming that this man should be in charge of such large sections of the nation's wealth and property.'

'These large companies more or less run themselves,' said Joanna. 'The man at the very top is so often a figurehead. Part of Carl's trouble is that he gets bored.'

'Gerald thinks something should be done about it.'

'Listeners may hear no good about themselves,' said Joanna, 'but they sometimes hear very useful things. Shall we meet and talk you know where?'

'Where's that?'

'Where I saw and admired Gerald's nice soft feet,' said Joanna.

'Ah, so that's what you were looking at,' said Angela. 'He thought it was his varicose veins. You sound much better.'

'Oh yes,' said Joanna, 'I'm better. I'm sorry about going on so the other day.'

'That's OK,' said Angela, of the hairy chin and thick legs, and the waist as broad as her hips, salt of a world fresh sown with salt. 'That's OK.'

42

'I'll be waiting at the corner
Of the bottom of the street,
In case a certain little lady goes by.
Oh me, oh my,
In case a certain little lady goes by'

sang Carl May. 'I wish I'd learned the ukelele,' he said, 'but in the circles in which I moved when a child it wasn't done!'

He and Bethany were in the May Gallery. The morning sun shone in the east window and made the place almost cheerful. Workmen – they wore glasses and were elderly – gently inched in from outside a large earthenware vat dating from the sixteenth dynasty, the great days of Egypt. The hieroglyphics were worn: it seemed to the untrained eye a rough-hewn if workmanlike artefact.

'Why's it so special?' asked Bethany. She wondered how many questions she'd asked in the last few weeks, in order to make Carl feel good by supplying her with answers. She wondered how she was going to get out of this. She wondered if Hughie Scotland could help. She was frightened of Carl May, who seemed to get happier and jollier with every day that passed. She didn't even correct him, saying, 'I'm leaning on a lamp post on the corner of the street,' and just as well, as it happened.

'This jar contains the dust of ancient liver,' said Carl May. 'Liver cells are rich in DNA. The ancient Egyptians mummified their dead to keep them in good shape for their journey to the next world. Nothing died unless you wanted it to in that fair land, under the wide Mesopotamian sky: everything went on for ever: so there was nothing to fear. The God Osiris died only as the sun set: he rose again. The priestess aroused the God and gave birth to the King and all was well in the world of men. And because there was no fear of death, no terror, simply a passing on, agreeable or disagreeable as it might be, all men were good, and all women too, and kind. Sometimes a bit stupid, of course. But they didn't shut their children up in kennels, or beat them, or torture them, or rape them, to express their disapproval of life, because life simply *was*, infinitely variable, infinitely long-lasting, and there was happiness upon earth. And the secret of it all lies there in the dust of all those livers, which are so very rich in DNA.'

'How do you know it's people's livers? Couldn't it just be dust?'

'Imperial Caesar, dead and turned to clay,' said Carl May, 'could stop a hole to keep the dust away. Dear little Bethany, we know it's liver because the hieroglyphics say so. Embalmers sucked the brains of the dead out through the nostrils, and the entrails out through I've forgotten where, including the liver, and saved them all in case of need in great big separate labelled jars like this one. This is a liver jar.'

Bethany felt quite dizzy and blackness made clouds around her. She'd never fainted in all her life, not even when her father had suggested she made a one-armed man happier than he ever had been in his life before – a service the complete in body must always surely be happy to render the incomplete – and she'd seen her father's choice for her had a hook instead of a hand, and she was only fourteen, but she thought she might faint now.

'I knew this existed,' said Carl May. 'That moony fellow Isaac King tried to say it didn't, but I knew he was lying. They had it at Liverpool University all the time. The pool of livers! I think we must get old Holly over and show him what we've found. Would you like that?'

Bethany hadn't liked the way Dr Holly had looked at her. She didn't much like the way anyone looked at her. At first she had thought the looks were admiration and envy; but now everyone seemed to think she was somehow cheating. She didn't know what she was supposed to have done. Carl May was being good to her. She was being good to him. Yet somehow she seemed to have stepped out of line. At home, there had never been this

207

particular feeling of *unrightness*. Things at home were sometimes sleazy and sordid; here they never were: servants cleaned the bath and changed sheets: cats never passed worms on the table: but luxury seemed to make things worse, not better. Nothing was real. Perhaps she was just homesick.

'I liked Dr Holly very much,' said Bethany. 'It would be good to see him.'

And Carl May wondered, now what is the matter with this fragrant girl, this Scotland hand-on, this product of the outer suburbs, this despoiler of my celibacy, this firm-fleshed luxury, this stirrer to pleasure, this brightness which flickers on and off like the sun behind a yew tree on a windy day, this little liar – what is the matter with her? I know what it is, she has a lover. She can't be bothered to turn the brightness on for me. She's thinking of him and anything will do for me.

'Is something the matter, Bethany?'

'It was the thought of all those livers mixed up, that's all; it made me feel quite faint.'

'I hope they're not too mixed up, Bethany, or we'll have a hard task in front of us. I hope they're still nicely layered so we can tell one individual from the next. Are you sure that's all that the matter is?'

'Well, Uncle Carl . . .'

'Don't call me uncle, Bethany.'

'Sorry. It's what I used to call my father's friends, back home. And talking about my dad, I had a phone call from him yesterday. He's not too well.'

Then he knew she was lying. She'd had no such phone call. Every morning at Britnuc Carl May was handed a private pink folder, in which were reported the substance of all phone calls made and received at Eton Square, the King's House, the Coustain residence, and many another household besides, not to mention industrial firms and government departments. Knowledge is power, as Carl May had been told at school: '*Scientas est potentas*'. Carl May the sceptical, Carl May the shrewd, looking up the original text, found '*scientas est potestas*' instead. Knowing is to be empowered. More like it. But, understanding why the misprint was preferred, he told no one; just hugged the empowering truth to himself. Truth was power. Truth was so disagreeable you could, if you had the stomach for it, keep it pretty much to yourself. Joanna his wife was one of the very few who understood these things; in her bones, in her blood, for no good reason: in her genes: Joanna May, Carl May's ex-wife, to whom he had trusted his being; here in this very room: this place, no longer young, no longer his, no good to him; but empowering him, proving yet again the world was what he knew it was, the empire of despair, beneath the little tent of blue that men call sky.

'She must die, or she'll go on to ruin other men,' said Carl May aloud, or just about. The removal men from Carling Antique and Rarities Specialist Transport let slip the giant jar – they felt it had a life of its own, sometimes, but hoped they were wrong – only a couple of inches, but it made quite a bang on the cold marble floor. Carl May seemed not to notice. They breathed again. Carling Transport was a subsidiary of Garden Developments. They specialized also in the moving of rare trees and plants.

'I'm sorry, darling, I didn't quite catch that,' said Bethany.

'Just something from *Othello*, my dear.'

'Oh. We didn't do *Othello* in diction.'

'No,' said Carl May. 'I daresay it's not often done in girls' schools.'

'Can I go home to see my dad, since he's poorly?'

'*Beauty and the Beast*,' Carl May said. 'Of course you can, my dear. But be back by five thirty this evening. Such a pity you can't come with me to the lido. I rather thought of going there this afternoon.'

'The lido?'

'The Brent Cross Lido. A charming place, prettily landscaped; though I'm afraid the chlorine fumes don't do the shrubs and flowers much good. Joanna's favourite place, it seems.'

'You be careful, my darling,' said Bethany, 'don't be outdoors too long. They say the fallout's dreadful: worse than Windscale. And to be frank with you, I'm not a lido sort of person. Now the south of France . . .'

209

Oh yes, she had a lover. She laid her hand on his arm, a pretty hand, long-fingered, each finger slightly trembling, promising pleasure, but promiscuous.

'I'll be back this evening,' she said and, suddenly giddy and happy again, whirled round the musky gallery, yellow skirt flaring, white shirt gleaming, gold shoes glittering, murmuring fond farewells to the embalmed remains of Gods and kings, waving goodbye to the stolid wooden funereal peasants, even dropping a quick brave appalled kiss on the crown of the liver jar, and then back once again to Carl.

'I don't think you got the *Othello* quote quite right,' said Bethany. 'But a good try, Carl-O-Carl! We didn't do it at diction, but my dad did take me to the theatre a lot. He said there was no need not to be cultured, just because I was kind.'

'Four,' said Carl, but Bethany did not even notice. Bethany said, 'And I may be the Beauty but you are not the Beast. You are not even a fiend in human form, you are just a little boy in a right old state, you silly thing!' And he was about to say 'five' – he'd given her to five – but Bethany was gone, emerald eyes and all, in a flash of yellow white and gold, and in strolled Jacko, Petie, Elwood, Dougie and Haggie so he let her go. The lads claimed to be a pop group. Theirs, they maintained, was a new close-harmony rock sound. They called themselves Barbers of the Bath. Carl backed them with recording studios, equipment, venues, wheels, even though they took little advantage musically of what was offered. Some people will do anything for money, the better to maintain the illusion that they have some purpose in life; and this failing, this conceit, suited Carl very well.

43

Jane, Julie, Gina and Alice.

————◦◦◦————

Gina left Julie in charge of her three children and went to visit her mum.

'You have let yourself go,' said Annette, kindly. Her hair was tight permed and blonde and her black plastic belt broad and close around a dieted waist. Bilbo had gone, Annette said. She was now with Nigel, an ex-policeman, something of a racist, but only thirty-five. It was over a bit of trouble with Bilbo, in fact, that Nigel had had to resign the Force. Bilbo was in hospital, more of a cabbage, said Annette, than a man. He'd suffered brain damage. A tragedy. She and Nigel were going to move to the country and open a pub. Start afresh. Nigel had quite a few enemies, Annette said, not without pride. She'd be sorry to sell up their little flat: could Gina take the cat, she'd always liked cats, hadn't she? How were the kids? How many did Gina have? She'd forgotten. She smelt strongly of sherry; a warm sweet smell which reminded Gina of her childhood.

'It was never your flat,' said Gina, 'it was Bilbo's flat.'

'Well, Bilbo's a cabbage, and what good's a fortune to a cabbage, and that's what this place is worth, a fortune. We can buy two pubs and still have some over.'

'Can we talk about me, Mum?' asked Gina.

'Little Miss self, self, self,' said Annette. 'Some people never change.' She looked closely at Gina. 'I told you not to marry what's-his-name,' she said, 'but you wouldn't listen. You never used to have a bust like that!'

'His name is Cliff,' said Gina, 'and you were all for my

211

marrying him. In fact you talked me out of a termination just to get me married and this place to yourself.'

'It was always just right for two, never for three,' said Annette. She kept budgerigars now, and the living room, with its view over the market, was warm and musty with the smell of birds, and birdseed, and the air stirred with the soft brush of feathers. 'And you mustn't be bitter. I'm sure you don't regret that little baby now! Mothers never do.'

Annette offered Gina tea and biscuits and when Gina accepted a biscuit raised her eyebrows.

'Mum,' began Gina, and Annette said, 'I'm sure I'm not old enough to be your mum, Gina. If you ask me I look more like your younger sister than your mother. I certainly weigh a lot less.'

'Don't worry, Mum,' said Gina. 'I'll be gone before your Nigel gets home,' and after that Annette was a little kinder.

'Mum,' said Gina. 'I met a woman who's exactly like me in all sorts of ways and we went to a clinic to be tissue-typed and it turns out we're identical twins.'

'What a peculiar thing to want to do,' said Annette. 'I expect all kinds of people are twins and don't know it. They certainly don't go rushing off to clinics to find out. It's rather like squeezing your breasts to see if you've got lumps: better not start or you'll only find them. A hit and miss kind of thing, I imagine, tissue-typing, whatever it is when it's at home, but you know what these clinics are. They told a friend of mine she had cancer and they'd got the slides mixed. She got the radium treatment and the worry while the other one stayed home happy and died. They'll tell you anything that suits them, these doctors.'

'Mum,' said Gina, 'I'm going to sit here until you tell me.'

Annette's mouth clamped shut, to demonstrate that she did not respond well to threats, but opened again soon enough.

'Don't you try and blackmail me, young lady.'

'I'm not blaming you, Mum,' said Gina. 'I can see twins are a real handful and my dad had thrown you out and you were very young and you couldn't be expected to cope. But I want to know. I have a right to know: was I twins?'

'No such thing as rights,' said Annette, acutely. 'Just such a

212

thing as it would be nice if only, only it usually isn't. All I can say is the doctor never said anything about twins to me. Mind you, I was under anaesthetic at the time. Anything could have happened. Anything. A girlfriend of mine was raped under anaesthetic, but would anyone believe her? No.'

She had some more sherry. She drank it by the teacup full. As she filled and refilled Gina's cup – and she proffered little thin china cups with saucers, flowered and gold-rimmed – with tea, she filled and refilled her own with sherry.

Gina wondered what Nigel was after: cosiness, or daftness, or pneumatic sex, or budgerigars, or just the money for two pubs and some over, or to have what Bilbo had, poor Bilbo, or perhaps it was true love, who could tell?

'You aren't telling fibs, are you?' she asked presently, hoping against hope for maternal reassurance, comfort. 'You didn't adopt me, by any chance? I wasn't some other mother's cast off twin?' to which Annette replied, 'No such luck. Split me coming out, you did; God knows why I did any of it. I must have been mad. All that fuss and trouble and pain and you not even my own child, from what I could make out, though I never could make out much. They talked so fast, the pair of them, and one of them not even a doctor. It was the end of my marriage, not the beginning of it, contrary to all their fine promises. If they were wrong in that what else were they wrong in, that's what I want to know. A twin! They should have told me that. If it was a boy you might have grown up to marry him. You'd have had to be warned. To tell you the truth I was glad when you got pregnant – at least it showed you were normal. I always had a feeling you mightn't be. Like a mule, that's the one, isn't it, or do I mean a donkey, the one that's a cross between a horse and a something else? At any rate, it's sterile. That's what I thought you might be. Sterile. Unnatural. I thought you ought to have that poor little baby. It might be your only chance. And Cliff wasn't so bad. You have to forgive me, Gina. I did the best I could.'

Gina sighed, amazed that she had once taken this woman so seriously, longed to please her, hoped to impress her, and with

213

the worldly competence that enveloped her like some cloud of embracing, protective mist the minute she was out of the children's company, soon had the details of her birth, and an old appointment card for Annette to see Dr Holly at the Bulstrode Clinic.

'I know you think I haven't a heart, dear,' said Annette, 'and sometimes I think you're right, but I kept that card as a memento. Time and time again, when the occasion arose to throw it out, I refrained. I knew it would come in handy. I've always done right by you. Didn't I come and rescue you from Granny and Gramps that time? Say what you like, when you needed me I was there.'

'Yes, Mum,' said Gina, 'you certainly were!' and was off to the Bulstrode Clinic by the next available Underground train. She went to Acton Central and took a bus down Acton Lane and found the Bulstrode Clinic. But it was now a lending library. A white car stood outside, all white, startlingly white. She noticed it. There were a lot of them about, these days. They must, she thought, be very hard to keep clean. Only very particular people would own them.

The librarian was of the old school, motherly, dustily dressed; she stood at the noticeboards and pinned up leaflets on rate support, rent rebate, family allowances and Citizens Advice.

'What do you want?' she said. 'We're about to close.'

'I want to know where the Bulstrode Clinic is,' Gina said. 'Where it went, if anywhere. Where Dr Holly can be found.'

'I've told you once,' said Mrs Avril Love, sublibrarian, for so her badge proclaimed her.

'No you didn't,' said Gina. 'I only just came in.'

Mrs Love looked at Gina more closely.

'I'm so sorry,' she said. 'I thought you were someone else. My eyesight is going, and then what use am I going to be to anyone? Mind you, all you young things look alike to me.'

She shut the library door, switched off the library computer; she offered Gina a cup of tea. She wanted company. She was in no hurry to get home: the later she got home the more likely someone else was to make the tea. Gina was the third young woman in a week to ask about the Bulstrode, after years and years of nothing. What was going on? Something finally come home to roost, the way things did? Birth would out, like murder. Funny things had happened up the Bulstrode, she'd always said so. They'd been fiddling around with women's eggs all that time ago, doing God knows what, the field even less regulated then than it was today. More people walking round who came out of a test-tube than anyone realized, said Mrs Love. She served tea in wholesome mugs, with biscuits. In the end the past caught up with you, said Mrs Love. No use running. She'd had an abortion there herself: she often wondered what they did with the poor dead foetus – and if it was dead. How could a woman know? They knocked you unconscious and did what they wanted: you couldn't object; what you were doing was wrong, illegal. She was sorry to have to speak like this, it sounded unhinged, but she'd never recovered from the experience, for all it was thirty-five years ago. She'd never married: the Mrs was a courtesy title. If Miss was on the library badge, the young mocked her and the old patronized. Ms didn't ring true, not for her. She never had more children: that had been her only chance, she'd blown it. Odd though, that she'd come to work in the very building where it had happened. Sometimes she thought life was just a pattern of spoiled expectations which you weren't allowed to forget. Was Gina a Catholic?

'No,' said Gina. Mrs Love said she nearly was. She'd taken a diet pill. It made her talkative. She was sorry. How old was Gina? Thirty? No. Too young to be her child grown-up. Because Mrs Love always had this notion that at the Bulstrode they'd take your baby away and just implant it in someone else's womb, like moving a fish from one tank to another. She hadn't killed her baby – somewhere it lived. Did Gina think that was possible?

Gina said she really didn't know. She thought it was more complicated, more difficult than that. She had begun to feel very tired. First her mother, then this.

'And to think,' said Mrs Love, 'I lost my baby here – well, gave it away, what kind of mother is that, to give her child away, hand it over to death, and now you lot come along, three of you, and say you were born here, and there's nothing here but books, books. Doesn't it make you feel funny? It did the

215

other ones who were in here asking. They were twins if you ask me, though they said they weren't.'

'Yes, it does,' said Gina, 'it makes me feel really very funny,' and went home feeling hunted and haunted, and told Julie she thought there might be more than just the two of them, and that she wasn't going to see Dr Holly on her own – Julie would have to come with her.

'In the meantime,' said Gina to Julie, 'it looks as if my mother's the one who had us. Yours just bought you in.'

———— ·•· ————

But Julie was in the honeymoon stage with the children: there were fish fingers and wet towels everywhere and she didn't mind one bit. She'd bought a tropical fish tank and set it up and called the vet to ask his advice, and he'd said he'd come round to see if it was fit for fish and she'd said OK but only to see the fish and he'd said of course and both knew different. She told everyone Gina was her sister. Her sister and her children had come to stay. Now when the neighbours talked about the price of children's shoes, so could she. Cliff called round, of course he did, and Julie wouldn't let him see Gina; Julie was cold and reasonable and said a cooling-off time was required, that was all, and he agreed but both knew differently. Cliff was intimidated by the cleanliness, the orderliness, the ordinariness of the house, the net curtains, the glimpse of parquet and framed prints when the front door was opened: this was how people were supposed to live, he could only imagine. He'd never somehow achieved it himself, or rather Gina had failed to achieve it for him. Weeds grew round his and Gina's door. What could he say, what could he offer? Cliff did not want to be a bad husband, he said so: it distressed him to be one: he was just too young to be a father of three: the wrong person to be Gina's husband, or else she was the wrong person to be his wife. 'Quite so,' said Julie, crisply, closing the door. 'Come back on Wednesday week and we'll see how things are. Who's right for who, if anyone.' He'd banged once or twice upon the door to prove a point and then left, apparently satisfied. No one had asked him for money.

'The more of us the better,' said Julie. 'There could be a hundred of us and I'd be glad.' As Gina had got thinner, she'd got plumper. They could wear each other's clothes.

When Alec rang from the airport she said, 'Look, why bother to come home? It's a long way. You'd rather be in an hotel.'

He said, 'There isn't an overnight laundry service.' After a short pause he said, rather pathetically, 'I'm sorry, Julie. I hadn't realized things had got so bad. I don't know what this is all about.'

She said, 'I do. If there aren't any children, there isn't any point.'

He said, over the noise of the airport, 'If only you *did* something: had a job. It's like coming home to a stage set. You hardly seem to exist.'

She said, 'But you didn't want me to work, you wouldn't let me. You wanted me there when you came home: you wanted proper home-cooked meals, you said you had enough plastic hotel food, airline food.'

He said, 'Did I say that? I can't remember.'

She said, 'I can hardly hear you. Why don't you check in at the Sheraton or the Holiday Inn –'

'– the Hilton,' he said.

'– and call me from there.'

'OK,' he said and he hung up, but he didn't call back.

'There could be a thousand of us and it'd be OK,' said Julie. 'The thing is, I'm not my mother's daughter. I thought I had to be like her, but I don't. I'm free to be me. Now everything can change.'

'You've still got to share,' said Gina. 'You got rid of her but now you've got me. You can still see your limits, your outline. And instead of your mother, you now have to put up with mine.'

'But it doesn't defeat me,' said Julie. 'How can I explain it to you? I don't know your mother, and since she didn't bring me up she doesn't count as my mother, and she's nowhere near as boring as the one who did. Boring, boring, boring. I thought I had to be boring, and I don't.' She danced about the house, elated.

Sue was wetting the bed; Julie didn't like that at all: it was smelly. She wanted to make Sue wash the sheets, but Gina said no, that made things worse. The children were upset. They'd lost their father. They were grieving.

'It can't be true,' said Julie. How could they miss a man like that!

'They were born loving him,' said Gina. 'And it's not so long since they were born.'

'There's such a thing as contraception,' said Julie. Women without children are smarter, tougher and more decisive than women who have children. Women with children are torn in so many directions they become kind, nice and hopeless in their own interests in the effort to understand themselves, let alone their children. Gina tried to be like Julie, and Julie like Gina.

The two grey cats slept next to each other on one or other of the children's beds, and Julie thought they ought to be in the kitchen.

'No,' said Gina, 'they need all the comfort they can get. Everyone does.' She missed Cliff; of course she did. Perhaps he'd change. If she went back now it might be different.

'No, it won't,' said Julie. 'You're just addicted, that's all. You've got pain and pleasure mixed.'

Little Anthony turned up the thermostat on the fish tank and one of the angelfish died. Julie slapped: the vet wouldn't like it one bit.

'Don't do that,' said Gina.

'What those children need is discipline,' said Julie.

'Don't you use that word to me,' said Gina. 'It was Cliff's favourite word. When are we going to see Dr Holly? We can't keep putting it off. It's getting on our nerves.'

And Ben said, 'Look Mum, look Auntie Julie, there's a man working on the gas main outside and there isn't gas down this street, only electricity.'

Ben had just started at a new school. They were hopeless at football which meant he was the best and to be the best player

218

in a losing team is easier than being the worst player in a winning one.

Ben said, 'He has a notebook and he writes things in it.'

Julie said, 'By the pricking of my thumbs, Something evil this way comes. There's more going on than meets the eye. We'll go to Dr Holly tomorrow. Ben, you'll have to stay off school and look after the little ones.'

'Oh, sh—' Ben began to say, and then, out of deference to his twin Aunt Julie, whom he had begun to quite like – he admired her toughness – 'Oh botheration. I don't want to miss too much school. I want to be a doctor. Or perhaps a vet.' He would be quite happy here if it wasn't for Sue, who kept getting on his nerves, so he'd start hitting her. He didn't want to, but he was sure she wet the bed on purpose, just to put everyone to trouble.

44

Jane, Julie, Gina and Alice.

———•••———

Jane went home and announced: 'I've lost my job and I've lost my boyfriend and it looks as if I'm going to lose my home. That's the good news. The bad news is I've found a twin. Which means, Madge, either I'm adopted or you had twins and gave one away. I need to know which.'

They were having Friday supper. Jeremy had met Jane off the train, and been late. She'd had to stand about waiting for him in the outfall from Chernobyl for a full twenty minutes. The waiting room had been too full of cigarette smokers to afford acceptable shelter. When her father did arrive, she scarcely recognized him. She was used to a tall, albeit gangling, man. This one seemed shrivelled and shrunk, old. She didn't like it at all. She liked it even less when he said, 'I'm sorry I'm late. We have little Tobias staying. Not so little, of course. He's thirteen.'

'Who in God's name is Tobias?'

'Laura's little boy,' said Jeremy. 'He's over from Toronto to stay with us. I'm sorry, he's in your old room. We didn't know you'd be visiting. You so seldom do.'

'What a Godawful name,' said Jane. 'Tobias!' She had learned the power of bad temper from Alice, and the value of non-smiling. She practised them assiduously.

'He always was called Tobias,' said her father serenely, 'but you weren't listening.'

'I was too busy trying to pass my exams,' said Jane. 'Well, it's a wise child knows its own father.'

But her father did not rise to the bait. She found Madge shuffling round the kitchen, wearing slippers. Madge had a bunion, Madge said. The glass in her pebble lenses was thicker than ever, but not so thick that Jane couldn't see love for Tobias shining out from behind them. How could she! Madge's eyes had always shone with emotions that shouldn't be there: good emotion, noble emotion, masochism triumphant. They streamed out from her in a bright trail of kindly confusion. Now Madge loved Tobias, her rival's child, because he was there, because he was her husband's, because she should. How could she be like this and still teach grown people? Didn't she understand the value of the negative emotions? Have I, Jane, ever understood them, come to that? Would she ever let me? It was my mother made me what I am, and what I am is what I'm not. So thought Jane, as she looked for forks clean enough to lay the table with.

It was the better to annoy and upset, no doubt, that Jane kept her announcement until Jeremy, Madge, Tobias and herself were sitting round the table eating shepherd's pie – a typical English dish, Jane explained to Tobias, who was a beastly clear-skinned, thick-skinned Canadian lad, very plain, with his father's short-sighted eyes (no doubt there, alas). By a typical English dish, Jane implied, though did not say, she meant improperly cooked, fatty, stringy, English mince, hopelessly old-fashioned, unhealthy, and awful: even Canada could do better: sometimes Jane felt Madge did it on purpose to persecute Jeremy. After the mince she went on to her parentage.

'Well,' said Madge, 'I'm glad you've raised the matter but I hardly think this is the time.'

'Why not?' asked Jane.

'We don't want to upset the child,' said Madge.

'Either he's my brother or he's not,' said Jane. 'And he doesn't look like it to me. My belief is I'm adopted. Do I look like either of you two? No I do not.'

'You're upset,' observed Jeremy. 'You'll get indigestion.'

'If I'm upset it's Madge's cooking,' said Jane. 'Tough old shepherds, these, Tobias. Tough and greasy. A great mistake to cook them, if you ask me.' Her parents were shocked into silence.

Jane felt terrible and began to cry. There was a kind of noise in her ears, as of breaking glass.

'Dear, dear, dear,' said Madge, 'it's as if she was six again.'

'She was like this at fifteen,' said Jeremy.

'But worse at six,' said Madge. And Jane had always had a vision of herself as a placid, easy, perfectly well-behaved child!

Madge made Jane go to bed in the spare room with a hot water bottle and sat on the edge of the bed, spare leg flesh swelling over the tops of her slippers, wispy hair awry – shouldn't she have hormone treatment, thought Jane, but she wouldn't, would she: she'd say she didn't want to interfere with nature; what she herself would have said, as little as a week ago, come to think of it. Since she'd met Alice she'd become a great deal less pious, but also a great deal more critical and, she began to see, really rather nasty. Alice had lent her a photographer for a bed companion and she'd found him so boring she'd asked him to go and buy a bottle of wine and then locked the door and pretended to be out when he came charging up the stairs again. She enjoyed that far more than she would the night in bed with him.

Madge said, 'Well, dear, to tell you the truth you're not quite adopted: I most certainly gave birth to you: your father isn't Jeremy: you weren't quite a test-tube baby: it wasn't quite artificial insemination by donor . . .'

'Stop it, stop it,' shrieked Jane. 'This is disgusting.'

'I don't think it's nearly as disgusting as sex,' said Madge.

'You always told me sex was wonderful,' said Jane.

'A child should think that,' said Madge. 'Just because it never went right for me didn't mean it would be the same for you.'

Jane opened and shut her mouth like a goldfish in a bowl hoping for sustenance, reassurance, information, nourishment, anything.

'So I must tell you that although Jeremy isn't technically your father – I was told he was a Harley Street surgeon – he really is your father in essence. What was it Brecht said in *Mother Courage*? "The child belongs to the one who looks after it."'

'Brecht is a man,' said Jane.

'I don't see what that's got to do with it,' said Madge, a little peevishly, Jane thought, in the circumstances. Surely she, Jane, was central to this drama. All the emotions should be hers.

'You mean you've never had sex with my father?' said Jane.

'No,' said Madge, 'and he isn't your father. It's all a long time ago and I think the best thing to do is go and see the Dr Holly who helped us to achieve you. He made a very good impression. I imagine that what's happened is that you and this other young woman share the same father. They may have used the same semen more than once.'

'Taken semen from the same batch, you mean,' said Jane.

'Well of course,' said Madge.

Jane was sick in the washhandbasin: she could not even get into the bathroom; Tobias was having a bath. The rest of the weekend went well enough. She got used to her father looking so old and her mother looking so soppy. She thought perhaps Brecht was right. These were the ones who had looked after her: these were her parents. She felt quite pleased, however, not to have to repress those qualities in herself she had always disliked in her father – the apathy, the sitting about, the slow movements, the grunts as his mind worked, as if some infinitely complicated inner machinery ground incessantly on. She could take of him what she wanted, and simply leave the rest. And the same went for her mother. She need take only what she fancied. She had been so amply served with a helping, she could well afford to be fussy.

She even took down Tobias's address in Canada and promised to write to him. But she didn't ask after his mother. She wouldn't go that far.

45

Jane, Julie, Gina and Alice.

———◦◦◦———

At 10.30 a.m. on the third Tuesday in May, Jane and Alice sat in Dr Holly's outer office, by appointment, and waited for Dr Holly to return from, or so his secretary said, an important meeting. They sat as far from one another as they could. Just because they were sisters or half-sisters, they did not see why they should like one another, let alone resemble one another: in fact, the more they thought about it, the less they felt they did either. For the occasion Jane wore a tweed skirt and jacket; Alice wore jeans and a pink sweatshirt. Jane's hair was now cut remarkably short; Alice's was pulled back from her yet higher forehead by a sweatband but cascaded down her back. They came in separate cars. When Dr Holly's secretary Sarah said, 'Identical twins?' and neither replied, she said, 'You both turn your heads at the same time at the same angle. It's quite funny really.'

She went back to her word processor and Jane tapped with her fingers on the side of the chair until she noticed Alice was doing the same, so she stopped.

'Have you come in for the study?' asked Sarah. 'Is that what you want to see him about? Because they're not starting till next month. He is very busy.'

Neither replied.

'Oh well,' said Sarah, 'no skin off my nose. It may not even get off the ground, I warn you. I get these letters from the Biomedical Ethics people. He leaves me to answer them. Never a dull moment.'

Alice and Jane stared into space; four pure-blue eyes staring at nothing, giving nothing away if they could help it. Jane had lost some weight since she had discovered her twin, confronted her mother, and gone, as Tom put it, finally barmy. He kept out of the way. Alice had put on a little, since she'd begun losing so much work, and slept alone.

'Most of the twins are babes in arms,' said Sarah, filling in the reproachful silence. 'Lots more twins being born these days. Mothers have their babies later, when twinning's more likely; and they're healthier, so they carry both babies to term. One used to just get lost, before the mothers even knew. We get triplets and quads quite often, and nothing to do with fertility drugs. So it's not as if you two are a rarity. They might not even take you on.'

The blue eyes turned slowly towards her.

'At least it's just brain cells, these days. He's stopped doing all that egg-cell stuff: he got frightened. I wouldn't do it, I wouldn't have my eggs taken away in the cause of science, no matter how much money they paid. I don't want to even *have* eggs, it makes me feel like a hen. I'd rather not know about them.'

She thought she'd better shut up and get on with the mail. She was being disloyal to her employer. She had hoped for a decent conversation but seldom got it. Perhaps there was something wrong with her. People didn't like her. She did say sharp things, she supposed. She couldn't help it. She wished she could: was there a pill which would make you likeable? If not, no doubt Martins was working on it. Would she take it if there was? Probably.

Two more of them came down the corridor: the eleven o'clock appointments, no doubt. Sarah could see them through the glass door. She worked out the number of eyes that were now going to stare at her in disbelief, dislike and reproach: eight. These two did seem jollier, however, than the two already in the room. Both wore pink sweaters and jeans. She was glad to see they were at least not quite the same height. Too much similarity gave her the creeps. Reared separately, no doubt, though they'd end up much the same in the end. The impact of the rearing environment wore away with time. In old age genes triumphed. Mind you, all old people seemed pretty much the same to her: as did small babies. People started out true to the broad human type, and ended the same way. Variation peaked in the child-bearing years.

'Oh, quads,' said Sarah, when the next two came in. 'That is a bit more interesting. But why didn't you all come in together? I'll see if Dr Holly can be brought out of his meeting.'

'You do just that,' said Gina, mother of three, accustomed to telling others what to do for their own good. 'And fast. We have a right to some kind of explanation.'

Like so many who have dealings with a beneficent but controlling state, she had a clearer view of her rights than many another, and was quicker to voice them. The others seemed stunned into silence. Not just two, but four. So far.

46

Gerald called Hamish Tovey of NBI – News Broadcast International – and said, 'The public are getting hysterical. They won't go out in the rain: they won't have picnics; I went to the lido with my wife and there was almost no one there, just us and a couple of friends. The farmers are complaining; the horticulturists are complaining; the fashion trade's complaining; and the Electric Power Authority are having kittens because the future of nuclear power is in jeopardy. Not only that, the vets are complaining of litters having two heads; I'm even getting tales of budgerigars exploding.'

'Budgerigars can explode if you feed them the wrong grain,' said the NBI man. 'We've just done a feature on it, nothing to do with Chernobyl.'

'Tell that to the public,' said Gerald, bitterly.

'That's what we are doing,' the NBI man pointed out, 'as best we can. But the public can't tell a roentgen from a rad, and to tell you the truth neither can anyone at NBI. If you could put some of your experts at our disposal to help our graphics team out, I'd be grateful. We've a world opportunity here and it's going to waste. It's sickening.'

Gerald said he thought Britnuc had some spare experts in the divinatory area, tested and proven in the field, and Hamish Tovey seemed as interested and grateful as a TV newsman can get: that is to say, he said, 'There just might be an interesting wind-up item there, I suppose. A light closing laugh. I could look into it. Now what can I do for you?'

Gerald said his Department could see the value of some kind of prize-winning news feature, fronted by someone from the commercial rather than the governmental sector – inasmuch as official announcements had lost credibility in this particular area. A popular yet authoritative figure, if such a person existed.

'Carl May?' suggested Hamish Tovey.

'Brilliant idea!' said Gerald Coustain.

'Did you see him drink that glass of milk on TV?' said Hamish Tovey, suddenly animated, 'defying the roentgens! Brilliant PR! How's he been since?'

'Fit as a fiddle, top of the world,' said Gerald. 'Perhaps we could get him to do something just as dramatic.'

'Or even more so,' said Hamish.

'So long as it's safe,' said Gerald. 'We don't want to lose him!'

'So long as the roentgens and the rads are as harmless as you lot make out,' said Hamish Tovey. 'I have my crew to think about, not to mention the union.'

'Back in 1957,' said Gerald, 'when Windscale caught fire and the instrumentation failed – twice round the clock and back again and no one noticed – the duty engineer lifted the lid of the pile to see what was going on. He stared right into the burning heart of the dragon. He's still alive to tell the tale. Head of the Nuclear Safety Inspectorate, as it happens.'

'Is that so!' said Hamish Tovey. 'Now that would be really something by way of a visual fix. Radiation's something we're all going to have to learn to live with, I guess.'

'I guess so,' said Gerald Coustain.

'Do you think Carl May would do it?' asked Hamish, wistful and dependent all of a sudden, like a greedy child lusting after a cream cake it knows its mother's purse can't afford.

'You can only ask him,' said Gerald. 'I have his personal number here, as it happens. He's not averse to publicity, of the right kind. If you took his astrologers and tea-leafers off his hands, he'd certainly feel obliged. I think his board aren't too happy about them.'

'I'll have to ask the boss about that,' said Hamish Tovey.

'I didn't know you had one,' said Gerald.

'When it suits me,' said Hamish.

'Mind you, these old Magnox stations of Britnuc's aren't the same as Windscale, or Sellafield as we call it now,' said Gerald, 'but I suppose they could raise a fuel rod from the pile and Mr May could clasp it to his bosom. How would that do? Or he could jump into the cooling ponds with his young companion: something like that might not go amiss.'

'Oh yes, the young companion,' said Hamish Tovey. 'I filmed her jumping into a trout pond with someone or other, once. Quite a looker. Amazing eyes. Now that's really interesting. It would have to be a zoom lens of course, this time. I don't see my crew with an underwater camera in a cooling pond.'

'Depends if they're running scared or not,' said Gerald, and left him to it.

Gerald was using the public phone at the lido. He knew better than to call from the office. He made a further call or so to contacts in Britnuc too low down the ranks of command to be directly under Carl May's eye, but men of action and responsibility, like himself. Then he went back to his family and friends.

The lido was almost deserted, in spite of the warm weather. Angela, Joanna and a brusque young woman with boots, who seemed a security risk of one kind or another, sat in the tearoom, under shelter. He didn't like them sitting out in the open: he'd asked them not to and they'd obliged. Angela had ordered the full tea for everyone – sandwiches, scones, cream, jam, muffins, cake. He went to join them.

47

Dr Isadore Holly beamed his goodwill towards the four Queens but they weren't having any of it. Interesting.

'Life,' said Dr Holly piously, 'is the only wealth, and I gave you life.'

'You did not,' snapped Cups.

'You just fiddled around in a test tube,' scorned Wands.

'Who do you think you are?' sneered Pentacles.

'God?' jeered Swords.

They had rapidly acquired the habit, now they were together, of dividing up a sentence amongst them and handing it out, with fourfold emphasis. So long, that is, as their emotions coincided, which fortunately was not always the case. They produced, or so thought Dr Holly, a kind of wave motion of feeling and thought, a trough in one giving way to a surge in the next. Alice had the sharpest peaks, the lowest troughs; Jane and Gina flowed more moderately in between: Julie was the smoothest, the most languid. He thought she was the most successful, or was this merely a sexist reaction in himself, what the man liked in the woman, a kind of acquiescence? More research, more research! But how could research into personality ever avoid the bias, the conditioning, of the observer? Interesting.

So God must have thought when the first sea creature grew a fin sufficiently strong to be called a leg and put his weight upon it – how much it hurt but how interesting!

Dr Holly sat on a swivel chair, and moved it gently to and fro in time with his thoughts; his short legs did not quite reach the ground; he had to use the muscles of his buttocks to provide the impetus for movement. He wished the women would go away and leave him alone with his thoughts, but they wouldn't. They came to ask questions, and stayed to nag. How much easier theory was than practice: how much more convenient the idea than the reality. And where was May, Carl May, whose theory, whose idea these women were, this multiplication of perfection out of technical ingenuity? He had thought to breed passivity and had manufactured its opposite. May should be here to witness this turn up for the books.

How they tapped their feet, how they drummed their fingers, these four handsome creatures, the clones of Joanna May; each one amounting to more than the original, by virtue – by virtue of what? What was it that gave the illusion that there was somehow more room in them than in their original, some sort of inner space not altogether taken up by flesh and bone, nerve, muscle, brain, blood; which gave them an energy, a freedom, a distinctiveness which Joanna May had never had? The life force skipped about in their bodies, toeing no particular line, if only because that line had opened out, widened, become fuzzy. These women were less the sum of their genes than was Joanna May, that was what it was, by virtue of being born into a later decade – as if time itself was a factor in the making of a personality, and ought to be included along with diet and education, and social expectation as a complementary building block. Each year its special character, as with wine, and due to something more than weather: rather some complex, so far undefined, pattern at work. Interesting. Except that it smacked of that insult to the civilized and rational mind, astrology.

'We're waiting,' said Alice.
'We've come a long way,' said Jane.
'We won't be put off,' said Gina.
'We have a right to know,' said Julie.
'Who our parents are.'
'What our relationship is.'
'Why this has been kept secret.'
'And are there more of us?' asked Julie, and a little breath of air stirred the air of the perfectly air-conditioned, even-temperatured room, as the other three drew their breath in surprise and alarm. More? It was intolerable.

'There is one more of you,' said Dr Holly, consolingly. 'But only one.'

Five of us!

They would not sit down. They moved about the room, their energy focused upon him. He had the feeling their energy bisected him. He expected their gratitude, but they had none to offer. Well, this was the fate of the prophet, the searcher after knowledge, the reformer, the artist, the innovator: he should not be surprised.

The room was acoustic-tiled, palest green: the light came from gently humming fluorescent tubes, the carpet was neutral oatmeal, the furniture pale ersatz oak veneer, the files a dingy yellow, computers, VDUs and faxes creamy white. No money had been spared: equally, none wasted. The room was male, male; straight-lined, hard-edged: he saw now what was wrong with it. No pot plants, no family photographs, no cushions – not an ashtray, not a coffee cup – nothing to bear witness to human frailty, everything to further unimpassioned thought, that divine inspiration, that necessary trigger if Utopia was ever to be achieved. And how else but by logical means, since all other ways had been tried, and had failed? Poet priests, and painter kings, all failed; empires crumbling as art and nonsense prevails: aspiration and practicalities always so little in accord: no, this was the way forward, through the digital clicking of information, the intricate matching of fact with fact, through memory forever retained, patching together the parts of wisdom to get at the wider vision: as DNA is logged and booked and coded and patched. Working up from minutiae rather than in from the macrocosm, for that could never be grasped in its entirety, only guessed at intuitively, and how much time and money you would waste if you got it wrong. Obviously, you had to start with the little bits and make them up into the whole. No wonder computers wrote such bad poetry.

'We're waiting,' or rather 'w–we–we'r–we're wait, waiti, waitin, waiting.' Odd, that; the ripple effect when they all said

232

the same thing at much the same time, just fractions of a second apart. Did it follow the same sequence as the initial cell division? Well, he would never know. He longed to know. How uppity they were, how irritating, these grown children of his invention. 'Which of our mothers had quins, then,' they demanded, 'was it a fertility drug, and who was our father? You?'

'Good God no,' said Dr Holly, shocked. 'You seem to be labouring under considerable misapprehensions.'

And Dr Holly explained to them the detail of their birth. ('Not birth,' snapped Alice, 'say genesis.') Afterwards they were silent for a little. He was glad he had shaken them.

'It isn't nice to be so unusual,' said Julie presently. 'To be implanted, not conceived.'

'We were so conceived,' said Gina. 'We were conceived in Harley Street sixty years ago. We are orphans. Our parents are dead.'

'Well if they're not,' said Alice, 'they needn't think I'm visiting them.'

Jane said, 'We were postponed for thirty years. We should sue.'

'I gave you life,' repeated Dr Holly. 'You should be grateful.'

They were not. Why only four, they demanded. Why not a hundred?

'We couldn't get more than four, in those days,' he apologized. 'We weren't in the business of swapping nuclei, shuffling genes, just parthenogenesis, and ex-utero conception.'

Then they despised him for a failure in ambition. He felt bad about it. He wished them out of existence, but they failed to dematerialize.

The clones turned their mind to Joanna May. They needed someone more exotic than Dr Holly to blame. She should never have let it happen. What sort of person could she be? How could you be cloned and simply not notice? Jane wanted to know.

'Easily enough,' said Gina, sadly, who had more experience of hospitals and doctors than her sisters.

'I don't want to meet her,' said Alice. 'She's so old we'd have nothing in common.'

233

But Julie said, 'You might learn something from yourself grown old,' and they pondered that.

Dr Holly rashly said sixty was not old, it was positively young, and they turned the energy of their attention back to him. They jeered.

'You have made orphans of us,' they said. 'Snatched away the ground from beneath our feet. We are unnatural, and all you can do is talk about yourself.'

Gina began to snivel at the notion of being unnatural. Alice slapped Gina: Julie comforted Gina; Jane restrained Alice's hand. They swirled around a little, touching, hugging, patting, settled down again.

'And now,' said Alice to Dr Holly, 'I suppose you think you're God and we should worship you. Well, we don't. We are much more likely to sue you.'

'The general opinion is,' said Dr Holly, kicking his feet against the central pillar of his chair, as if he were a little boy, 'that God is dead.'

He felt himself grow tall: his legs extended to the floor and below; his head to the ceiling and beyond. He floated. He felt himself swell, he thought he would burst. It was a most unpleasant feeling. Still his mind worked, computer racing, information pitted against wisdom. Interesting! The Gods were dead, starved to death by lack of belief, and when the Gods died the Titans returned, and he was a Titan untrammelled. Dr Isadore Titan Holly, suffering from gigantism of the head: outside the laboratory windows were the chimneys, the puffers, the suckers, the spitters and nibblers of Martins Worldwide Pharmacopoeia, patents taken throughout the universe, through all eternity, nothing too small, nothing too short, just everything, everything buzzing and whirring and blinding, swifter, faster, cleaner, neater, smarter, richer, glossier exploding markets, expanding universe, stretching time, smash, crack, ecstasy, smack, the cocaine culture, a faster mile, bigger muscles, sweeter smiles, shorter skirts, up their own arse and out again, he was part of it, feet through mud and head through clouds – and splat, he'd fallen flat on his face. The breath was knocked out of him. He was having a fit: a bad one: perhaps this was the one which would carry him off?

Not one of them helped him up, these, the women of his creation. Not one of them loosened his collar or made his tongue safe. They stared down at him, watching him froth and twitch, waiting for him to die, or not, as the case might be.

'He can't die now,' said Alice eventually, brutally. 'There's more we need to know.'

He felt better, as if having been given permission to survive. He tried to speak. He couldn't. But his limbs moved now of his own volition, not of his brain's convulsion. That was something. Perhaps he should crawl out to Sarah? But they closed in on him. He thought they might kick him, even to death. Supposing they felt as entitled to end him as he had been to begin them? What would happen to his research? Had he remembered to put away his own dehydrated DNA? Yes, of course he had. A loss to humanity, otherwise. A multiplicity of ingenuity was what he had, and others had not. So much to be done, so very much it had frightened him off: nothing to do with Carl May. He had wanted the grant cut: he had wasted time unforgivably. Brain transplants: memory transfer: personality shuffling: all waiting for his attention. He of all people needed to be cloned, properly. Effective genetic engineering; not a hopeless dream: just a great deal of money and international cooperation. Another fifty years would do it. It would not be personal immortality for him, even so. It couldn't be. Just look at these four to know; to know what? Not one soul to go round, but a soul apiece and more to spare, and man, woman, was more than the animals, and God was there, and to find out that was enough for a lifetime. But had he told Sarah where his DNA was? Where he'd put himself? Would she remember? Oh fallible, fallible! So much industrial security in a scientific arena; records always so secret: things got lost. Death was something you never expected. Four straight noses bending down. Perfect noses. Beautiful eyes. It couldn't be bad to have achieved this. He was proud of them. At least he was down to proper size. Little size, almost child size. Four short upper lips, four rather thin lower lips. Better breed clones than rely on finding twins: why had he doubted it! He would do what Carl May wanted: it was what he wanted. He was decided. He would take all the money and get going again. If they let him live. They did.

'What did you say?' asked Alice.

'Interesting,' managed Dr Holly, and they fetched Sarah.

'He had some kind of fit,' said Jane.

'Epileptic,' said Sarah. 'He must have forgotten his tablets. He'll be OK now. I expect you exhausted him. He's not as young as he was.'

The clones left, still angry: they blamed the bearer of bad news for the news: and the bad news was they were not who they thought they were, and that is always difficult to accept, no matter how little you may like being who you thought you were. Dr Holly had given them life and they'd drained the life out of him to the point of death, exhausted him, to punish him for every unpleasantness received and recorded during that life. Children do it to parents every day of their lives, to pay them out for not providing a perfect world to live in. They felt their own unreasonableness and it made them irritable rather than guilty. They felt the inherent guilt of the female, but not powerfully; being four that guilt was quartered. The soul was multiplied, the guilt divided. That was a great advance.

The realization cheered them up. They thought they should celebrate. The clones went back to Julie's house as soon as they could because Ben couldn't be left alone with the little ones for too long. A mild obligation, when divided by four. Alice said, at first, she wouldn't come, she wasn't interested, but in fact she did, she was. The others understood quickly that though Alice needed persuading, she was not difficult to persuade.

Julie and Gina went in Julie's small automatic Volvo, Jane followed in her Citroen Deux Chevaux, Alice in her Porsche. They were glad not to have chosen the same car.

'Alec likes Volvos,' said Julie.

'Tom only believes in Citroens,' said Jane.

'Mine's just more expensive than my brothers' cars,' said

Alice, cheering up. 'At least they're not really my brothers. Thank God, it wasn't incest, that on top of everything.'

'I never had time to learn to drive,' said Gina.

48

Carl May sent for Jacko, Petie, Elwood, Dougie and Haggie.

'Tell me about the clones,' he said. It was Thursday evening.

Carl May looked at his watch as he spoke, unusually conscious of the tyranny of time. So much to do, and so few years to do it in! The skin on his right calf itched; his circulation was bad. Would Bethany return of her own free will, and by five thirty, as she had promised, or would she have to be fetched? The hands of the watch blurred: the most expensive watch in the world, sleek, unobtrusive, infallible, but still the hands blurred. It was bitter. The fault lay in his eyes. They had tears in them. He wanted Bethany to return to him of her own free will. If she had to be fetched, he would feel discouraged and end up removing her from his scale of reference: that is to say from the material and current world. She would not die, or only so far as friends and relatives were concerned, and up to a point herself – though what that death experience was, who was to say? No, she would merely be put off to some other time, as Joanna's gardener had been. A pity for the genes of that particular talent, greenfingers, to be lost to the human race. The experience of Garden Developments plc was this, that – forget science, nutrients, temperature, humidity, and so forth – plants simply grew better in the care of certain individuals than in others. Greenfingers. He thought perhaps Bethany had pink fingers. See what happened to his circulation when she went away. He had been happier, calmer, of course, when married to Joanna. White fingers. But white fingers betrayed, strayed. If Bethany did not return, if Bethany removed herself from Carl May and the world – for were not the world and Carl May the same thing? – then perhaps one of the younger versions of Joanna May would do: white fingers he himself had made tolerable by tingeing them with youthful pink: redipping the faded stuff in stronger dye.

But Jacko was delivering the report on the clones. He was dyslexic. He held folders but spoke from memory. They were in Carl's penthouse office suite at the top of Britnuc's tower. Carl May sat in his architectural chair, and tried to find it comfortable. He thought for the first time that it was a young man's chair: it was uncushioned: it demanded resilient young flesh for its proper occupancy. The Barbers of the Bath did not sit, however, no matter how resilient their flesh. Their layered trousers were too bulky, or the chairs too narrow, to make it possible. He stared at Jacko's trousers: a ragged hole in dusty black cotton gave way to ripped green wool tartan, which showed slit red satin beneath, and that was patched and pinned. Three of them smoked: ash fell unnoticed on their clothes and on the pale floor. He would be glad when he was finished with them. He would not use a rock group again: they were easy to buy, easy to bribe, so unnecessarily cynical were they about the ways of the world – citing 'everyone does it' as cause and justification of their actions when of course the truth was everyone did *not* do it – and they were certainly stylish, but he felt more at ease with professional villains, who could make a proper distinction between criminal and ordinary citizenship, and stood their toddlers in a corner if they swore.

Jacko recited the qualities and lifestyles of the clones, rather as a nervous waiter recites a memorized menu, babbling a little, eyes to heaven. Carl May was accustomed to nervous waiters.

Carl May looked at his watch. He still could not make sense of it. Haggie took out his Victorian pocket timepiece 'Five thirty-five, sir,' Haggie said, rounding to the nearest figure, as people always used to, in the old world. Carl May was surprised that the lad could tell the time from a handed watch. So many of the younger generation could not. In the four Magnox stations under Britnuc's control, all clocks had of necessity been converted to digital display, at considerable expense. A wave of despair made Carl May catch his breath. All to no avail, all efforts on behalf of the human race; how could science hold back this tide of stupidity, flesh and blood rioting, breeding uncontrollably, surplus upon surplus, so excess a quantity that quality went out the window, more and more and more, this plague of unthinking, all-feeling humans, no better than a plague of locusts, chattering, devouring, destructive, monstrous. To no avail, this latest heaven-sent breakthrough of the geneticists: the happenstance in nature of a dehydrating fungus, so that henceforth the nuclei of mammals could be treated and transferred unharmed, the building blocks complete. And not just transferred, but multiplied a million times in the E.Coli vats, so the shuffling of DNA, the improvement of physique and personality, could now be done at will. Jacko, Dougie, Haggie, Elwood, Petie. What could you do to them? Require the skill, refine the spirit, make *good* not bad. Too late, too late! Too many now. The random creations of nature would overwhelm the desires and designs of thinking man. Five thirty-six.

Carl tried to listen to Jacko's report. For the hors d'oeuvre, Alice, light and astringent (but too much lemon). For the fish, Julie, tentative and delicate (but a little stale, a little flat, too long out of the water). For the entrée, Gina, full-blooded but overcooked. Jane, a delectable dessert except salt not sugar had been put in the topping.

Faithful, monogamous? The Barbers of the Bath allowed themselves sounds of derision, close-harmonied snorts. Promiscuous at best, lesbians at worst. Carl May said perhaps it was because they had never met the right man, and the four young men shuffled their great Doc Martens eighteen-hole boots and looked uneasy: they had not expected words for the defence spoken by the prosecutor. They had understood their task to be to report adversely.

'So what's the message, sir? What's the next step?' Jacko asked.

Gina and Jane, meat and dessert. Too rich and indigestible. He had an old man's gut, it had to be faced. Those two would have to go. Alice and Julie would replace Bethany, one or the other. Which would he choose? Hors d'oeuvre or fish? One too lemony, one a little stale. Why not both together? They'd consent. They'd do as he asked, as Joanna always had. They'd love him, as Joanna had. Of course they would: they were Joanna. When he multiplied her he had not so much tried to multiply perfection – that was a tale for Holly – he had done it to multiply her love for him, Joanna May's love for Carl May, multiply it fourfold: to make up for what he'd never had: Carl May, the bitch's son. But love was strong, when it came to it: you couldn't stand too much of it: Joanna had been more than enough. It took Bethany, a sorbet between courses, tasted, relished, to restore a jaded palate, a tired appetite. Alice and Julie it would be. Five thirty-seven.

He tried to speak. His voice shook: he stopped.
'Instructions, sir?' asked Jacko. They sang the word, in inefficient close harmony. Inst-instr-instruct-instruction-instructions. He wished they wouldn't. His leg began to itch badly. There was a whining and whuffling in the air: it was the snuffling harmony of a bitch and her litter of pups. He'd lived amongst the excrement and the noisy, messy warmth of the litter and got quite fond of it. The need to love, for a child, is stronger than the need to be loved. When he was hungry, he'd sucked from her. But that had been when he was very small: he'd been told that: he didn't know if it was true. Five thirty-eight.

'Oh yes, instructions,' said Carl May. His voice came back, and his will. He told them Jane and Gina would have to go. Julie and Alice would be fetched. Their ten eighteen-hole Doc Martens boots marched out, blurred by a flurry of dangling fabrics.

241

49

When Bethany went home to Putney she found her father weeping and alone.

'I knew there was something wrong,' she said. 'I knew I wasn't lying. What's the matter?' Patsy had gone, torn the flowers from her greying hair, been born again as a Christian, and given up her life of sin, said her Dad. Now Patsy was living in an hotel for born-againers, going from door to door, converting as she went.

'But, Daddy, it wasn't sin,' said Bethany. Empty coffee cups stood around, and biscuit crumbs, and sugar bowls with mice droppings in them, and piles of stained sheets on the floor. He needed her. Upstairs there was the sound of revelry. 'It was never sin. Sometimes I'd wish I'd been brought up differently, sometimes I thought that you didn't know what you were doing, the pair of you. Sometimes I was so scared – you and Mum never knew quite what was going on, you thought what they did was just ordinary sex, but sometimes it wasn't, you have no idea. I tried to be kind, I tried to be loving, I tried to bring happiness into other people's lives, especially the disabled, but, Dad, they sometimes sure as hell weren't bringing happiness into mine.'

'Don't you start,' said Dad. 'I've had a bellyful. We had good times, didn't we? Don't take that away from me along with everything else. Your mum will be round here before long, trying to make me believe in Jesus Christ, and I can't, I just can't. Remember how he cursed the fig tree?'

'Well, I can't either,' said Bethany, sadly. 'I can't believe. We went to the theatre too often. You made me read too many books.'

'I suppose you hold that against me too,' he said.

'Of course I don't,' said Bethany. 'Let me help you get this place cleaned up before Mum comes back. She'll just die if she sees it like this.'

'You will stay, won't you?' said Dad. 'This is where you belong, your proper home.'

'I don't know,' said Bethany. 'I really don't know.'

It was three o'clock.

'Who's upstairs?' Bethany asked.

'That's another thing,' said Dad. 'I think I'm getting old. People don't seem to go. Once I used to tell them, quite quietly, it was time to get dressed and go, and they went.'

'You always were a big man,' said Bethany.

'I don't register that way any more,' said Dad. 'It's got worse since your mother moved out. Now I tell them to go and they don't: or worse, they turn up and walk in and use the bedrooms without so much as a by your leave, any time of day and night, as if this was Liberty Hall, and don't even put money in the box. I don't know who's up there, Bethany. You've got to help. I need you here.'

'But, Dad,' said Bethany. 'Carl May needs me too. I'm only on leave of absence, as it were.' And she cooked him a meal. Only omelette and beansprout salad, because of course he didn't eat meat, but better than boiled eggs and toast, on which he lived. It was four o'clock.

'Beauty and the Beast,' Bethany's father remarked, watching her clear and wash up. 'I must say you're looking good. Why bother with a beast? I'm proud of you. We were right about sex, weren't we, your mother and me? We grew you proud and true.'

Bethany's father had a cavernous, grizzled face. His thick hair had turned greyish since last she saw him. He reminded her of Father Christmas, the kind she'd been taken to in stores when little and on whose knee she most hated to sit; agony shone out from behind the joviality. You had to not notice, for fear of hurting feelings. To hurt feelings was the real sin. It was four thirty.

'We'd better put locks on the doors,' she said. 'And the front door, and the back door, and get a dog.'

'I don't believe in locks,' her father said. 'Lock the door and get robbed. The only time I ever locked my car was once in an underground car park and when I got back someone had broken into it and I had to get a new door.'

She'd heard the tale a hundred times, and taken many a lesson from it. If you kept the door unlocked, as it were, you didn't get raped. Some personal doors, alas, were on permanent lock; she sighed. Her father, for all his experience, for all his principles, was an innocent. She'd had stitches twice, and neither she nor her mother had liked to tell him. She was glad her mother was born-again. She hoped she was happy.

'We can't have strangers coming and going,' Bethany said. 'Things have got to change.'

'I don't like it,' he said. 'The world goes round on love and trust. I've always believed that. Besides, we have nothing to steal.' He made a concession. It was his principle to make concessions, save face wherever possible. 'But a dog, now . . . your mother always wanted a poodle.'

'I'll get you an Alsatian pup,' she said, and ran down the market and did so once she'd cleared up the rest of the house. The bedrooms were disgusting. It was five thirty-five. She'd said she'd be back at Britnuc at five thirty. She could feel Carl thinking about her. She didn't want to feel it. He spooked her. 'For a young man he is young, And an old man he is grey,' she sang as she cleaned, as much to dull the puppy's lamentations as anything else: it had been torn too young from its mother. But where was the young man? Where were they all? They so seldom travelled First Class and she so seldom Standard Fare. They never met.

'Don't lose your trust, Bethany,' her father said, petting the puppy in a way which once would have made her jealous, but which no longer did now her father was old. 'My little girl. Don't ever forget how to love. Keep the flag of faith flying.'

She said she'd try. Somehow there seemed no place between the two of them, Carl May and her father, where she could properly dwell. It had to be one or the other, and she didn't like cleaning, so that settled it. It was five forty-six. She called Carl May, and said she'd be late back, but she would be back. She was on her way.

50

How desperately I, Joanna May, tried to be myself, not Carl May's wife. Even in exile, even divorced, I was married to him, linked to him. She married to him is so different from he married to her. She occupies a little space in his head; he surrounds her, encloses her, as a white leucocyte surrounds some invading cell: if he puts his penis in her it's just to test the breeding warmth: he's really there already. He can escape, she can't. She is squeezed in there, in his head, without room to manoeuvre. Even in Isaac's bed, his uncomfortable, lumpy-mattressed bed, his comfortable arms, I was Carl May's wife, his employer's wife, source of his funding: he was my illicit lover. Therein lay the excitement, the pleasure. I could understand Carl's rage, I could understand my guilt, but not his jealousy. How could he be jealous when what I was doing could hardly be acting, could only be reacting? When Carl divorced me and Oliver climbed into my smooth, firm, clean and luxurious bed, Oliver was my comfort, my consolation, because Carl May had eased me out of his life, as the head's squeezed out, eased out, of a pimple. If Carl May did it painlessly, it was for his own sake, not mine: he didn't want any nasty, unsightly inflammation left behind.

When I acknowledged my sisters, my twins, my clones, my children, when I stood out against Carl May, I found myself: pop! I was out. He thought he would diminish me: he couldn't: he made me. I acknowledged fear – what would they think of me? I recognized shame – I am old, so old. I faced my rage – how dare they exist. I felt desire, and a great swelling energy, a surging pleasure, the joy of being one of a million million, part of the life of the universe, in all its absurdity, its tremulous glory: I was part of a living landscape, and the function of that life was to worship and laud its maker, and the maker was not Carl May: he had not made me: wife I might be, but only part of me, for all of a sudden there was more of me left. The bugles had sounded, reinforcements came racing over the hill; Joanna May was now Alice, Julie, Gina, Jane as well. Absurd but wonderful!

Carl May could not go on. I let Angela know, who let Gerald know; a man may murder his wife's lovers, but cannot be mad in charge of four nuclear power stations. I was no longer just a wife; I was a human being: I could see clearly now.

If thine eye offend me take a good look at yourself. If thine I offend thee, change it.

It's not lies that kill the soul, it's the effort to believe the lies, especially your own. Carl's dead, white face on the TV screen alarmed me, and should have alarmed the world sooner than it did. The walking dead can't be in charge. There is no room for zombies.

That day at the lido Gerald had a word with someone, who had a word with someone, who had a worker in the field, of course he did.

Sometimes accidents, or events as they are called, do occur without prompting in relation to the fuel rods of the old Magnox stations. Are bound to. The spent fuel rods – fissile uranium wrapped in magnesium – are removed from the pile when they've worn out their usefulness, are no longer capable, poor tired things, of sustaining a reaction. They're taken out, in sequence, en bloc, as they went in – some thirty at a time. But sometimes rods which are not quite spent, may even have quite a vigour to them, get in with the others: they too get dumped in the cooling ponds – square concrete-sided pools, open to the air. Such events do happen – it hardly seems to matter much. No one's going to swim in the pools, are they! What does it matter, if the dials do go round a second time, a third time, a tenth time, and no one notices – or in this particular case, cares to notice, gets paid not to notice; who's to say what goes on, no skin off anyone's nose, unless, that is, the owner of the nose is vain enough, proud enough, sufficient of a scorpion to sting himself to death. When it would be the scorpion's fault, no one else's. The old-fashioned dial readouts should have been converted to digital display long ago, but if management is mean, mean, whose fault is that? Management baying at the moon – snapping, howling: how dare you shine so bright! It doesn't stop the moon.

Accidents will happen. No such thing as an accident.

I, Joanna May. Or perhaps now, just Joanna.

51

Joanna, at the age of sixty, chaired the first meeting of her life. Her clones appointed her chairperson. The meeting took place in Julie's house, where Mavis had led her. On arrival they found a Volvo, a Citroen and a Porsche in the drive. They could hear the sound of children playing, or squabbling, not to mention TV-set, radio and hi-fi all turned up loud.

'How very peculiar,' said Mavis, who wore for the occasion a long brown woollen coat of amazing plainness. 'My report says this one, Julie, lives very quietly, and has no children. Isolated, rather the way you are. An "executive wife" is what they call this particular brand of woman.'

'Perhaps she's had no choice,' said Joanna. 'Or perhaps she lacked the courage to have friends. Look how brave I have to be to have Angela!' Joanna wore a nice little black suit and high heels to give herself confidence, or perhaps to annoy Mavis.

'Perhaps they've found each other already,' said Mavis.

'Yes, perhaps that's it. All of a sudden, like you, she has a family. And noise and drunkenness breaks out!'

Mavis rang the bell, because Joanna hung back, and knocked, and tapped upon the window, and finally was heard. The door was flung open.

'Mother!' cried the clones, elated and irreverent, 'it must be Mother!', as Joanna May stood in the doorway, startled. They crowded round, inspecting, touching, laughing. Even Joanna, accustomed to sobriety, could see they'd been drinking. But she was relieved they had recognized her with so little difficulty: had no doubt at all but that she was theirs.

'Mother!' she said. 'Oh, I see. I'm to be mother, am I!' She looked them up and down: she hushed them and tutted them.

She felt like her own mother, disapproving; she felt a flicker of forgiveness for the poor dead woman. Mother! The girls would have to take the consequences, the general brisk comment and interference for their own good. Joanna May, mother, refused champagne, fearing alcoholism; she accepted tea. (Mavis took what remained of Alec's whisky from the mahogany-and-glass cabinet.) Wildly, the clones asked Joanna for her opinion of them: they insisted, insisted. They wanted a proper mother's report – at last, they would have what every daughter wants, a mother to wholly appreciate them.

'I see,' said Joanna May. 'You want my true opinion, do you? My maternal view? Then here it is.'

She, Joanna, didn't like one bit the way Alice had taken back her hairline; it was vulgar; she felt Julie's sweatshirt was too informal considering this was her house and she had guests, and what is more she didn't care for the patterned drink coasters, they were common; she thought Jane should comb her hair properly – and it was much too short – and Gina should lose some weight and stop smoking. She couldn't help saying these things. They were true: she was right about them: they must listen to her. It was for their own good. She had been around longer than them: she *knew*.

Joanna felt resentment rising in her daughters; they were oppressed: they wanted her to go away, and yet she'd hardly said a word to them, had she, nothing that wasn't necessary. Just she didn't like this and she didn't like that. Which was true. And for their own good. And look how they drank – alcoholics, every one! They drummed and tapped with their fingers: they were one split into four: they defended each other: to attack one was to attack all. Joanna May stopped as suddenly as she began. She had shocked herself as well as them.

'I'm sorry,' said Joanna May, 'but this is the penalty of daughterhood. I remember it well. The mother must make the daughter as much like her as possible, unthread, unknit, the father in her. In this case, as it happens, my father is your father: you *are* me, so there's no point in me doing it, but still I can't help it.'

'I do it to Sue,' said Gina. 'I can't help that either. I don't do

250

it to the boys: I let them be themselves, I could never work out why. I suppose that's what it is: you try and unravel the father out of the daughter. How else can she be properly female?'

'Worm and the sperm!' said Jane.

'Disgusting,' said Julie and Alice together.

'I will not be your mother,' said Joanna May. 'I hereby renounce the role. If this is motherhood, save me from it. I always wanted it, but this is all it is! Nag, nag, nag!'

'She can't be our sister,' said Alice scornfully. 'She's much too old.'

'She'll only get jealous,' said Jane, 'of the way we are.'

'She does age well,' said Gina. 'I suppose that's something to look forward to.'

'I don't want to look forward,' said Julie. 'I want to live now.'

They allowed Joanna May no authority: she had disclaimed mother, she must take the consequences: they would not even accept her status as originator. They looked her up and down, inspected her, now their equal, their equivalent, but somehow dusty with it. So that was what the passage of the years did – it made you dusty. They resolved never to wear black. It did not suit them. They were in a manic state. As for Joanna, she wanted their pity, all of a sudden, their acknowledgement of her wrongs, but they'd allow her none of that. An easy life, a quiet life! Married for thirty years! To Carl May, the famous Carl! They had all been wronged, more than she, each one claimed. Joanna of all of them had her proper place in the world; she'd been born at the right time. They were a generation out. No wonder they'd been lonely: their lives had been in a mess. They could see now that was the trouble – they'd been lonely. They used men to stop them being lonely. No wonder it all went wrong. Now they had each other, nothing need be the same. They were delirious, giddy. It was absurd, wonderful. Joanna thought they were far too young, far too noisy, far too energetic. She wanted to be alone. She said so. They wouldn't have it.

'We'll make her chairman,' said Julie. 'That's what we'll do. That should keep her happy.'

'Chairperson,' said Jane. So that was what Joanna May consented to be: someone who controlled an agenda but couldn't vote. Mavis watched, and said nothing, but every now and then looked out the window, uneasily.

Ben came into the room and said 'Mum', and Julie and Gina both looked up. 'Those men are back,' he said. 'There are five of them this time, and if you don't do something about it I'm going to take Anthony somewhere safe. And Sue too, I suppose.'

Jane said, 'You let him watch TV, Gina, you shouldn't,' but Joanna said, 'No, we have to be careful. You don't know Carl.'

'I'd rather like to meet this Carl,' said Julie. 'Can it be managed?'

'At last,' said Alice, 'a man worth loving.'

'What everyone wants,' said Jane.

'If you did, Joanna,' said Gina, 'so could we.'

'To be able to love!' said Julie. 'Truly love.'

'He's a demon, a monster,' protested Joanna. 'It wasn't love I felt. Something else! He doesn't deserve to live. He is wicked, he is mad. It took me a lifetime to see it.'

'All that happened,' said Alice, 'is that you grew old.'

'Lost energy,' said Gina.

'Got the worst out of him, not the best,' said Julie.

'Any of us could manage him better,' said Jane.

'How would you do that?' asked Joanna.

'By not taking him seriously!' said Jane, and they all crowed with delight, and poured more champagne, and Joanna turned to Mavis in alarm.

All Mavis said was, 'I didn't think about the back,' and tried the telephone but there was no dialling tone when she lifted up the receiver.

Ben said, 'It's OK, I've already called the police. All the times I wanted to call the police, Mum, and never dared, because it made it worse for you.'

Jane, Julie, Alice and Joanna were shocked. They turned and looked hard at Gina, and Gina said, 'I know, I know, I can't cope, I'm an awful mother, I don't want to be a mother, please help me.'

Mavis and Ben seemed to understand each other, to comprehend that the world was a desperate and dangerous place. Police

252

sirens sounded. Joanna said, 'Why did they come so quickly?' and Mavis said, 'It depends what Ben said,' and Ben said, 'Well, I'd better get it over,' and went out, and Mavis followed.

Alice said to Gina, 'Why don't you go after him, he's your son?' and Gina said, helplessly, 'Well, he's a boy,' and Alice said, 'This can't go on; personally I hate children but after all he is my nephew. Something has to be done about this.'
'About Gina, you mean,' said Jane.
'I'd like to help,' said Julie.

Mavis came back and said Ben's wonderful; he told them this tale of child assault, sex assault, five men in the car, and they believed him, and they took the men away; now they're going to have to talk themselves out of that. Ben's got to go down to the station. Someone ought to go with him.
Gina didn't stir. It was Julie who said, 'I'll go,' so that decided that.

Joanna, Jane, Julie, Gina, Alice.

52

A memo reached Carl May from the Divination Department: his PA thought it advisable to let this one through. The department was becoming an expensive joke, rumours of its existence having reached the media. The memo took it upon itself to warn Mr May fairly and squarely that the auspices for the day of the projected PR event in Wales were bad indeed. The common pack had produced the Ace of Spades 40 per cent above probability: the Tarot pack the Tower 90 per cent likewise; the *I Ching*, the Chinese Book of Oracles, that normally sedate and encouraging book, had come up with No.23 (Splitting Apart) four times running with mention of Tears of Blood; the prophetic dreamer had wakened screaming, the encephalic discs popping off of their own accord; so far undiagnosed telekinetic forces in the office had shredded the Welsh map, and the teacups came up repeatedly with coffins on the rim.

Carl May laughed aloud. 'Gobbledygook,' he said, and to the gratification of his PA dictated a memo back to Divination: 'If you have foretold anything it is the death of your own department: the end of your payslips,' and told his PA the Welsh PR event was now on and he himself would graciously participate.

A couple of days later, Hughie Scotland ran his finger down the M's in his private address book, and once again got straight through to Carl May.

'I take that back about you being a dry old stick,' said Hughie Scotland. 'I understand you mean to jump into a cooling pond to prove radiation's safe. Young Bethany has certainly brought you back to life. I hope you're grateful.'

'Moderately,' said Carl May, who sounded buoyant, almost

happy. 'It's the TV producer's idea. I must make a fool of myself, it seems, to bring the country to its senses.'

'I jumped into a trout pond for the same reason,' said Hughie Scotland, 'to popularize freshwater fish. These days we men of power must make sacrifices.'

'I thought you were drunk,' said Carl May. 'Bethany told me you did it because you were drunk.'

'Bethany tells lies,' said Scotland. 'How is Bethany? You know my wife's in Nigeria? Is Bethany jumping in the cooling pond, too?'

'The TV man says yes,' said Carl May. 'We're in his hands. And Bethany is looking forward to it.'

'What is a cooling pond exactly?' asked Scotland. 'Is it safe?'

'I wouldn't be jumping into it if it weren't,' said Carl May. 'It's where they put the old spent fuel rods to cool off, lose any short-term radioactivity they might have picked up in the pile, before they're carted off to Sellafield. No harm in them at all. The water's filtered and purified, monitored daily, just to be on the safe side, to keep the local populace happy.'

'I'd rather Bethany didn't jump in it,' said Hughie Scotland, 'all the same. I find I'm very fond of Bethany. Does she ever talk about me?'

'No,' said Carl May, 'and she is indeed jumping into the cooling pond with me. It can hardly be worse than into a trout pool with you. Personally I find freshwater fish unnatural. Our streams and rivers are a great deal more polluted than our seas, even the North Sea, and that's saying something. Well, good to speak to you, Hughie. I take it your men will be there in force, cameras and all. If one's going to do something like this, one might as well make as big a splash as possible.'

A joke too. Hughie Scotland winced.

'As it happens,' added Carl May, 'Bethany and I are getting married.' And he put the phone down. That last would stir up Scotland and his media troops.

Carl May told his secretary to confirm detailed arrangements with the NBI. He did not think he would marry Bethany, when it came to it, not even to annoy and upset Joanna. What he did not want, what he did not like, what upset him, was Bethany

255

staying away of her own accord. But when she was there, he could do without her. He could never win in his own head, only in the outside world.

Bethany looked up briefly from her computer game.

'I have the highest score ever,' she said. 'There's this little figure you have to guide through rooms full of demons and ghosts. I'm really good at it. What was that about you marrying me?'

'Only for the press,' said Carl May. 'We want them all there, not just the science boys. Why, do you want to marry me?'

'Of course I do,' said Bethany, but she wasn't sure. It would take her too much out of circulation. You could never divorce Carl May, and if he divorced you you'd be lucky to be alive to collect your decree absolute. The Barbers of the Bath might sing you to death.

'It was Hughie Scotland on the line,' said Carl May, waiting to see how she'd respond.

'That's nothing to me,' said Bethany, and for once she didn't lie. She had a short emotional memory which, considering her life, was just as well.

53

The journey to Britnuc B, in the heart of the Welsh hill country, impressed and awed as many of the journalists and newsmen who travelled down, by car, by train, by helicopter, to cover the media event of the year (for that, according to Britnuc's PR, was what it was) as it troubled and depressed others. The wild beauty of the hills, their sheer scale, the overwhelming presence of nature unorganized and unconfirmed, the indifference of the shaggy cattle, the unkempt quiet roads, the general dwarfing and rendering risible of mankind, inspired as much deference to nature as resentment of it.

Britnuc B had been carefully landscaped so as to offend the aesthetic sensibilities of landscape lovers as little as possible. Some – on the whole those with country cottages – shuddered as they approached the power-station complex, and their radios crackled and faded beneath the marching pylons. Others were thankful that something sensible, profitable and organized had at last, thanks to Britnuc, enlivened the rural torpor of the area.

Green grass grew wherever possible inside the security fence: the massive containment unit was so placed that it was all but dwarfed by the flat rock face that reached up to the sky behind it. Birds wheeled unconcerned above it, delighting in updraughts and downdraughts, the low, interesting, steady thunder of the heavy steam-driven turbines. As Carl May loved to say, 'What is a nuclear power station but a gigantic kettle? All we do here is boil water!'

Only the security gates themselves, the high fences, the handing out of security badges, the requiring of passes, the writing down and checking of names, made matters appear the least unusual: that here was the focus of a nation's terror, the very fount of paranoia.

Britnuc's PR teams made coffee, poured drinks, handed out booklets. Chernobyl could not happen here, the Russian designs were *other*, all *other*, hopelessly old-fashioned, and even if it did, would be no worse than a coal-mine explosion – less horrible, in fact, less likely to be a lethal accident. Nuclear power plants were the opposite of labour intensive! Carl May himself wished to make this very point. And if this proved too technical for the mass-circulation papers, middle rather than front page stuff, why, Carl May was engaged to be married – yes, he was free to marry – yes, he was divorced: a matter of mutual consent many years back: there would be a press handout presently. In the meantime, international TV was present on this wonderful day: a cinema film was being made, not just TV – though we're glad so many TV stations are represented here today: we really do have to get this message across to the general public. Yes, the film was to be part-funded by Britnuc: of course, why not? Part of the PR job – and look here, mementoes for everyone, on this splendid occasion. Choose from a genuine leather-bound Filofax or this genuine Barbour – if the rain should just possibly fall no one must get wet – and of course there'd be a buffet lunch after the event. Telephones, telex and fax facilities all available in the press office – and out, everyone out into the beautiful fresh air of Wales! The show's beginning. Carl May, nuclear magnate, and Bethany his bride – well soon to be his bride: no, the date wasn't quite fixed, but the press would, of course, be informed the minute it was – would ceremoniously jump into the cooling pond to prove low-level waste was no threat to anyone, and the future of nuclear power, clean, efficient, safe, would be assured.

And all trooped out into the clean, bright, windy air: a good day! A long way to come but at least Britnuc knew how to organize things.

'Do I have to jump?' asked Bethany. She stood on the edge of the concrete bunker looking down at the clean bluish water below. She'd felt the water with her long, nervy, trembly fingers. Pink fingers, as Carl kept saying. Pink fingers. It made her uneasy. The water was just nicely warm. Bethany wore a yellow bikini, with polka dots; it was cut high up the thigh to make her long legs longer. Her red hair flowed out in the wind. Her bosom was only just encased in yellow, polka-dotted fabric.

'This is really something,' murmured Hamish Tovey. 'Get a look of that!'

'This'll travel round the world,' said someone from a newspaper not in the Scotland chain. 'This'll really hit headlines.'

The Scotland chain were concentrating on the copycatting angle. They were rerunning the Scotland/Bethany trout-farm pics, to go out side by side with this one, inviting the reader to decide whether Bethany was going up or down in the world.

'Focus on the girl,' said Hamish, as Carl May joined Bethany on the concrete ramp. He wore black swimming trunks and was in good trim condition for a man of his age. But he was shorter than she was. 'Forget him.'

Carl looked Bethany up and down: he was elated.

'She wore a teeny weeny ultra-teeny
    Yellow polka-dot bikini –'

he chanted.

'No, Carl,' said Bethany. 'I'm sure it's not ultra-teeny.'

He pushed her in.

'Oh Christ,' shouted Hamish. 'What are you playing at? We'll have to do that again!' Though most of the press had got it, he wasn't yet rolling.

'We'll do it without the girl,' said Carl May. 'She's irrelevant,' and so they had to, because Carl May said so. The mood of the day changed. The media became bored and sour: what a waste of time: all the way to the Welsh mountains to get one old man, who had to hold in his paunch, jumping into a pond, top executive or not. Carl was in and out of the water six times before NBI was satisfied. They did not make it easy for him. As for Bethany, she'd scrambled to the side at once and had a really good hot shower straight away, and washed and dried her hair, and then sat gently crying. Carl May had finally really upset her. She hadn't wanted to do it in the first place: she had only said she would for the sake of the nation, for their moral health, as Carl put it: to keep the flag of faith flying, as her father did: doing the kind thing which was the right thing. And now Carl was angry, swimming around in the water, doing stupid things for a camera, not himself – where was his pride? Where was his integrity? She had more than he had when it came to it, and now she was frightened again: Carl had taken the name of marriage in vain and would be punished for it: yet he knew no better. She found she was sorry for Carl, which was almost worse than being bored and she hated the countryside: green hills closed in around her. She wanted to be back in the city.

A man came up to her and said he was Hughie Scotland's PA: Hughie had said if she wanted a lift home, he could give her one. Bethany was doubtful. Then she looked over to where Carl May still thrashed about in the water of the cooling pond, white head bobbing.

'Hughie says not to worry,' said the PA, who was young, broad-shouldered, good-looking and interested. 'Hughie says he'll look after you. If you know what I mean.'

'OK,' said Bethany. 'I seem to remember what he means.'

She sat next to the PA in the car on the way back to London, not in the back as he'd expected. She felt shivery and a little sick presently, but it soon passed. She took out her contact lenses.

'I like your eyes grey,' he said, his own eyes off the road.

'Do watch where you're going,' she said, 'or you'll kill us both,' but she was pleased. Presently she started humming to herself:

'I do, I do, I do,
And I ain't going to tell you who.
But I belong to somebody,
Yes indeed I do!'

and felt positively brave and cheerful, and as if her life had begun anew, which indeed it had.

54

Carl May sat amongst the Pharaohs and wept. 'I am a stranger in my own land,' he thought. He shivered and felt sick. Painted eyes stared at him, oval, beautiful and calm: the carved and soulful eyes of strange beasts, but there was no one to talk to. His impatience had driven them away. His own easy irritation, his flashing anger, his unreasonable demands, had seared a burnt and blasted space around and no one came near him. Why should they? He wouldn't if he were them. He lived in a kennel, and barked. If he'd been his own mother, he'd have put himself there.

He was dying. He did not care. Only that none of it had been what he wanted, none of it what he meant. He hoped Bethany would be all right. Death, he could see, was too great a punishment for the habit of correcting someone out of turn. Nausea made him feel kind: as if you needed strength to be cruel and kindness was just the easiest, most natural thing. There was no more time to investigate the notion. The mind had to die, that was the dreadful thing: bodies were two a penny, but that all the buzzing speculation of the individual mind had to go – therein lay the tragedy. He should never have got involved with the Barbers of the Bath. That had been insanity. He wished to apologize to the clones of Joanna May. But he didn't have the strength. Too late.

After he'd got out of the pond, towelled and walked back to the VIP room, the meters – the ones put in to reassure the visitors – had started to chatter. The area had been cleared, more or less. Media men will risk anything for a story, even stay round chattering meters. What a fuss! They'd wanted to put him in the isolation room and start emergency treatments, but he knew already it was no good. It had been foretold. Let them suck out as much bone marrow as they wanted, he was finished. Philip drove him back to Eton Square. Good for Philip. He'd make the alarms chatter now, too. He wondered if it had been an accident. Probably not. Who had fixed it? Coustain? His own Divination Department? Joanna? He wouldn't blame her. He wished she was with him. In spite of everything, he wished she was there. He thought Isaac was in the room; he hoped he was: it would be somebody to talk to. But there was no one, nothing animate. No sound at all, unless he was deaf. He would have to take his own journey through death, so alone, without servants, without friends; stand at the Throne of the Most High, and make his explanation there, without support, without witnesses. What could he say? I wanted to know what would happen next? Was that enough? There had not been time: he had been clapped like a bird in full flight, soaring. Fate was unkind, but just.

It wasn't Isaac. It was Joanna. He saw her blue eyes. He shivered so much he could hardly speak. He said, 'No, don't come too near.'

She said, 'I never did, I never dared. I should have been more brave.'

He said, 'I know all that. I know. My fault.'

She just stared at him, but at least her eyes moved. They weren't dead. He had, after all, spared her, saved her. Now he had his reward.

'Joanna,' Carl May said, 'take me, remake me. For God's sake, remake me.'

'All right,' said Joanna May.

55

That was a year of strange events, some wonderful, some terrible: and there are stranger years ahead, no doubt. They don't frighten me; even death has lost its sting. The future shouldn't alarm us: how could it possibly be worse than what's gone before? Little by little, wisdom replaces ignorance, self-knowledge overcomes stupidity, awareness gets the upper hand of cruelty. It is the past which is so terrifying, with its capacity to spoil and destroy the present. That can't get better.

Little Carl runs round my feet. He's three years old, an energetic, noisy little boy, with thick pale hair and bright red cheeks, interested in everything, bored by nothing. He can read and write already, and even recite nursery rhymes, which he loves to do, never getting them quite right. If I correct him he has a temper tantrum: he is beside himself with upset and indignation – I have failed to recognize the difficulties he has overcome, the achievement; so great a task for one so small – and his small frame cannot contain such passion. His whole body turns as red as his cheeks, he flails and kicks and beats the ground, the door, me, anything; and then I, hurt in mind and body, have to carry him, as best I can, to his room and shut him in until we both calm down and can begin again. I could beat him black and blue, and am still sometimes tempted to, to punish him for what he did to me, for the unlived life he gave me, so many years of it, the guilt he made me feel, the loss he made me endure, for the deaths of Isaac and of Oliver. Except this innocent has done nothing: I know he could, that's all, and knowing what he could do also know what I could do, sufficiently provoked; and so I have to forgive him, both in retrospect and in advance.

Easier not to correct him, one way or another, to avoid the confrontation, to let the error go unchecked. 'Spoiling,' Gina calls it. Now she has given her children away, how quickly she has taken on Julie's former role, and become censorious. But I'm older, I know better, I no longer fight for fairness, truth and justice. I just say, 'That's wonderful, Carl, how clever you are!' We christened him Rex, Alice and I. King. Why not? But Julie was against it – a dog's name, she said – and it soon drifted back to being Carl, little Carl.

Alice, of all of them, Queen of Cups, was the one who volunteered to give birth to little Carl, on condition she didn't have to rear him. Dr Holly, back in the business, used his own tried and tested techniques of nuclei transfer to bring it about. Alice proved a good and dutiful birth mother: didn't smoke, didn't drink, watched her health and her moods – trained as she was in keeping her body well under control. She relinquished the baby to me at six weeks, without protest – glad of a decent night's sleep, I daresay, and happy enough to let the simple pleasures of narcissism prevail over the more complicated snakes-and-ladders game of motherhood; anxious to get back to work; and knowing I'd bring up the child pretty much as she would. How could I not?

Julie, Queen of Pentacles, is happy bringing up Ben, and little Anthony too; Alec, their adoptive father, comes and goes. He is resigned to the noise, the mess, the constant upheaval; consoled by the sense of present and future, so long as he can fly off from time to time, leave it all behind and tread the clean and flattering corridors of world class hotels until such time as his strength returns and his self-esteem is restored.

Jane, Queen of Wands, no longer toys with the idea of working in film: she has settled happily and quite profitably as a journalist – the work suits her better, being more about facts, less about fantasy. She felt obliged to take Sue in because three was too much for Julie, and Alice had done her bit by actually giving birth to little Carl, and Gina wasn't fit, and a child will take any clone, it seems, for a mother. The essential nature is the same, after all: only the frills are different. Sue then felt the lack of a resident father, so Jane, running comfortably on only a quarter guilt, finally consented to allow Tom to move in. Jane is always out and about so Tom does much of the childminding and cooking, grumbling the while, but the three of them, Jane, Tom, Sue, seem happy enough. Sue sees her birth mother from time to time, of course, but prefers the Jane rather than the Gina version, or at any rate, she'd rather have Tom for a father than Cliff.

Gina, Queen of Swords, now childless, is at medical school but back with Cliff. He still drinks, he still hits her, but not so much or so hard. Pain is indeed addictive, and perhaps the effort of curing it is hardly worth it, if there are no children about. If it's pleasurable, why not? We've had so many oughts and shoulds, all of us, we've all but given up being critical of one another. Good for her, say we.

We would have been perfect people if we could, but our genes were against us. We would have been faithful, kind and true, but fate was against us. We are one woman split five ways, a hundred ways, a million million ways.

It's autumn. I, Joanna May, am out in the garden, raking leaves. I keep things tidy, and growing, in memory of Oliver, and besides, I like to do it. Little Carl runs round my feet and all but trips me up, and falls headlong into a pile of leaves. 'Careful,' I say, 'I'm not as young as I was,' and I pick him up and set him straight, and he laughs cheerfully and rushes off to set to flight a flock of seagulls, rashly gathered on the lawn: and when the wicked deed is done, and the birds have risen crossly and unwillingly into the air, where they hang around to wheel and squawk their reproach, he stands stock still, amazed at what he's done. I do love him. Never stopped.

Fay Weldon

Life Force

Into the lives of Marion, Nora, Rosalie and Susan erupts Leslie
Beck, an old flame not quite extinguished. Recently widowed,
though somewhat weepy Leslie is still a man with the Life Force.
To the four friends he is Leslie the Lucky, Leslie of the
magnificent dong – his force forever pulls. Old secrets stir, old
rivalries are resurrected and scores are settled as the friends are
catapulted back into their murky past.

This copulative story of passion, jealousy, fidelity and faithlessness
is Weldon at her most provocative.

'Weldon's funniest novel yet' *Cosmopolitan*

'Weldon sends up all the novels of sex 'n' marriage 'n' kids in NW3
by triumphantly writing one of her own that is witty enough to
finish off the breed' *Mail on Sunday*

'Fay Weldon's *Life Force* is a scathing indictment of rampant seed-
shedding and moral vanity. Through the voices of women Beck
has seduced, Weldon joyously wields the scalpel, cutting deep into
the sexual psyches of both men and women' *Woman's Journal*

'A breezy book, often very funny and, as can be expected, full of
energising satire' *Times Educational Supplement*

'Weldon at her most wicked' *Elle*

'Everywhere is the unmistakable zippiness of her narrative style'
Daily Telegraph

'Fay Weldon can tease, tantalise and scandalise better than any
other writer today . . . Not recommended for the faint-hearted with
something to hide' *Financial Times*

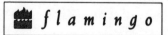

Fay Weldon

Darcy's Utopia

Scandalous Eleanor Darcy, wild young wife of a world-famous economist, sketches her vision of Utopia to two journalists, Hugo Vansitart and Valerie Jones. In glorious detail, she describes an earthly paradise of peace, love and technological progress where sex is plentiful and money does not exist. Such is Eleanor's charisma that, to their own astonishment, Hugo and Valerie abandon their families and set up home together in a Holiday Inn . . .

'This is a dazzling tour de force from one of Britain's most inspiring and intelligent novelists today'   Kate Saunders, *Cosmopolitan*

'To read Fay Weldon is like drinking champagne'   *The Times*

'A crash course in philosophy, religion, politics, idealism, with sexual passion, love and the nature of betrayal thrown in'
Woman's Journal

'Prolific and provocative, Fay Weldon shines brightest in the league table of British women novelists'   *Time Out*

'Weldon is a gifted tease of a writer'   Penny Perrick, *Sunday Times*

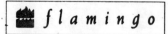

Fay Weldon

Growing Rich

Bernard Bellamy has done a deal. He's sold out to the Devil, in all his forms. In return, he is promised that all his wishes will be granted, all his desires fulfilled. One of them, young Carmen Wedmore, is proving to be quite a challenge.

Carmen lives in the new town of Fenedge, East Anglia, near her former schoolfriends Laura and Annie. The three girls dream of the day they'll escape their dullsville existence. While Annie flies off with a fluttering, blipping heart to the snowcapped peaks and frothy rapids of New Zealand to join the man of her dreams and Laura marries, capably moving the population graph a few notches higher, Carmen stays in Fenedge, under the powerful clasp of Sir Bernard and Driver, the Devil's agent. Disguised as a suave chauffeur, Driver cruises in his plush, shiny, sinister limo, stalking her every move.

But Carmen becomes ever more determined to ride out the temptations laid in her path and not to sell her soul. Will she eventually succumb? Or will the Devil, for once, not have everything his own way?

Fay Weldon's *Growing Rich* is a turbine-driven fantasy of love and revenge, values and morals: a witty and compelling elixir.

'Fast, funny . . . a glorious entertainment for the Nineties'
Woman's Journal

'Breathtaking . . . catches its reader up in a gale of good spirits and devilment that keeps on blowing from beginning to end'   *Observer*

'A typically Weldonesque tale of cleverness, with tongue-in-cheek asides'   *Good Housekeeping*

'Another Fay Weldon classic'   *New Woman*

'As exuberant as ever'   *Daily Telegraph*

'Absolutely hypnotic'   *Irish Press*

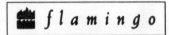